EVERYONE CAN'T BE WRONG

PRAISE FOR *EVERYONE CAN'T BE WRONG*

"No one has dramatized the push-and-pull of being an immigrant child, the way family and cultural duties swallow up individual wants, as well as Sonal Champsee does in her funny, warm-hearted novel *Everyone Can't Be Wrong*. Champsee writes with compassion, authority, verve, and never wastes your time."

—Kevin Chong, author of *The Double Life Of Benson Yu*

"With her distinctive warmth, wry humour, and subtle incisiveness, Sonal Champsee conjures the anxious feeling of being trapped inside our own second-guessing, following everyone else's ideas of who we should be until we no longer recognize ourselves. *Everyone Can't Be Wrong* pushes back against the endless "supposed-tos" that too often stand in the way of truly knowing—and loving—who we really are."

—Jessica Westhead, author of *Avalanche And Worry*

"*Everyone Can't Be Wrong* is a gorgeously written novel by Sonal Champsee. Champsee is a longtime champion of upcoming Canadian writers, and her depth of knowledge of the craft is clear in this book. Descriptions shine, luscious details sparkle. Every metaphor is multi-layered. Sharp dialogue gives great insight into each characters' motivation and desires. I truly admire the way the author approaches her reader with openness and trust, inviting us fully into every scene.

The main character of the novel, Payal, is one of the most loveable I've met in fiction. Payal is so deeply caring, a perpetual people-pleaser, and yet her insecurities are painfully exploited by those around her. The protagonist is flawed, messy, imperfect, and wonderfully relatable.

This gorgeously written story will feel familiar to anyone trying to balance multiple cultures and their competing pressures, anyone who has felt torn between individual self-fulfillment versus the demands of a collective. It is a book for anyone who has felt how the pressure to live up to expectation can be consuming.

From the first line, this novel never lost my attention and when I finished it, I only wished for more. I won't forget these beautifully rendered characters, who, for a time, felt like my family too."

—Kirti Bhadresa, author of *An Astonishment of Stars*

The publisher gratefully acknowledges the support of the Canada Council, Ontario Arts Council, Ontario Creates and the Canadian Government.

Canada Council for the Arts Conseil des arts du Canada

ONTARIO ARTS COUNCIL
CONSEIL DES ARTS DE L'ONTARIO
an Ontario government agency
un organisme du gouvernement de l'Ontario

Canada

Cover design: Pei Yuan Li

Any references to historical events, real people, or real places are used fictitiously. Other names, characters, places and events are products of the author's imagination.

Library and Archives Canada Cataloguing in Publication

Title: Everyone can't be wrong / Sonal Champsee.

Names: Champsee, Sonal, author.

Series: Inanna poetry & fiction series.

Description: Series statement: Inanna poetry & fiction series

Identifiers: Canadiana 20260235202 | ISBN 9781834210292 (softcover)

Subjects: LCGFT: Novels.

Classification: LCC PS8605.H3546 E94 2026 | DDC C813/.6—dc23

INANNA
PUBLICATIONS & EDUCATION INC.
TORONTO, ONTARIO, CANADA
www.inanna.ca

Printed and bound in Canada

Inanna Publications and Education Inc.

210 Founders College, York University

4700 Keele Street, Toronto, Ontario, Canada M3J 1P3

Telephone: (416) 736-5356 Fax: (416) 736-5765

Email: inanna.publications@inanna.ca

Website: www.inanna.ca

EVERYONE CAN'T BE WRONG

SONAL CHAMPSEE

For my father, Motilal (Mac) Champsee, 1942–2019.

It's unlikely that he would have read this book, but he absolutely would have talked everyone into buying a copy.

TABLE OF CONTENTS

CHAPTER ONE

November 2010, Toronto

IT WAS TOO CHILLY FOR ME on the balcony, but still I leaned on the railing and looked below at the city getting on with its day. People grabbing coffee and heading to work, cars and delivery trucks creeping through the narrow streets while bicycle couriers slalomed between them, people walking, parents pushing baby strollers—but I looked away from the strollers and curled both my hands around the steaming cup of coffee to warm my fingers. I could have gone in for a sweater but instead I stood out there and pretended I was fine.

I heard the sliding door open and then shut behind me. Bryan. He was still in his boxer shorts, unbothered by the autumnal chill. "Where do you want to grab brunch?"

"We could try Petit Dejeuner?" It seemed popular with the hipsters; it showed up a lot on Yelp and UrbanSpoon. Plus it was near our condo. There were a lot of restaurants in our area, but we hadn't tried many of them in the six years we'd lived here.

"I was thinking we could check out somewhere near our new place." He stood beside me and put his hands on the railing, surveying the streetscape as if he was looking for a brunch place from above.

"Is there anything there?"

He laughed. "It's suburbia, not the tundra. I'm sure there'll be an East Side Mario's or something nearby."

There would be no hipsters at East Side Mario's.

He continued. "Besides, I don't think we'll have much time to stop between appointments."

I sipped my coffee, and kept looking down at the street, not wanting to think about either appointment. We were due to finalize finishes on our new house, the one we bought pre-construction four years ago, but before that we were seeing our fertility doctor, whom we'd met three years ago.

"It'll be great," said Bryan. "A new plan. A new hope. Our new house."

I blinked to prevent rolling my eyes. "It might not be good news."

"You have to try and stay positive."

"Bry," I started. "You've been staying positive for three years now." Our official diagnosis was "unexplained infertility," which Bryan took to mean that an explanation was forthcoming, whereas I saw it more as a science experiment on my body that no one understood.

His face dropped. "Do you always have to be so negative?"

"Sorry."

"Like, why are we doing this if you don't think it will work?" He gripped the balcony railing and stared over the edge, but I could tell he wasn't looking at anything.

My cell phone rang before I could apologize again. Mom. I answered.

She didn't say hello. "Where are you? We have a meeting."

I turned away from Bryan. "I took a day off."

"It's just one meeting."

"I arranged this weeks ago." The balcony felt quiet. I knew Bryan was listening, and that he knew it was my mom, because who else would it be?

"You think business stops because you have the day off? You can't do one simple thing like come in for a meeting?"

I tucked my hair behind my ear, and swallowed. "What's it about?"

She steamrolled over my words as if I hadn't spoken at all. "This isn't IBM. This isn't some big-big company, okay, I don't show up, no problem, no one notices."

"Mom—"

"Do you think Daddy gets a day off? When it's your company, there are no days off. The poor man, breaking his head building a business, and all you care about is a day off? Do you know how lucky you are that you have a father with his own business?"

"Mom—"

She kept going. "We work night and day building this for you, and for what? You can't come for one meeting? So irresponsible. Just like your brother."

"Mom—"

"Even worse than your brother; Amit is coming to the meeting. Shruti is already here. Why can't you be more like your sister?"

I held my phone away from my ear and let my mom rant into the air. I put the mouthpiece close to my lips and spoke as loudly as I could without shouting. "What time is the meeting?"

I glanced over at Bryan in time to see his shoulders sag. A moment later, he went back inside and sat on the couch. I sorted out the details with Mom and hung up the phone, and then followed Bryan.

"I can still make it to the appointment afterward."

"It's your day off." He put his feet up on the coffee table, thumping them down one a time, almost like he was stomping.

"I have a meeting."

"Did you forget what 'day off' means?"

"Are we doing this again?" I headed to the bedroom to get dressed for work, but turned to face him at the doorway. "There are no days off when it's your company." Inside, I cringed hearing my mother's words coming out of my mouth.

"It's not your company; it's your parents' company."

"Same thing."

For a moment, I thought we might end up in another fight, but he only shook his head, shaking off the inevitable stalemate. "So much for brunch."

I dressed quickly, layering fleecy tights under a wool skirt and a thermal cami under my button up shirt. Today's appointment was pants-on.

Bryan wandered in while I was brushing my hair. He was smiling a little; Bryan was always easy-going. I'd never seen him stay mad for long. "When we go by the new house, we can start planning out the baby's room. Manifest success."

I ran my fingers over my hair to crackle the static out. "You know it might not be that easy."

He nodded. "But you have to visualize. It helps. The positive energy can make things happen." He put his arms around me, a reverse bear hug. I leaned into the warmth. "Who knows, maybe we'll be one of those couples who get pregnant the day they start treatment?"

"We started treatment three years ago."

"The new treatment; whatever the doctor tells us about today."

It would not happen. Bryan and I hadn't had sex in a long time. Somewhere in the middle of infertility treatment, all of that started feeling clinical. Was this a hint?

"Picture it," said Bryan, stretching his arm out as if pointing to the scene. "A baby crawling over the hardwood floors in our new place. A crib in the corner. Toys all over. It'll be perfect."

I tried, but in my mind was a magazine photograph, posed and pristine and featuring two white models as smiling parents. Not us. But even if I couldn't see it, surely things would be better. The pressure would be off. We would have done everything we were supposed to do to be happy. I should be happy then. I should be happy now.

I shivered a little.

"Don't tell me you're cold," said Bryan. He started laughing. "It's barely November and you have seventeen layers on."

I pulled out of his embrace. "I have to get to work."

* * *

I dashed in and found my sister, Shruti, sitting at reception. I could tell from the blue reflection in her eyes that she was looking at Facebook.

I was annoyed. "Where's Amit?"

She shrugged. "Not in yet. Don't you have the day off?"

"Don't you have better things to do than answer phones?" We didn't need a reception desk anymore. It was a relic from years ago, when the office was full of keyboards clicking and phones ringing and dot matrix printers clatter-buzzing through reams of connected paper. But Dad wasn't ready to let the reception desk go, and in any case, it was one of the few tasks my older brother Amit was capable of doing. He'd come back from LA earlier this year to start working for Dad.

"I don't mind." Shruti was a competent bookkeeper, but she'd been increasingly checked out since she'd gotten married. Eventually, I suspected she'd go part-time or quit and become a housewife.

"Do you think Amit can do some real work yet?"

"Mom doesn't think he's ready." Shruti said this in a neutral voice, but our eyes met and I knew we were thinking the same thing: Amit was milking the situation through perpetual training.

"He can update Shannon's books." Shannon was Amit's girlfriend. His sole contribution to the business was bringing her on as a client. I wrinkled my nose. "If he messes that up, he'll be able to smooth it over."

The door jangled. Amit. With one fluid motion, he dropped a fresh Tim Horton's coffee in front of Shruti, flipped a box of Timbits in the air and caught it with one hand, and hip-checked the door to Dad's office open. He raised his own coffee in my direction. "Meeting time, don't be late." He disappeared inside.

"Nice of him to bring me a coffee."

Shruti shuffled out from behind the desk. "You weren't supposed to be here." She handed me hers. "Take it, I'm off coffee."

We pulled chairs up to Dad's desk. Dad was staring at his computer and frowning a little. Behind him was the large family photograph from when he opened the accounting practice. We were standing in front of the reception desk, Dad's arm around a ten-year-old Amit in a too-big suit. Shruti and I wore matching pink dresses, with Mom behind us in a smoothly pleated sari. Her face was serene, revealing no trace of the yelling she'd done moments before, when Shruti and I had been picking at the gold embroidery in her pallu.

Mom brought in two cups of steaming chai, plus a plate of Parle-G biscuits. I peeled the lid off my Timmies and dunked a biscuit, pulling it out quickly before it disintegrated.

"Since we're all here," started Dad, taking a sip of chai, "I wanted to talk about the future of this business. One day, we're going to die." He chuckled a bit. "I wish it wasn't true, but everyone dies." He explained this as if this were new information.

Out of the corner of my eye, I could see Shruti lifting a hand to smother a giggle, but Amit still looked blandly attentive. At least he could use his acting skills.

"But it's time to step back and ease into retirement." He glanced at Mom. "Mom too. I had hoped Amit would take over instead of getting involved in this acting business."

Amit smiled back tiredly. "Is it already time for your daily reminder that I'm not going back to school for accounting?"

"You only have to try, beta," said Mom, using an affectionate pet name. It was a word used for both sons and daughters, but Shruti once told me that it actually meant 'son.' Mom reached for the plate of cookies, took one, and handed it to Amit.

I wished they'd give up on Amit. Accounting was one of those things that nobody cared about, but if no one did it, nothing would run. Responsible people like me did the accounting.

"I thought Payal was taking over when you retired," said Shruti.

"Payal will keep everything running, yes," said Dad. I was the only qualified accountant, aside from Dad. "But it isn't fair that the whole company goes to her. I built this business for the three of you. Equal partners, equal shares."

This had always been the plan, but it made me uncomfortable. Dad's advice when we helped clients with estate tax planning was to honour their intentions. But was it fair when I was the one doing most of the work?

He began running through the tax planning scenarios, and I could see Amit's eyes glaze over. Shruti was texting. I could see how things would go in the future. Why had I been called in on my day off for this? Bryan would be pissed off when he found out.

I interrupted him. "So I run this place by myself, and Amit and Shruti own the majority?"

"Don't be selfish," admonished Mom.

"Amit will help you. Maybe Shruti too," said Dad, nodding at each of them.

Amit sighed loudly. Shruti gave a slight nod without taking her eyes off her phone.

If Dad retired, I'd have more choices. We could expand beyond bookkeeping and tax preparation. Offer advice, maybe be the unofficial CFO for so many small businesses that needed us. I checked my watch; I could still make the appointment if we wrapped up quickly.

Dad went through every detail while the rest of us pretended to listen. As soon as he finished, I gathered up my bag to leave, but Mom grabbed me by the back of my shirt to hold me back. "You need to go see Shannon. Today."

"I'm sure Amit can handle it." I had no idea if he could handle it or not, but whatever he did, it would be no worse than what Shannon would do on her own. I started putting on my coat.

Mom shook her head. "Amit's not ready."

I glanced at Amit, hoping he'd protest, but instead he shrugged with mock helplessness and left the room.

"It's my day off. Shruti can do it."

Mom waved this off. "I have some work for Shruti. You have nothing else to do."

I wasn't going to tell her about the fertility appointment. Maybe I could just pick up the files and do it from home tonight. "What's so urgent?"

Mom looked around to make sure no one was in earshot and lowered her voice. "This is the first girl Amit has ever been serious about. We can't let him screw up her business."

"So?" I doubted that this was the first girl he'd been serious about, and I wasn't even sure how serious Amit was about any girl, but Mom didn't need to know that. I crossed my arms. "I'm pretty sure she's not into him for his accounting skills."

She sucked her teeth. "He's too old to be unmarried."

Amit was only thirty-four, but if I suggested this was not unusually old to still be single, I would be told that I was too young to understand. I didn't even like Shannon. She was one of those yoga women who greeted people with "Namaste." If she left Amit because he screwed up, we'd be better off. "Fine. I'll go."

Shruti was back at the reception desk, and I paused to throw out my empty coffee cup in the garbage under her desk. "Guess who got stuck doing Shannon's books?"

"Seriously? You're a CA."

"At least when I'm in charge, I can make Amit deal with Shannon himself."

She snorted. "Like that'll happen."

I was confused. "You'll be on my side, right?"

She stared at me. "You know Mom and Dad will never really retire. They'll still be around every day telling us how to run things."

I could feel all the anger and irritation drain out of me as a heavy black weight settled on my back. I'd hoped this was only a paranoid thought, not a truth that everyone else around me had accepted. "Surely they have to let go a little."

She turned back to Facebook. "Have fun at Shannon's."

* * *

Bryan didn't hear me dash in. He sat alone, head in hands, among the other couples in the waiting room. Closest to him sat a man in a grey suit next to a woman with a quilted Chanel purse on her lap; they were staring off in different directions. Another woman with coppery highlights in her impossibly shiny hair whispered to a man who kept jittering his leg. His silver watch flashed as he checked the time. Everyone seemed to be in their own private worlds. I took a moment to smooth my hair with my hands. Bryan looked okay in his Dockers and dress shirt; I hoped to be equally unobtrusive, to blend in.

I slid into the padded chair beside him; he jumped slightly. "Ready for the big news?" He clapped his hands against his thighs a little too loudly and winced at the sound.

"I guess."

"Think positive."

I smiled slightly, hoping to convey positivity instead of creeping dread. At least this was a talking appointment. No wrapping myself in paper sheets in a darkened room while the tech dug the wand around inside me.

I told Bryan about the meeting. He nodded somewhat absently. "So you'll be in charge at last?"

I rubbed my eyes. "Something like that." I paused, trying to decide how to tell him I was going to Shannon's next.

But Bryan spoke first. "Better you than me. I'd way rather be told what to do and not have to worry about anything."

I made an agreeable noise, and we lapsed into silence. Bryan began bouncing his leg up and down; I could feel it vibrating through the chair. He was nervous. I'd tell him about going to Shannon's after the appointment.

The doctor came out leading a couple through the waiting area before returning to her office. One woman wiped her eyes with the back of her wrist, revealing her red and blotchy face. Bryan's face tightened; he had noticed too.

Our names were called and we went in. The doctor began running through the numbers, the tests we'd done, the procedures and protocols we'd undergone: a full catalogue of our repeated failures over the years. Bryan kept nodding earnestly, not listening but waiting for the new plan. I couldn't look at her face so instead watched her fingernails, perfectly oval-shaped, a reflective dull rose.

"I'll be blunt," said the doctor. "There's not much more we can do."

I glanced at Bryan, but he seemed frozen. "What do you mean?"

"We can't help you conceive with your own eggs. I'm so sorry." She sat, leaning forward on her elbows, watching us, waiting for our reaction.

My eyes felt hot and I shifted my gaze to the orchid on her desk. I studied its waxy whiteness, the way the backs of the petals were tinged with pink, the way the curved face in the centre of the flower was stained yellow, the water spots and dust on the succulent leaves. Bryan stammered through the things we had been told, that we were young and had excellent chances, that testing hadn't revealed any problems. Surely a change in protocol was all we needed.

She answered calmly and patiently, reminding us of our diagnosis of unexplained infertility, going through our test results again and our many failed attempts at timed intercourse, intrauterine insemination, and IVF. His voice and hers began to blend together, like they were underwater. Like I was underwater.

We were out of protocols to try, she explained. It didn't matter if all the test results looked fine on paper, sometimes things just didn't work.

I remembered meeting our doctor for the first time and noting that she was Asian, and then wondering if she had immigrant parents like mine, and if being a doctor was her choice or theirs, or if the line between what she wanted and what they wanted was impossible to see. Were they pleased? Or had she still disappointed them in some way, just as I had done all my parents wanted me to do, and was still a disappointment? And now I would disappoint them again by failing to have kids.

The orchid petals weren't smooth, but veined with shadows. Not something you'd notice with each flower so perfectly arranged along that simple, delicate arc. An arc that began to blur into a white smear as the tears rose and filled my eyes without spilling over.

"Pi?" said Bryan.

The doctor was staring at me, her sad but helpful expression somehow reminding me of a Labrador retriever.

"Sorry."

"Nothing to apologize for." She gave a brief sympathetic smile before briskly turning to pull a thick red folder out of her file drawer. "But I wanted to know if you'd considered donor eggs as an option."

I shook my head and blinked to shutter back the tears. This was not the time for crying. A calm and logical person would ask for more information, but my mind was blank. I scrambled for a question to demonstrate that I was okay. "How does that work?" Inside, I swore. It was an amateur question, we'd been doing IVF long enough to know this.

The doctor pretended not to notice. "It's like IVF, except we use someone else's eggs."

She began to explain about higher success rates and the steps in arranging a donor cycle, legal agreements to be made, counselling sessions to attend. I made notes without paying attention to what I was noting. I didn't look at Bryan.

"Do you have any female relatives, Payal?"

"Yes, a sister." Mom would be delighted if Shruti was my egg donor. One more reason why she was perfect. I crossed my legs.

"Good." The doctor leaned back. "If you can work with family or friends, that makes finding a donor easier, especially with your ethnicity."

I had a familiar sinking feeling.

She continued. "The problem is that there are very few South Asian donors available. But in those cases, we find selecting a Hispanic or Native donor usually comes out close enough."

I squirmed in the uncomfortable chair, recrossing my legs in the other direction. Bryan opened his mouth to say something, but I put a hand on his arm to quiet him, and he stopped. I knew what she meant; that a future child would resemble me enough that there would be no questions. But I also knew that it meant that as long as appearances were fine, nothing else mattered. And that we had to be okay with this because we had no choices.

Not we. I.

I didn't have choices.

Be professional. I straightened my back, looked the doctor in the eye and thanked her. "I think we need to talk all of this over."

She nodded. "It's a lot to take in." She handed us the red folder and stood up, ending the appointment. "All the information is in here. Let me know what you decide."

We were hardly in the elevator before Bryan started in. "Wow, can you believe she said that? Close enough? Really?"

I looked at the elevator buttons, pausing before pressing P2. I should have said something, but what? I leaned against the metal walls of the elevator, feeling the coldness through my jacket. I wished I had the orchid plant with me, that I had stolen it from the doctor's office, so I could shred the petals one by one until the stem was bare and empty.

"Don't say 'I told you so,'" said Bryan. "I know you're thinking it, but not now."

Anger snapped me upright. "What were you expecting? Balloons and party streamers? You see all the worried people in the waiting room every time we're here. That crying woman before us?"

"Well, screw me for being positive."

"I told you it wasn't going to go well."

The elevator doors opened and Bryan strode out ahead of me into the parking garage. I scurried after him, the red folder still in my hands. We got into the car silently and Bryan pulled out of the parking space before I even had my seatbelt on.

He turned south out of the garage towards the highway. "Wait, I have to go to Shannon's shop."

"Since when? The builder is expecting us." He glanced over at me.

"I have to go for work. It's important."

"So's our house."

"You can handle it without me. Just call me."

"Whatever," he muttered, and flipped his turn signal on.

We drove in silence. The early afternoon traffic was light but the streets were still busy with people, cars, and cyclists. I could see the red and yellow and green signs of old Chinatown, the sidewalks filled with sandwich board signs and small market stalls of food, priced with handwritten signs on neon Bristol board. I'd always meant to explore the area but I still hadn't. The city landscape soon changed, getting slicker as we passed by the Eaton Centre and Yonge-Dundas Square. Traffic slowed as more pedestrians stole across the street from between parked cars, and soon we were stuck behind a streetcar.

"About Shruti," started Bryan. "Are you going to talk to her?"

My mind skimmed over everything the doctor had said. If we didn't go through with this, we would never have children. But if Shruti came to the rescue, I'd still fail. My mom would know what we were doing and the advice would begin. All the reasons none of this would have happened if I'd listened to her more and been more like my sister would start and never end. It wouldn't matter that none of it was true. "We can't ask Shruti."

Bryan was in the middle of merging into traffic to get around construction, and it took him a second to reply. "Why not?"

"It would be a nightmare."

"But the doctor said..."

"I know what she said."

"So are you saying that we stop the process right here?"

I turned to the window, looking at my faint reflection instead of the cityscape going by. That was a choice we could make. I knew other people got married and didn't have kids. But before I could even picture it for us, I could hear my mother's voice in my head. *What would people say?* "Don't tell anyone about this."

"This is important," said Bryan. "We should talk it over with our family."

"No."

"I mean, if Shruti does this, the kids' aunt will sort of be their mother. Isn't this some kind of a family discussion?"

"No, and we aren't asking Shruti."

Bryan smacked the steering wheel with his palm, and then immediately grabbed the wheel again to swerve around a bike courier cutting across the road. "Fuck!"

I opened the red folder and pretended to read the papers inside. Bryan hated driving downtown. He'd be a lot happier when we moved out to the suburbs, to our own cookie-cutter house with its flat, barren lawn. The housing market was holding up; I could try to find some satisfaction in that.

"So if Shruti is off the table," said Bryan. He sounded calmer now. "What do we do? Stop, or try for close enough?"

"I don't know." I glanced down at the folder on my lap. "Maybe there's another option for us?"

"Of course," said Bryan. "We should explore all our choices." He glanced over his shoulder and changed lanes. "Are you sure you can't get out of this Shannon thing? It would be best if we went through the house together."

I pictured Bryan in our house, imagining furniture, people, our lives. Making plans, as if plans were reliable. We'd bought the house on the assumption that we'd be on our second child by the time it was move-in ready, and that we'd be outgrowing our tiny condo. I'd pictured us congratulating our past selves on the smart planning, and now we were going to go to look at a house full of empty rooms with no purpose to them.

"I really can't," I said. "Mom would kill me."

* * *

The tea shop was in West Queen West, one of those hipster neighbourhoods where every other store sold cupcakes or dog accessories. Shannon was talking to a customer when I walked in, but gracefully folded her hands and said "Namaste." I suppressed an eye roll and nodded slightly at her. The fresh white and green in the shop made her red hair pop in contrast.

I made my way to the back of the shop and down the stairs to the cramped closet that Shannon used as an office. It barely fit me and the computer, let alone the receipts and papers she'd left me. This should be Amit's job and not mine.

I booted up the computer and started QuickBooks. Even if Mom thought her precious Amit wasn't ready to do real work, he couldn't do worse than what Shannon had done on her own. The shop was doing well, but behind its bright, cheery fake-yoga face, her books were a mess.

But it was all basic bookkeeping. Shruti had gotten a lot of it tidied up; there was no reason for me to be the one doing the mundane data entry.

The red folder from the clinic was in the side of my laptop bag. If Bryan and I had kids, would they take over the business too? The thought was heavy. It had been a heavy day already, with all the expectations on the horizon: house, career, kids. I'd hoped the weight of these would lighten as I checked them off the To-Do list for my life, but they only seemed to get more complicated.

I could hear the creak and thud of people walking in and out of the shop above me, but I couldn't hear any of their voices or the lame sitar-like music Shannon had playing. No one up there had any idea that I was down here, breathing in the scent of damp basement and floral teas. I pulled out the folder and flipped through the pages, most of them advertisements for donor registries. I picked one and brought up the website, all pictures of delighted couples with babies giving those wet, gummy smiles that only babies could do. I wondered why I didn't have that melting feeling you're supposed to have. I had read so many articles on the Internet, late at night while Bryan was asleep, about how children weren't everything, how women didn't need children to fulfill them, how nobody should have children unless they really, really wanted them. But there were so many images of families with babies and small kids, joy emanating from all their faces. I wanted that feeling.

We can't have children, I thought, and whispered it out loud. I wanted it to sound worse than it did. It should be devastating.

There was no reason why I felt so grey. Nothing terrible had happened to me. I had done everything the right way, the way I was supposed to. The only thing missing were kids, and aside from that, wasn't this having it all?

Was emptiness the same as wanting something?

I set the folder aside and began tearing open the shop's bank statements and bills, relishing the loud *r-r-r-rip*, dropping the envelopes into the recycling and unfolding the papers inside, before sorting and smoothing them into neat stacks. I would get it all in order.

A knock startled me. Shannon stood at the door holding a vintage floral cup. "How are you doing down here?"

I glanced at the folder. Its cover was blank, anonymous, nothing that would raise questions. "Just trying to make sense of everything."

She shoved aside one of my carefully made stacks and set down the cup. "Thought I'd check in."

I wiggled the mouse and brought QuickBooks back to life. "Shouldn't you be upstairs?"

"They can handle it." She gestured at the tea. "New mix. Tell me what you think."

I didn't like herbal tea. Tea for Indian people was a hot, sometimes spiced, always overly sweet milky drink with some black tea-like flavour for balance. I held the cup's delicate handle and sniffed; the orange scent was promising, but the flavour was like acid in my mouth. I tried not to grimace. "Astringent."

Shannon laughed. "Good. People never trust health teas that are too sweet."

"Do they work?"

She laughed again. "They won't cure cancer. But this one is great for general immune function. Full of antioxidants. I call it ImmuniTea."

I tried very hard to not to grimace.

"Are you okay?"

"I'm fine." I picked up a bank statement and studied it. The numbers swam together on the page.

"How's my business running?"

I glanced at QuickBooks on the screen. The columns of debits and credits, the transactions and journal entries, the trial balance were clearly organized on the screen. I had done all the accounts right, everything by the book. But the numbers weren't making any sense right now. "It looks fine."

There was a tiny barstool beside the desk. Shannon pulled it into the doorway and perched on it. "Are you sure you're okay?"

"I'm fine."

She pulled a tissue from the pocket of her dress. "You seem a little upset."

I took the tissue and blotted my eyes. "It's the dust." We sat silently for a moment, both of us pretending I hadn't made a lame excuse.

She leaned towards me. "I know we don't know each other that well, Payal, but you're Amit's sister. Doesn't that make us family in your culture?"

According to my parents, it wouldn't make us anything at all, since Amit and Shannon weren't married, they were only living together. But I knew that Shannon would see it differently. I would see it differently too, except that it was Amit she was living with, and who knew if he was serious about her at all? But I nodded to avoid explaining.

"I'm a really good listener," persisted Shannon.

I gestured at the papers. "I have a lot of work to do."

"Can I help?" She reached for the papers on the desk and picked up the red folder.

I snatched it back. "I have a system. Don't mess it up."

She raised her hands as a peace offering and backed out of the room. "I'm sorry. I'll let you get to it."

I listened to her creak up the basement stairs. I shouldn't have left the folder out. If Shannon saw what we were doing, she'd probably have suggestions for some sort of bullshit tea. FertiliTea. What would a tea do that we hadn't already tried? The Vitamin D and the CoQ10 and yoga and eating pineapple cores and high-protein diets and taking cough syrup. None of it would change a medical impossibility.

I opened the folder again and flipped through the shiny pages. There was no harm in looking. I minimized QuickBooks, opened up a browser and signed up for one of the websites. It reminded me of an online dating site, with picture after picture of happy faces and personal statistics, except there were also childhood photos, degrees, and hereditary conditions. I clicked on random profiles in the sea of white faces. "Scottish and Italian background, musically talented" read one. "Mostly Scandinavian, athletic" read another.

I was neither musically talented or athletic. Maybe I could improve on things. Maybe if I were more confident, more outgoing, things would have been easier for me like they were for Amit. Or maybe my mother was right and I should be more like Shruti; everything was always effortless for her.

The website allowed me to search by race and country of origin. I searched for India. Zero hits. I tried again with Pakistan. Zero hits. Sri Lanka. Zero hits. Bangladesh. Zero hits. I picked South Asian. Zero hits. Nobody who looked like me or came from the same part of the world. I looked up Arabic. Zero hits. Not even a neighbouring part of the world.

I thought about what doctor said about close enough. Maybe it didn't matter. Maybe as long as the surface looked okay, it would be enough. My stomach churned; was it the tea? I looked up Hispanic and Native. Zero hits. Close enough was still very far.

I flipped back to "Mostly Scandinavian, athletic." As a child, I'd always wanted blond hair and blue eyes. I pictured myself with a white, blue-eyed baby. Posing for pictures with Santa. Taking the baby to the park. I would be mistaken for the nanny.

I tried another donor registry and another, but they were the same. Zero hits. One had an option to sign up on a waiting list. There would be other couples on the same list, willing to take the first donor that came up. People who knew they really, really wanted a child instead of me, who was so stupid I didn't even know what wanting one felt like, except that it was the only answer I had. I could feel a small tight ball in my chest, where my heart was, and feel my body shrinking into itself while tears spilled out. I cried as quietly as I could, so that if Shannon creaked back down the stairs, I wouldn't have to explain that I was crying for no reason.

CHAPTER TWO

September 1985, Toronto

"AMMAJI IS COMING SOON," said Mom.

"Who?"

She cuffed me on the side of the head. "Your grandmother, how come you don't know?"

I rubbed my head as I wandered up to my room, but I was excited. I quietly repeated, "My grandmother is called Ammaji," to myself to learn it. We had just done a unit on family trees at school, and the class had sat in a circle to say the name for their grandmother.

"Nanny."

"Gran."

"Bubbie."

"Nanna."

"Oma."

But when my turn came, I didn't have an answer. All of the kids stared at me. "You don't know your grandmother's name?" said Rachel.

I shook my head, enjoying the feel of my hair sliding over the back of my neck. "I've never met my grandmother."

"Neither of them?"

I shook my head again, this time short and quick, hoping it

would be a smaller no. She was looking at me like I was weird. I knew, because people always looked at me like that.

In my room, I pulled out the green construction paper tree, a Y with each branch split into another Y. In the middle, where the Ys came together, was me. I was glad there had been no room for Amit or Shruti on the tree. It was mine and mine alone.

We were supposed to put pictures of ourselves and our parents and grandparents on the tree. I ran my fingers over the blank green tips. I had no pictures of my grandparents that I could glue to the tree. Mom and Dad had some black-and-white ones in the photo album, but there was no way they'd let me take them to school. They were small pictures anyway, my grandparents sitting stiffly beside each other in Indian clothes.

I didn't get in trouble for not finishing my tree, but my teacher put it up on the board with everyone else's with colour pictures of grandmothers smiling with their teeth showing and grandfathers in knitted sweaters. No one else had blank spaces.

It was like the first day of school, when the teacher tried three times to say my name and made me say it out loud in front of the whole class, and then repeated it and asked me if it was right. After a while, I nodded, even though it was still wrong. She said it "Pay-yal" and that meant the whole class called me that too. I came home and make the mistake of asking my mom why she didn't give me a normal name like Jennifer or Sarah and then she slapped me and told me Payal was a beautiful name. I didn't believe her. No Jennifer had to say her name out loud in front of everyone.

No Sarah didn't know the name of her grandmother.

But now I knew, and she was coming for a visit, so maybe I would get a colour photo for my tree.

The day Ammaji was supposed to arrive, Mom cooked a lot. Mom always cooked a lot, but she even kept cooking after dinner. "Ammaji might be hungry when she gets here."

"Is she bringing me a present?" Lots of kids in my class had grandmothers and grandfathers visit and they all got presents. Plus more on Christmas and birthdays. But others had grandparents they saw every week when they went there for dinner, and they didn't get presents, so visiting grandparents seemed like a better idea.

Mom cuffed me on the top of my head.

Shruti giggled from her playpen. "Pi bad!"

"So selfish! Your ammaji is coming all the way from India to see you, and all you ask about are presents? What would people think?"

I'd gotten that wrong too. Wrong at home and wrong at school.

I tried to stay up late to wait for Ammaji but I feel asleep in the living room. I dreamed of my grandmother. She floated down in a puffy white cloud like the snow white puff of hair curled around her head. She wore pink lipstick with a matching fuzzy sweater and smelled like chocolate chip cookies. "I love you, sweet pea," she said, and handed me a huge, red box with a silver bow, and when I opened it, a puppy jumped out and licked my face.

I woke up in my own bed hearing voices in the kitchen. One was my mother's. The other was sharp and sounded like it was coming out of someone's nose. They were speaking Gujarati, so I didn't understand what they said.

I crept halfway down the stairs in my Strawberry Shortcake pyjamas and sat. In the kitchen were Mom and Shruti, and with them was a woman in a white cotton sari. I'd never seen such a plain sari. Mom only wore them to go to parties, taking them out from the high shelves in her closet where they were wrapped in cloth, but those saris were shiny and bright-coloured and covered in gold and silver threads. This one could have been bedsheets. Old bedsheets. I could see her from the back, her hair in a long, thin grey braid. I felt my own hair. It was tangled and I'd never worn it in one braid. I couldn't do it myself and Mom said it took too long to do it for me, especially after she'd pulled Shruti's hair into two ponytails. The woman was barefoot, and I could tell from the hand gestures that my mom was trying to convince her to sit down and she wouldn't. Shruti sat on the floor, pouring pretend tea into a blue plastic cup.

I edged down one more step but Mom saw me. She waved me over. "Payal! Come." I glanced up the stairs, but Amit's door was still closed. The woman in the white sari turned around. She was old and wrinkled and her face looked caved-in at the cheeks. I shook my head.

The woman spoke sharply to Mom, who repeated her order to come in a louder voice, so I uncurled my legs and came down the stairs one at a time.

"This is your ammaji," said Mom, leading her to me. "Page lagavum. Touch her feet."

I looked up at Mom. "I know what it means."

"So do it," she said, pushing me.

I bent down and touched the woman's feet. They were old and dry and wrinkled, and her toenails were turning yellow. I stood up and folded my hands. Mom breathed out like she was relaxing, and Ammaji put a hand on my head and smoothed out my hair. Then she spoke in Gujarati.

"She's saying you are very big," said Mom. They spoke to each other for a moment, and then Ammaji looked at me and spoke. Her voice went up at the end, so I knew it was a question. She said it again, slowly. She had a big diamond in her nose. Mom had a small diamond in her nose. I rubbed my nose, all skin, no stones.

Mom translated. "She wants to know why you haven't come to India for so long."

I shrugged my shoulders.

"We could put you in the suitcase and she could take you with her."

I didn't know what to say. Mom was smiling like she loved the idea, but I didn't want to go. I looked at my feet. They were small compared to the brown kitchen tile. I lined up my foot inside one.

They spoke a little more and then Mom sat me down for breakfast. "Ammaji has brought laddu from India for you."

Laddu. We had to go all the way to Gerrard Street for laddu, deep orange balls of sweet. I never got to eat them for breakfast.

Ammaji brought a small cardboard box, edged with purple diagonal stripes. She lifted the lid off, and a sweet, spiced smell came out. Inside were brown balls.

"Take one," said Mom.

I looked up at her. "They're supposed to be orange."

"Those are orange laddu. These are brown laddu."

"What if I don't like it?" I wasn't allowed to not finish my food, because all the Indian grown-ups always told me that if I didn't finish, it was going in my hair. Mom, Dad, all the uncles and aunties at Indian parties. But they always put too much food I didn't like on my plate.

Mom took one out of the box and set it in front of me. "Ammaji made these for you." Her voice was coming out louder and faster. Shruti began crying, because Mom wasn't taking the pretend tea she was offering, but Mom just stood over me and waited.

I picked it up and looked at Ammaji, who was looking at me and not Shruti. She didn't seem mad at all, not like Mom. Her eyes met mine steadily, and then she smiled. I took a bite. It was sweet, but not as sweet as the orange ones. It was cold but tasted warm like gur, which was a sticky brown Indian sugar, and a little bit hot—taste hot, not temperature hot—but not too hot like when Mom gave me Indian food full of fat pieces of ginger. It was good. I chewed and swallowed and took another bite, a big one this time. And then another and another and it was gone.

Ammaji smiled again and put another brown laddu on my plate. She spoke softly to me in Gujarati, saying my name but nothing else I understood, and stroked my tangled hair.

* * *

I followed Ammaji like a shadow, even when she was fussing over Amit and Shruti. I showed her my room and all of my toys, especially my favourite Barbie dolls. She helped me braid their long hair and tie the ends with bits of yarn. I didn't even mind that we had to eat Indian food for every meal, though I asked Mom if we could have pizza instead. She got mad for a second and told me that I loved Indian food, though I didn't. She used a smiley voice, and looked at Ammaji when she said it. But I loved pizza and maybe Ammaji would too.

Ammaji sang songs to me in Gujarati which I didn't understand except for "ek, be, tra" which was "one, two, three." So I taught her the same words in English, repeating them over and over until she got it. Maybe if I repeated every word I knew, she'd be able to talk to me.

Every night I fell asleep leaning against Ammaji in the living room, the sandalwood smell of her white cotton sari in my nose. But Monday morning rolled around and Mom shook me awake and told me I was going to be late for school.

"Do I have to go to school?" But Mom didn't answer.

I forced myself out of my cozy pyjamas and into my favourite pink corduroy pants and stripey sweatshirt, before sleepily making my way downstairs.

Ammaji asked questions, which Mom answered and translated for me. "She wants to know where your school uniform is. When we were little, we had to wear a uniform to school every day. And our hair had to be in two plaits."

"Plaits?"

Mom searched for the word on the ceiling. "Braids."

After breakfast, I sat cross-legged on the floor in front of the couch, waiting for Mom to brush my hair. I was nervous for the hair brushing, because my hair was always tangled and Mom always pulled hard and I always cried, and then Mom always yelled at me for crying. Then she'd tell me that Shruti never cried when her hair was brushed, which was not true, but there would be more yelling if I said that.

Ammaji sat cross-legged on the floor and gestured for me to sit in front of her. She spoke to Mom, who came back with a white jar with green letters on it. She gave it to Ammaji who opened it up and let me smell it. Coconut.

"Do you know what this is?" said Mom. I shook my head. "Coconut oil."

"It doesn't look like oil."

"It's for your hair," said Mom. "Your ammaji puts coconut oil in her hair every night. And when we were little, she would massage it into our heads and then plait our hair for school."

Ammaji scraped a soft white lump out of the jar, and rubbed her hands together fast. She pulled them apart, and the white was gone and her hands were oily. She put them on my head and began to gently rub. Her hands felt soft and warm and strong, and made my head feel pillowed, like in that moment before you fall asleep, snuggled down under soft blankets. Except I was awake.

"It's good for your hair," said Mom. "Keeps your head cool and your hair soft."

Ammaji ran her fingers through my hair without catching anything. No tangles! Surprised, I combed my own hair with my fingers, feeling it smoothly slide against the webs of my fingers. Nothing caught or pulled. I smelled coconut on my hands. Ammaji took the hairbrush and stroked it through my hair. "It doesn't hurt at all!"

"Thank God," said Mom.

Ammaji parted my hair in the middle and pulled it into two braids, finishing them off with elastic bands. I swung my head back and forth, pleased at the new feeling of two small ropes of hair hitting my shoulders.

Amit walked with me to school, Ammaji waving to us as we left, but once we got to the school yard, some of the big kids shouted his name and he ran off the join them as usual. I stayed near the edge of the playground until the bell rang.

The other kids didn't say anything about my braids when we were lined up to go in, or even when we first got into class and sat at our desks, but as the day went on, they were looking at me and whispering.

Rachel told me why during recess. "Everyone wants to know why your hair is greasy. Don't you wash it?"

"I wash my hair!" My eyes stung a little bit.

"But why is it dirty?"

"It's not dirty," I said. "There's coconut oil in it."

She looked at me, puzzled. "Why would you put oil in your hair?"

My head was getting warm. "It's something Indian people do." She kept looking at me, like I was a half-squished bug. "My grandmother did it."

She wrinkled her nose at me. "You shouldn't go around with dirty hair. You'll get bugs. Then I won't be able to play with you." She walked away to play with some other girls. I didn't dare join them.

All day, everyone looked at me. I couldn't hide my head, and when Amit came to walk me home I ran ahead of him the whole way to get home fast. Mom had barely opened the door before I screamed at her. "Why did you send me to school with oil in my hair?"

She looked to Amit for explanations, but he only shrugged. I cried and shouted, words coming out in pieces. Ammaji stepped forward, tried to grab hold of my hands to keep me still, but I shouted at her. "I don't like you. Let me go."

Mom slapped me. "How can you say that? Respect your elders."

I looked at Ammaji for help but she said nothing. She didn't do anything except try to hold me still. I pulled away from her and ran into my room. No one understood. I could hear them talking in Gujarati downstairs and couldn't understand them either. Still crying, I picked up my Barbie dolls and started undoing their braids. Their hair fell loose and untangled, silkier and blonder than mine would ever be.

CHAPTER THREE

November 2010, Toronto

I SPRITZED THE WHITE PLASTIC BALCONY CHAIRS with more Fantastik, and then blew on my cold fingers before rubbing the worn, blackened scrubby against the seats. Water and pollution had pooled and dried where the backs met the seats. There was no way these would ever get clean.

I sat back on my haunches and surveyed the street below. The roads were oddly empty; barricades had been placed on either side in preparation for the Santa Claus Parade. Bryan and I were preparing to host a viewing party for our families.

Bryan came out onto the balcony. "No one is going to do surgery on those chairs."

"They look grimy."

"We could have gotten new ones."

We'd had this discussion before. I pushed my hair out of my face with the back of my wrist. "There's no point in getting a couple of new chairs when we'll need a full patio set for the new house."

"Summer stuff's on sale though. We could have found cheap ones."

"Cheaper than free?" Mom had given us these chairs. She had dozens of them stacked in her basement to use for parties. All of them had been spotless.

"I'll deal with the chairs. Go in and warm up."

I handed him the dirty scrubby and the Fantastik bottle and squeezed past him. Bryan had arranged the room while I was fussing with the balcony chairs. He'd put out our small tabletop tree on the computer desk. The cookies I'd made were on a plate beside a supermarket tray of veggies and a shrimp ring on the coffee table. Bryan was more excited for this party than I was, even though it was technically my idea.

Last week, after we'd seen our fertility doctor, he'd been upset that I cancelled on our appointment to go over finishes at the house instead of cancelling on Shannon. "It's like you don't even want to move."

"Of course I do!" I pushed away the little quiver of a question starting to form in my brain. "It'll be so great. We'll have so much space for—" I didn't want to say *children* "—parties and gatherings. The open concept will be perfect for that." I gestured around our condo. "This place really isn't big enough for having people over."

"We used to make it work," said Bryan. He had slumped on the couch, staring out the balcony window at the greyed-out sky.

He had been right; we used to have people—mostly Bryan's friends—over for game nights or drinks, or we would go over to their places. It was like being on *Friends*, with everyone eventually coupling up. But over time, our friends starting having kids, and getting together became difficult, especially as they began moving to the suburbs.

"They're leading different lives now," I had said. "You remember what it was like—everyone had a kid's birthday party, or swim lessons, or it was nap time." I hadn't wanted to see our old friends anyway. We were falling so far behind other people, and every gathering, with its conversations about daycares and baby sleep and questions about when we were having kids, had only made me more conscious of how I was failing at life.

"It doesn't have to be a party-party," Bryan had said. "We could have our families."

The idea had worried me. What would my parents and Bryan's parents even talk about? How would we entertain Bryan's niece and nephew without any kids' toys? What would we feed everyone? My mom already thought I was incompetent in the kitchen; she'd be extra critical of my inability to cook dinner for a group.

"We can't," I had said. "We couldn't fit a table big enough for everyone to sit properly in here."

"It doesn't have to be dinner. We could have people over in the afternoon." He'd sat up straighter.

"And do what? Have tea? Greg would never go for that." Bryan's brother-in-law was a beer and hockey guy.

"No, but—"

"Or watching the game? My parents don't watch sports. Watch the Santa Claus parade?"

"We could do that," Bryan had interrupted. His face had brightened up. "The kids could watch from the balcony."

"It's too much work."

"We'll do cookies and hot chocolate," Bryan had said. "How much work could it be?"

And so here I was, trying to scrub grime off balcony chairs. I went into the kitchen to wash cleaning spray off my hands and surveyed the room. Barb, Bryan's mom, considered our tiny little tree a half-assed effort. Her home was like the Griswolds: every square inch lit and decorated, and yet she always found room for new decorations. Even my parents would have strung up lights for Diwali and left them up through the Christmas holidays. On the coffee table was our meagre offering of food. They'd find all this very uninspiring.

I tried rearranging the food to make it look more abundant on the table. The cookies I'd made looked terrible. I couldn't get the Santa icing coloured right and it had all flowed together to make pink and white blobs. At least the trees looked somewhat like Christmas trees.

I straightened out the vegetables on the tray, lining up the sticks of celery and pale lumps of button mushrooms. We should have taken it out of the plastic tray. Bought some glass serving dishes at Winners, some kind of a segmented circle around a dip bowl like the ones my mom had. Next to the veggies were the shrimp; the circle of fleshy pink bodies bothered me, which meant they would bother my mother more. She'd never touched meat in her life. I picked up the ring and moved it to the breakfast bar. Was it odd to not have it with the rest of the food? Would someone move it to the coffee table anyway for convenience? Would it end up like our wedding, everyone siloed on their side of the room, with Bryan's family gathered around the shrimp ring and mine by the veggies, leading to a disastrously stilted and boring party? I moved it back to the coffee table.

Bryan came in and flipped on the lights to our tiny tree. There was a soft whir as the LED rotated and lit up the plastic strands in different colours, red, blue, green, yellow, white, and then red again. He picked up a paper crane from the small pile on the red folder and stuck it into the tree. He picked up another.

"Just toss those out." Folding cranes was a nervous habit of mine. I began rotating the veggie tray to see if I could find the best angle, as if that could make a supermarket tray of cut vegetables look better.

"I like them."

"They're made of scrap paper. It's junk." I should have thrown them out earlier. Or not made them at all.

He shrugged and pulled them out of the tree, but dropped them back into the pile on the desk.

I scanned the room. "Do you think it's Christmassy enough in here?"

"Just one more thing." Bryan clicked his iPod into the speaker dock, and Christmas music filled the room. "Perfect."

The music made the room feel sadder, the overhead lights too bright and the condo walls too bare. In six years, we still hadn't managed to put up any pictures. "It looks like Christmas was only an afterthought in here."

Bryan squeezed my shoulders and went to get dressed. "The party is going to be fine."

Christmas put me on uncertain ground. All the TV shows I'd grown up with made it clear that Christmas was a big deal. As a child, we would occasionally have a token celebration with a few gifts and perhaps a tree. We'd have a family dinner of some kind, mostly because the holiday gave us an excuse to have dinner together. But it was a little bit like playacting. There was no tradition to it, no excitement, nothing special that we looked forward to all year. No recipe for cookies that grandma used to make. No ritual for how and when presents were opened. No real feeling behind it, just a checklist of a few things to do so that we could say that we had made a gesture.

Still, nothing I'd imagined about a real Christmas celebration quite matched up to the reality. I remembered being excited to try cranberry sauce the first time I'd gone to Christmas dinner at Bryan's parents' house. I'd been confused by the glass plate of jellied slices from the can.

I brushed the cranes off the red folder and into the garbage. We still hadn't talked about the appointment or what we were going to do. I picked up the tree and slid the folder underneath, knocking over the Christmas cards from Barb and Bryan's sister Lindsey. Sending out cards was another thing I'd failed to do.

My sister was the first to arrive, carrying a platter. She set it on the counter and turned on the oven so she could warm the food, but first she peeled back the foil to reveal samosas arranged in a Christmas tree, with round kachoris placed as decorations.

The pastry was even tinted green and red. "Naresh is bringing up the rest. He's just looking for parking."

"Did you make those?"

"It's easy." She started re-arranging the plates on the coffee table and then pulled out a package of Santa napkins from her purse. "I saw these at the Dollar Store and thought they'd be a nice touch. Cute, right?"

I'd forgotten about napkins entirely.

She circled the condo, and stepped out on the balcony. "Do you have one of those Magic Eraser things for the chair?"

I joined her outside. The chairs were just as grimy as before, and the cleaning supplies were exactly where I'd left them. Bryan hadn't done a thing. "I don't think so."

She considered the chairs thoughtfully. "Get some blankets and put them on the chairs. It'll be cozier that way anyway."

By the time I'd dug out some extra blankets from our over-stuffed closet, my parents and Naresh were inside and on the couch complaining to each other about the road closures and parking difficulties. Shruti had taken the samosas out of the oven and moved on to adjusting the decorations on our small tree; she'd thankfully left Bryan alone to start the kettle and set up an assembly line of mugs.

My mom waved at the pre-cut carrots and celery. "You didn't cook?"

"I made cookies." Mom inclined her head slightly, saying nothing. "It's not that kind of a party."

"You invite people to your home, you should feed them."

I waved at the food on the coffee table. "We have food."

"You should feed them properly." She picked up a samosa. "At least Shruti brought you some food." She took a small bite, chewed a moment while appraising it, and nodded. Acceptable. "Shruti, this is too much trouble. Even I don't make samosas."

"It's no trouble," said Shruti.

Mom started rhyming off stores that sold good samosas. Dad picked up a Santa-shaped cookie, questioning the smeary pink and white icing with his eyes before taking a cautious bite. His expression never changed as he chewed disinterestedly, as though he was only putting in time before moving on to a more important task.

Bryan brought out the tea and drew my parents into conversation. He was better at talking to them than I was. Shruti eventually stopped fixing the decor and sat beside Naresh. For a moment, we were a TV family, chatting, snacking, having a pleasant time.

Bryan's sister Lindsey arrived with her kids and her husband, Greg. The kids, Ethan and Madison, barged in. "Uncle Bryan! Uncle Bryan!"

"Hey rugrats!" He picked them both up and turned them upside down while they screamed in delight. Tomorrow, he would complain that his back was sore.

Greg headed to our fridge, taking a Canadian out of the six-pack he'd brought and putting the rest away. "Hey, Bry guy, you want one?" Bryan didn't answer. He and the kids had collapsed in a giggling heap.

Bryan's parents, Larry and Barb, arrived next, and within a few minutes, we had a party. Lindsey and Bryan took the kids out on the balcony to watch the parade, and soon the adults were running out with snacks and hot chocolate, and the kids popping in to express their excitement or their boredom at seeing the floats and marching bands. Dad and Naresh began talking about business. Larry and Greg set themselves up next to the shrimp ring and were praising the newly elected mayor, Rob Ford. Meanwhile, Barb started talking to my mom and Shruti about her new Shark steam mop and how it compared to her old Swiffer WetJet. Mom agreed with her animatedly, even though she hadn't had anyone but her cleaning lady touch her floors in years.

I began to worry if my floors were clean enough, and excused myself to the kitchen. I tried to look busy, wiping down the already clean counters.

Shruti's samosas and kachoris were steadily disappearing. Hardly anyone had touched the cookies. In the kitchen, I had a container that I had set aside with the extra-terrible ones that were a little bit burned. I tried a bite. Rock hard.

Bryan came in from outside, blowing on his hands to warm them up, smiling and joking with everyone on his way to join me in the kitchen. "What are you doing here by yourself?"

"Just tidying up."

He took the cloth from my hand and dropped it in the sink. "It's a party, enjoy yourself." He led me over to everyone else.

"Hey Bry guy," said Greg. "How come you're still using an iPod? You should get one of those new iPhones." He pulled it out of his pocket and brought up a map. "Look, it knows where I am." He tapped it a few times and raised it to his mouth before tilting his head back, and the phone screen showed amber liquid tilting and emptying as a pint glass would. "Check it out, I'm drinking a beer!"

"Not like we haven't seen that a million times," said Lindsey.

"I have Angry Birds too," said Greg. "One sec." He began jabbing away at the phone.

"Payal," started Mom. "I need your passports." She nodded in Bryan's direction. "Both of yours."

"What for?"

She pulled out a large gold envelope from her purse, and from the envelope, a series of glittering gold cards, decorated with red elephants and red writing, and left them on the table. I recognized it as an invitation to an Indian wedding. "Malika got engaged."

"Who?" asked Bryan.

"My cousin," I said. "In Mumbai." I was annoyed that he didn't know this already.

"The wedding is excellent timing. Christmas holidays," said Mom. "Nothing open, nothing to miss."

"Tickets are more expensive," said Dad, resettling himself on the couch.

My mind began running through the checklist of tasks that were needed to make this happen. If Shruti pitched in with some of the actual accounting, and Amit didn't make a hack job of all the admin, and I got all the critical files onto my laptop for some remote work, we could probably manage shutting down the office for a couple of weeks.

"This Christmas?" said Barb. "So soon?"

"There's no reason to wait," said Mom. "It's a good match."

"Shotgun wedding, huh?" said Greg. Everyone ignored him.

"Don't they need time to plan the wedding?" asked Barb.

"What's to plan?" said Mom. "In India, it's very simple. They call the caterer, they call the tailors. Everything is easy."

I thought back to my own wedding, the number of fights I'd had with Mom, who would simply call the caterer or the florist without telling me. Every single time I found out, I'd protest and she'd look at me blankly and say "You don't know how to do things properly. I'm only making things easier for you." And then I'd have to explain to Bryan no matter what we'd decided on, things were different now, and he would in turn have to explain to his mom, who would call me, confused by the changes, and ask me to make sense of what happened. And I'd have to explain my mom's decisions to her, as if I agreed with it, because how would it look otherwise? The bridal magazines kept saying this was my big day, but no one was having that.

Bryan was still confused. "Why do you need our passports?"

"To arrange your visas," said Mom. "Oh, and you need to get photos done."

Barb turned to Bryan. "You're going to India? It's Christmas."

Of course we are, I thought before realizing that I was the only one who considered this trip a given.

"We aren't going," said Bryan.

"It's Malika's wedding," said Mom. "I've already booked your tickets."

Bryan set his mug down with a loud *thwap*.

"You can't go on vacation over Christmas," said Barb.

"It's not a vacation," I said. "It's India."

"You knew about this?" asked Bryan.

"No." I was taken aback.

"We can't just pick up and go." He stopped himself before saying what I knew he was thinking: *because your mother wants us to.*

Mom began explaining to Barb. "You see, in our culture, weddings are important."

"They're important for everyone. So is Christmas."

I knew there would be no talking Mom out of this, only talking Bryan into it. But I had no explanation for him that went deeper than "it's our culture," which gave me an uneasy feeling of using something that was mine but didn't belong to me.

Bryan hadn't given up. "I can't get the time off."

"Just explain to your boss it's a family wedding," said Mom.

Naresh smiled. "It doesn't work that way here."

I could feel the weight of the explanation I would have to have with Bryan settle on my shoulders. I would have to make him understand why we could not miss this wedding halfway around the world, for a cousin I rarely saw or spoke to but was close family nonetheless. There was no excuse for missing any wedding in our community, except possibly to attend another one, and even that was dicey. Plus the entire community had to be invited when your child got married and then others were obligated to reciprocate by inviting everyone back when it was their child's turn. During the matrimonial season in Toronto, my mom would often go to the ceremony and lunch for one wedding, and the reception and dinner for another, every Saturday and Sunday, weekend and after weekend. Consequently, when I married Bryan, the small event we'd wanted had ballooned in size as my mother satisfied her many social obligations.

"Ammaji hasn't met Bryan," said Mom. "Who knows how long she has left? This is the perfect time to go."

There was a knock at the door, and I scrambled off the couch to get away from the discussion. Amit and Shannon strolled in. "I'm so sorry we're late." Shannon pulled off her knitted toque and smoothed her curls. "The shop was crazy today." She passed me a small box. "This is for you. Special holiday blend. I call it FestiviTea."

I sniffed. It smelled pepperminty. What on earth were we going to do with this?

"Hey Hollywood," said Greg. "You land any big roles?"

Amit's face grinned, but there was an edge to his voice. "I'm taking a breather. Helping out Dad. Oh, and Payal too."

"If you can call it help," I muttered.

The kids slid the balcony door open. "Uncle Bryan, can we watch Treehouse?"

"You don't want to wait for Santa?" asked Bryan.

They came in and grabbed the remote. "Mom's outside. She'll tell us," said Ethan.

"It's too cold," said Madison.

This party was going well.

Greg beckoned Amit over. "Tell me again about that time you spilled water on Cameron Diaz."

I left the living room and joined Lindsey on the balcony; I didn't need to hear Amit's inane star stories again. She smiled at me, so I pretended to busy myself re-arranging the blankets on the chairs. The sun shone brightly but the balcony was cold and felt empty. The astroturf poked through my thick socks. The cold was calming. I pretended to admire the view, the buildings that formed the city skyline, the crowds on the sidewalk watching the parade. The city was always so full, people everywhere. I tried to imagine what they did with their lives. Went to work and went home and what else? What else was there? Because surely there had to be more than this, than work and marriage and obligations.

I wished I was down on the street among them, breathing in the wintry air and breathing out smoky-looking vapour, finding my own place to stand amongst the kids screaming for Santa, or reaching to shake hands with the upside-down clowns. I wished I was one of the clowns.

Lindsey made a pretend smoking gesture, blowing out a cloud of vapour and then smiling. "Cold out here."

"Yeah."

The marching band below playing Good King Wenceslas covered up the silence. Lindsey and I had never chatted much. Somehow, Amit had befriended Bryan's entire family during brief interactions with them at our wedding, but I still couldn't get past small talk.

"How's your journey?" Lindsey glanced through the window at the kids, still watching TV.

"My what?"

"Like how are things going?" She patted my arm. The carol music faded off, and a new song that I couldn't quite place was trying to make its way in. "I know it's hard to talk about, but I wanted you to know that I'm here for you."

I was both confused and cold. "Sure."

"Did you know that Sarah Jessica Parker used a surrogate? And she had, like, twins. Isn't that awesome?"

I nodded slowly. If Lindsey wanted celebrity gossip, she'd be better off talking to Shruti. Or Amit. I was sure he had some kind of a Sarah Jessica Parker story. The song from the next float in the parade was now clear: the Christmas song from *Alvin and the Chipmunks*.

"I've been giving it a lot of thought since Bryan told me, and I just wanted you to know that I'd be honoured to be your surrogate. And I totally hope it's twins too, because how cute would that be to have matching clothes?"

I blinked rapidly, torn on what to explain first, that we didn't need a surrogate but also that she wasn't supposed to know any of this. And also that twins meant a high-risk pregnancy. She pulled me in for a hug, but I remained a statue, and she kept yammering on about baby stuff she'd kept for us and twin outfits she'd seen. "Lindsey," I interrupted her. "We don't need a surrogate."

"But Mom told me that Bryan said—"

Barb knew too? I interrupted her again. "We don't need one. At our last appointment, our doctor told us—"

"Oh my God, are you pregnant?" She shrieked and hugged me again. "Am I the first to know?"

"Lindsey—"

The sliding door banged open. Greg. "Who's pregnant?"

Lindsey ran in from the balcony. "It's a Christmas miracle! Pi is pregnant!"

The room erupted into a chorus of congratulations and conversations, with Greg loudly repeating "I'm just glad it's not me." Mom's complaints that I hadn't told her blurred with Barb hoping for a girl, Shannon recommending a tea, and some kind of a cartoon blaring from the TV that the kids sat watching, ignoring all the commotion in the room.

Bryan looked at me in confusion as I stepped back inside and slid the door shut behind me. I shook my head and mouthed *Do something.*

"Hey everyone!" he shouted. "Hold up a second." The room quieted but for the TV. "Pi has something to say."

They all turned towards me, and I had no choice but to disappoint them. "I'm not pregnant."

"So I can be your surrogate," asked Lindsey.

I glared at Bryan but he looked away.

"You want to carry your brother's baby?" said Greg. "Gross."

"It's not, it's beautiful."

"How come you need a surrogate?" asked Mom.

"We don't need a surrogate."

"So what are you doing with the fertility doctor?" said Barb. "How come there haven't been any babies in all this time?"

Bryan still said nothing, and I wished I had something to throw at him, something big and heavy, if only to get some sort of a sound out of him that might lead to an explanation.

"Payal, you never told me you were seeing a doctor." Mom rearranged herself on the sofa. "Who is your doctor? How do you know if they any good?" She turned to my Dad. "Who is that doctor Kishor's son saw? Payal should go see him."

"My doctor is fine."

"How can you know? You have no children yet."

"Did you try IVF?" asked Shruti. "I hear that works really well."

I glared at Bryan for starting this conversation where I would have to answer everyone's naive questions about the problems and failures we'd been living with for years, but that they didn't understand. When we'd first started wondering if we needed medical intervention, we'd thought the fixes would be simple. The movies always made them seem simple. Waiting for my temperature to go up. Bryan wearing boxers. Lying with my legs up after sex. The Internet advised eating the core of a pineapple for five days after ovulation. We'd thought IVF was an extreme measure, but that it would be a sure thing. We'd spent the last few years chipping away at all our illusions about this process, that everything we'd seen in the movies was bullshit, and we were left with the hard kernel of truth: medical science had very few solutions.

"Isn't that what all the celebrities do?" Greg flipped a bottle cap at Amit. "You have any connections for this, Hollywood?"

Amit rolled his eyes.

Any moment now, one of them was going to tell us to just adopt, as if we'd never considered that before, and without considering how complicated and hard that process was.

"I really loved being pregnant," said Lindsey. "I'd be a great surrogate. I'd have had another baby, but Greg doesn't want a third."

"We're broke enough," said Greg.

"They have excellent surrogates in India," said Mom. "The best. Premal Aunty's daughter, that's what she did."

Lindsey kept talking. "But it would be so beautiful. We could have a baby shower."

"There's no shower for your third baby," said Barb.

"But it would be Payal's first," argued Lindsey.

"It's a good system," said Dad, nodding. "They do everything for you. Even the Canadian citizenship. It's very easy."

Shannon spoke up. "Isn't that exploitive?"

Mom shook her head. "Oh no, they get paid very well. They live in a separate hostel so doctors can take care of them. They get rest from housework and all their other children. It's a very good system."

Lindsey and her mother kept talking about pregnancy etiquette for a surrogacy that we didn't even need. Shannon changed topics with my mom to talk about Ayurvedic methods and herbal teas for fertility, yoga poses I could try. Shruti and Naresh spoke quietly to each other. Greg harangued my brother with stories of how much the kids were bleeding his bank account dry. Our fathers nodded along, adding little to the conversation, Larry taking the opportunity to inhale the shrimp. The kids laughed at the blaring TV. And Bryan said nothing, and somehow the silence from him was the only thing I could hear.

The lights on our small Christmas tree, the one sitting atop the red folder, blinked out, not that the room could be less festive. I couldn't even throw a Christmas party right.

I interrupted everyone to explain what we had tried, what our doctors had said, and where we were now.

"So what's the problem?" said Mom. "You get an egg donor, you're done." She made it sound like we could pick one like a dandelion from a field, as if half the DNA of our child didn't matter.

"You guys need to get going on the grandchildren," said Barb.

Bryan spoke up at last. "There aren't many South Asian egg donors." As if it were my fault this was so difficult.

"Oh," said Mom. "Simple. Shruti will donate her eggs. It's all the same thing."

I saw Shruti ever so gently rub her belly, and the knowledge of what she would say hit me like a rock to my chest.

"I can't," said Shruti. "I'm pregnant."

The room once again erupted in congratulations, and I took the chance to approach Bryan and angry-whisper in his ear. "I thought we weren't telling anyone."

"I thought we weren't spending Christmas in India, but apparently we have plane tickets." He pushed passed me before I could speak, and headed out on the balcony. I stared at his back, willing him to turn around, but he stared out over the parade.

The party carried on. Lindsey and Barb told Shruti all about their childbirth stories. *If we don't have children, I don't have to go through that.* Greg managed to cajole the kids away from the TV and took them back out onto the balcony. The plate of cookies slowly started emptying once Naresh discovered that dunking them in tea made them edibly soft.

Shannon came around and sat next to me. "You okay?"

"I'm fine." She didn't say anything for a moment. I picked up one of Shruti's samosas. I'd barely eaten all day, and she was a way better cook than I was.

Shannon gathered up her hair in her hands, twisted it up into a bun, and then let go, stretching her arms up as her hair unfurled. "I had a thought," she said.

I took a big bite of samosa and chewed as visibly as I could.

"If they have surrogacy programs in India, surely they have egg donors there too." She tucked a stray curl behind her ear. "Maybe it's still exploitive, I don't know. But there has to be a lot more Indian egg donors there, right?"

I swallowed quickly, gagging a little as the too-big mouthful went down. Could this solve everything? Questions rose in my mind about the practicalities. How long would we have to stay in India? What about medical records, what would they need? How would we get them there?

"And since we're all going soon anyway, maybe you could check out a few clinics. There have to be reputable places in Mumbai."

"You're coming too?" My forehead creased as I turned over questions in my mind. How long had Amit known about this India trip? Did Shruti know before too? She would have told me if she had. Wouldn't she?

She squealed and did a little tap dance with her feet. "I've always wanted to go to India. And a wedding too! Indian weddings are so vibrant." She nattered on, telling me about a supplier of hers that was able to get her a room at the Taj Mahal hotel.

"You're staying at the Taj?" Of course Amit would get to stay at a luxury hotel in downtown Mumbai.

"But I'm totally looking forward to seeing some of the real India with your family," she said earnestly.

I made a noncommittal noise. I bet all of her expectations for India were based on *Monsoon Wedding*. Did Mom even know that Shannon was coming? I glanced her way. She was chatting with Shruti and Lindsey. She looked calm; it seemed unlikely that she knew.

The balcony door slid open with a thud. Bryan stood in the doorway and looked around the room, skipping over me. "It's Mrs. Claus. Santa's up next." Everyone pulled themselves up and shuffled out. Bryan stepped inside to make more room on the balcony.

"Bryan," I started, but he shook his head and turned his back to me to watch the parade through the windows, even if there was no way he'd be able to see.

CHAPTER FOUR

January 1992, Toronto

MISSING A MONTH OF GRADE SIX sounded great, except I had to spend it in India. My teacher had been way more enthused about the trip than I was.

"How long has it been since you've been home?" she asked after I told her. She pushed her glasses up her nose, and her pale blue eyes magnified.

I wanted to explain that India wasn't home, since I'd never lived there, but so many people acted like it should be home, including my mom. So instead I worded my answer carefully. "It's been five years since we last went."

"Are you excited? I would be."

I nodded because going along with her expectations was safest.

"I've always wanted to go to India. Just the colours are so beautiful and exotic. Are you going to see the Taj Mahal? That's been a dream of mine."

I shook my head. "We usually just visit family in Bombay. The Taj Mahal is in a different city." I didn't know any Indian kids who'd gone to see the Taj Mahal. Everyone always just visited relatives.

She looked vaguely disappointed. "It's the most beautiful building in the world. You really should make time to go."

I smiled and tried to look forward to the trip, because clearly there was something special about India that I didn't see. But a few days in, I was so bored. All we did was visit people who were related to me in ways I could not remember, who would force me to eat Indian food and tell me I should learn to speak Gujarati.

"How much longer until we go home?" I already knew the answer because I'd asked yesterday. Even school was better than this.

"Stop asking." Mom collected the sheet I'd been sleeping under and started folding it. "Everyone is already up. Even Shruti is ready."

I sat up on the bed I shared with her and my sister. My dad had left India early to take care of the business at home, and Amit got to leave with him because he was in high school and not missing classes mattered more. I was going to start junior high next year, didn't that matter?

"Don't forget to use bottled water to brush your teeth."

"You don't have to tell me fifty million times."

I had to walk past the table to get to the bathroom. Shruti was still eating breakfast, but even my aunt, Geeta Mami, had sat down. She usually didn't eat until after serving everyone else first. Thankfully my cousin Kaushik had already left for school. I was usually stuck with him because we were almost the same age, but most of the time, he was busy studying. I didn't get much homework in school yet, but he had pages and pages to memorize.

The bathroom itself was like a long hallway. Mom told us we were lucky because my uncle, Chandu Mama, had a Western-style toilet instead of a drain to squat over like at other people's houses. It didn't always work, though, so sometimes I had to fill up a bucket and pour it all down. There was no bathtub or shower either, just two taps at one end with a piece of pantyhose attached to the faucet. Water flowed through the pantyhose into a big bucket, then you took a smaller pitcher and dumped water from the bucket over yourself. And you had to turn the hot water on fifteen minutes before you wanted to use it, so once somebody "showered," everyone had to shower. At least the sink was a regular sink.

I wondered if this was what my teacher would call *exotic*.

By the time I got to the breakfast table, I was the only one eating. I grimly looked over the thepla and small metal cups of dahi. Nothing but Indian food. Mom had packed dry pasta and canned sauce so we could eat normal food sometimes, but we were always visiting some relative and had to eat Indian food anyway. There were too many people and I didn't know any of them, and every time they saw me they would say "Payal! Do you remember me? Last time I saw you, you were only this big." I couldn't even remember who we'd met yesterday. Everyone blurred together.

"Do you want toast?" Mom held out a plate of square-shaped bread glistening with butter. It looked a little weird, but it tasted like bread.

After breakfast, Mom announced that I was staying home to play with Sushma—a neighbour—and her friend Poonam. "You girls will have such fun."

"Can't I go with you and Shruti?" Mom was taking Shruti to some aunty's house to do arts and crafts. I was going to be alone with these girls.

"We arrange a visit with friends for you, and this is how you act?"

"Sushma and I aren't friends." She'd come over once or twice, but we had little to say to each other. "And I don't know Poonam."

"Of course you're friends," said Mom. "She's a nice girl. Both of them are."

Poonam, fortunately, liked to talk, and easily filled all the silences from when it was just Sushma and me. We sat around the living room, the girls in their school uniforms while I squirmed in jeans. It was too hot for jeans, but I wasn't allowed to bring shorts to India, and I wasn't going to wear the dumb long skirts Mom bought for me if I could help it.

Both girls had their hair in braids, but mine fell all over the place. Poonam began brushing her hands through it. "How come your hair is all loose?"

I shrugged. "I like it this way."

She began braiding it anyway, like I was some sort of doll. "Your hair is very nice. Silky smooth."

"It never stays in braids. It always falls out."

She began pulling sections of my hair tightly. "I can fix that."

Sushma just watched. "Poonam is very good at hair styling. But for school, we have to keep it like this." She pulled her braids, one at a time.

Poonam examined my face critically. "I know! A French plait." She pulled out the half-done braid and began again from the top of my head.

They began talking about movie stars, all of whom seemed to have the last name Khan. Poonam had a lot of opinions about which ones she liked and didn't like, but I had no idea who she was talking about and couldn't keep any of it straight. I hadn't seen any Bollywood movies, and so soon the other girls talked to each other while Poonam yanked my hair this way and that.

It reminded me of my friend Rachel after she came back from summer camp and started talking about Mark-Paul Gosselar and Jonathan Taylor Thomas like she knew them. We'd ride bikes to the convenience store and she bought magazines instead of candy. Her room was covered with posters of boys. We were supposed to start junior high next year, but it felt like Rachel was already there.

Poonam tugged at my hair to get my attention. "Payal?"

"What?"

"You are in a dream, hanh?" said Sushma. "At what age should we get married?"

I turned in surprise and Poonam lost her grip on my hair, which immediately began slipping out of the hairstyle she'd been crafting. "Aren't we a little young to be talking about that?"

"I don't want to get married too young," said Poonam. "At eighteen, nineteen, okay. But not before then." She began trying to fix my hair.

She spoke with such sureness that I hesitated. "In Canada, no one gets married that young." No one I knew, anyway.

"Here, other girls, they are getting married even younger." She tugged firmly on sections of my hair, and I stiffened my neck to keep my head still.

Sushma protested. "Older too. Even up to twenty-five."

"That's more like Canada."

"But why so old?" asked Poonam. "Why wait so long?"

"There's school," I said. "And university. And you need to start a career first."

"But so many steps before your life can begin?" She gave up on trying to fix my hair and pulled everything out to start over again.

"Does everyone have to get married? My teacher isn't married."

Poonam grimaced. "If you wait too long, there will be no one good left. You'll be stuck with someone no good at all."

"But what if you just didn't get married?"

"What would you do instead?" asked Sushma.

I shrugged. My teacher always talked about trips she'd taken or wanted to go on, but that didn't seem like much of a reason, since if you were married, your husband could travel with you.

Poonam began to vigorously brush my hair. "No. No. No. Everyone must get married." She pointed her brush at me. "You have a younger sister. If you wait too long, she has to wait for you."

"She doesn't." I winced as Poonam yanked at the knots in my fine hair.

"But how does that look?" said Sushma gently. "Everyone will ask, what's wrong with the eldest sister if the youngest is married first? And then they will wonder about the youngest, what if she has the same problem as the eldest? "

"And then, who will you marry?" Poonam tugged and twisted my hair decisively, now aiming for a fancier style than a French braid. "Indian system is better."

I wondered how Rachel would answer the question about when she would get married. She'd already told me about her dream wedding, right down to the off-the-shoulder lace sleeves and blush pink petals in her flower girls' baskets. I didn't know what my dream wedding was. Would I have to marry an Indian boy, and have an Indian wedding?

Poonam tried a few different things in my hair, and arrived at some complicated arrangement of braids where every strand of hair was twisted into a bun. No matter which way I turned my head, every hair stayed put.

Mom was impressed. "Your hair looks very good."

"My head aches."

"You just aren't used to it."

The adults began chatting in Gujarati and pointed at me, but smiled.

"What?"

My aunt, Reshma Masi, translated. "They're saying when you get married, this could be your bridal hairstyle."

I shook my head firmly. "I'm not getting married."

Everyone chuckled, the same way they chuckled at Shruti when she made cups of pretend tea.

"When you grow up a little," said Mom. "Right now is time for studies."

Reshma Masi nodded in agreement. "Then you can be married and have a happy life." She glanced at Mom and then grabbed my chin. "Don't worry, beta. We'll find you someone good."

CHAPTER FIVE

December 2010, Toronto

THE VISA OFFICE FOR THE INDIAN CONSULATE was in a strip mall near midtown; ironically, all the visa processing had been outsourced. Mom had been nagging me for our passports so she could get the visas for us, but I kept "accidentally" leaving them at home so I wouldn't have to tell her that Bryan wasn't convinced of the necessity of coming at all.

"Who buys tickets to India for people without even asking if they want to go?" said Bryan, the day after the party. We were tidying up the living room, cleaning the plates and glasses and vacuuming up the aftermath. I'd been too tired to pick up after everyone had gone home, and Bryan had been too angry.

"It's not about wanting to go," I told him while loading dishes in the dishwasher. "We have to go."

"Why?" said Bryan from the living room, where he was wiping up the coffee table.

"It's my cousin's wedding."

Bryan stood straight, hands on his hips and still clutching the damp cloth. "Your cousin that you never talk to. And it's Christmas."

I finally convinced him a week later to get a five-year visa by telling him about Shannon's idea over dinner. "We may as well get the visas done now. I need one, and it'll be one less roadblock down the road anyway."

"If we decide to do it," said Bryan, forkful of pasta still in the air.

"Of course."

He still held the fork aloft. "And this doesn't mean I'm going to India. And you don't have to go either. You have to draw the line with your mom eventually."

I backed down about pushing the trip to India and focused on what I had gained in getting Mom off my back about the visas. Bryan was just mad about my mom, but once he cooled off, he'd see that it was easier and better to go. There would be much less pressure. Plus, Mom would finally be able to introduce Bryan to Ammaji, and that would be a source of guilt alleviated for both her and me.

I'd booked an appointment on the consulate website so we could skip to the head of the line, but when we got there, I was confused to only see one line. I told Bryan to stand in it while I looked around for someone in charge.

"Madam! Stand in line." A woman from behind the plexiglass window at the counter pointed at me and gestured to the line.

"Appointment line?"

"Madam? Please Madam." She kept pointing at me and then at the line where Bryan stood, using hand gestures as if it would overcome a language barrier, even though we were both speaking English. I started backing away, and she began smiling broadly, nodding at me, all the while still pointing to where I should go.

I took my place next to Bryan on the industrial grey carpet. "I guess we wait here."

He looked around. "Are we in the right place?"

"I think so?" The room was full of Indian faces, largely from my parents' generation. Bryan was the only white face in that room. I wondered if he had noticed.

The line moved slowly. People were talking amongst themselves or on cell phones. I guessed they were mostly people going back: either home, or to see much-missed family, or something else they were looking forward to. We weren't here for any of those reasons. We'd sit around my uncle's flat in Ghatkoper, a suburb of Mumbai, and at some point go visit a different uncle's flat in Mulund, a different suburb of Mumbai, where we'd also sit around. At best, we'd go to a shopping mall as a big trip, since nice malls were still relatively new in Mumbai. I'd been to India several times, and I'd never seen much more of it than that.

Was that the kind of local, real India that Shannon was expecting?

What would it be like to really travel in India? To see anything other than another relative's flat? Non-Indians would ask me about the Taj Mahal, but I'd never been there. Every trip I'd taken to India had been arranged by my parents, and everything we did while we were there was arranged and negotiated by them, and all I did was follow along like a good little duckling. How would I even travel through India alone? My parents and grandmother and uncles and aunts and cousins would completely freak out. And people in India would see me and expect me to be Indian, to know the language and what to do and where to go, while I would be clueless, and then they'd think I was an idiot. It was easier for white people.

"Sure is a long line," said Bryan, looking around the room. "Should we come back?"

"We're already here." I scrounged through my purse, making sure I had our passports, the filled-in application form, the new pictures for our visa. "You got your pictures done, right?"

"Was I supposed to?"

"Bryan." Mom was going to kill me. Already, the timeline was tight for getting our visas approved. "It was in the instructions."

"We could come back another time."

I thought about sending Bryan off to do his photos but I didn't know if he'd come back. "Maybe they'll take the paperwork now and accept the photos later?" I suggested.

"What's the big deal? We aren't in a rush."

"I still have to get my visa." A gap opened up in the line, and people shuffled forward. "Anyway, the line is moving again. We may as well stay."

If we had kids, would I have to drag them to India too? Keep up with a web of people a world away? It was barely manageable with my mom around to explain things to me. Would I have to take more of an interest now so that I would be able to explain it to my own kids? Would we need to explain the egg donor's culture if it was different from my own? One that I knew even less about?

I tapped Bryan. "So about Shannon's idea."

"Was it a magic line-ending tea? Because I could really use one of those right now."

"Stop. You know what I mean."

He shifted his weight from foot to foot. "I still don't think we need to go to India when we could look locally."

"I looked. There's nothing online."

"We could wait. People must sign up all the time."

White people signed up all the time. Brown people did not. I couldn't see how any Indian daughter would be able to convince her parents to let her donate her eggs. And how would she hide the injections, the side effects, the clinic visits, the surgery and recovery? But I didn't want to argue with Bryan about it. Who knew if any of the aunties and uncles at the visa office knew my parents? If they would report back that they'd seen me arguing with my white husband in public? And at even the slightest whiff of a problem, my mom would take the opportunity to dig in and tell me what I was doing wrong, and how I should change everything about myself.

We shuffled forward in line again. "My mom said something," said Bryan.

"This is why I didn't want to tell anyone."

"No, it's just, what if..." We took a tiny step forward in line, although it hardly seemed worth it, since we were basically in the same place. "Like, what if the universe is trying to tell us something?"

"The universe? Was your mom talking to Shannon?" I smiled brightly at Bryan, but his face stayed serious.

"It shouldn't be this hard. What if it's not meant to be?"

"Your mom said this?" I thought of Barb, the number of times she'd asked about grandchildren, and what was taking so long.

"I think the egg donor thing threw her."

"She didn't seem thrown."

He shrugged broadly. Was I imagining things, or did this seem a little rehearsed? "Different generation, right? But it got me thinking. Maybe we should leave things up to fate for a while. See what happens."

"We know what happens. Nothing happens."

"We don't know."

"You were there when the doctor told us."

"Doctors are sometimes wrong."

The words were building up in my head, a protest march of words trying to get organized. All the explanations we'd been given, hearing the doctor tell us the news in her expensive office with that damned orchid, all the words tumbling together into a riot, wanting to explode out and explain and re-explain what Bryan already knew. "We are literally in line for a visa to India."

"We don't have to go."

We do. I turned away from him. "We agreed to keep all the options open."

"Not doing it at all is an option too."

No one in the room was paying attention to us, but I still spoke softly. "You don't want kids?" For a moment, I thought he would say "Not anymore" and for a second I felt something in me ease. But then I filled up again with worry. How would we explain it to everyone, especially now that we knew how to solve the problem but then chose not to do it? What would my mom say, seeing me fail again where Shruti excelled, and how many bizarre ways would Mom find to make this my fault, like how she blamed my teenage acne on everything from not tidying my room to cutting my nails at the wrong time of day?

"Of course I want kids," said Bryan.

I relaxed as the familiar pressure settled back in. "So what's all this?"

He held up his hands peaceably. "It's just an idea."

The line dragged forward. "Bryan," I started. "We've been through years of this, and you were fine. Now we have a real shot at making it all work, and you want to quit?"

"Who said quit? I just want to talk about it."

"We've talked."

He stared at me. "This is a lot. We're talking about medical care in a third-world country—"

"India has excellent medical care."

"— and we're looking for some stranger to be involved in our own child's conception? It's a lot."

People were starting to look at us. "This is our one shot at success. Don't you want to try?"

He muttered something and I pretended it was agreement. Maybe I'd been pushing too hard.

When we got to the front, the guy at the counter checked my application and photos, and then turned to Bryan. "Sir, visa photo?"

"He's forgotten," I said. "Can we drop them later?"

"We can do this another time," said Bryan. "There's no rush."

My mom would ask me tonight about the visa application again, and I would have to tell her about Bryan's photos, and then listen to her lecture me on my incompetence. And it would be more proof that she should have done this for me, and that even at nearly thirty years old, I could not be trusted to take care of anything. And it would be even worse if she found out why Bryan wasn't in a hurry to get a visa to India.

I turned to the counter guy. "I'm so sorry about this. Is there anywhere we can quickly do photos nearby?"

He rapped the plexiglass shield and pointed to a slightly crumpled laser printed sign. *Optional Services. Photos $15.* "No problem, Madam."

"Credit card?"

He shook his head. "Cash only."

I started rummaging through my purse. Bryan opened his wallet and shook his head, and then turned to show it to me, putting his back to the counter. "Does this seem shady to you?" he whispered.

There was a twenty in my purse. I held it up. "Do you have change?"

The counter guy shook his head.

"Pi," whispered Bryan.

I didn't want to reply. I couldn't start an argument here, with everyone looking. Instead, I grabbed Bryan's wallet. "There's a ten in here." I looked in my purse again. "I might have a toonie."

"Pi!"

"Look through your pockets."

The counter guy waggled his head once. "No problem. Just give me what you have."

I put the ten and the toonie on the counter, and he pulled out a digital camera from the desk, and gestured at Bryan to stand against the blank wall. He snapped a photo and told us to come back in five minutes and it would be done, and then handed back all our documents and a number. We stood off to the side to wait.

"That was easy," I said.

"Assuming the photos are okay." He shuffled his feet. "Maybe it's another sign that we shouldn't be doing this."

I didn't challenge him, but instead looked around the room again. There was now one white couple in line, grey-haired. Probably planning a trip of a lifetime. Probably excited. I wrinkled my nose slightly. India didn't have much appeal for me even if I could go as a tourist.

Would Bryan and I travel more if we didn't have kids? This was our first trip anywhere since our honeymoon at the all-inclusive resort in Punta Cana.

When our number was called, we picked up the photos and went to a different counter. The woman there took our documents and typed into the computer. "Why did you come so late? Your appointment was half an hour ago."

"We were here," I said. "We were in line."

"You should come earlier in case there is a line."

Bryan tugged at my elbow. I ignored him and took a deep breath to push the pit in my stomach away.

The woman at the counter gluesticked one of Bryan's photos to the application, then pushed the other photo back at me.

"Don't you need this?" I asked.

She shook her head.

"But he took two photos." I pointed at the other counter. "And the instructions say bring two."

She shrugged and started typing on her computer. "Photos are an extra service. I have nothing to do with photos."

"I knew it was shady," muttered Bryan.

"But are the photos okay?" I could feel anxiety spidering up my back. If we screwed this up, I would never hear the end of it from Mom.

She paused and studied both Bryan's photo and mine. "Should be okay."

After a few more minutes of typing, she took my credit card payment, then gave me a receipt and confirmation number. We were done. Bryan and I headed out the door, passing the grey-haired white couple. I caught words "anniversary" and "so colourful." White people were lucky they could think of a trip to India as a fun adventure.

We stepped outside and were hit by the cold air and the whir of traffic.

"So I guess going to India is on the table," said Bryan. He scanned the strip mall. "Should we try to grab lunch somewhere?"

He was starting to soften his stance, I could feel it. "Bryan, can I ask you one thing? About the wedding?" I reached for his hand, but he stepped off the curb and started walking to our car before I could make contact.

"We talked about this," he said without looking back.

I scampered to keep up. "I know, it's just…" I'd mistimed it, but maybe I could smooth things a little bit. "You know how my mom is. She's going to be so pissed if we both don't go."

"She bought tickets without even asking."

"You know how she is. She just assumed she was doing us a favour."

He stopped and turned to face me. "And why is it always about your mom? My mom is going to be so upset if we miss Christmas. She's already upset that you won't be there."

"I know, but it's a wedding."

"Who has a wedding at Christmas anyway?"

"It was probably the astrology. This must have been the most auspicious time."

"Now who's been talking to Shannon?"

I laughed. We'd reached the car, but neither of us had reached for the door handles yet. It was a good sign that he was still talking, still joking around. "It's Indian culture."

"You've never really cared about that, though."

"We might have to start."

He beeped the car open with his key fob but didn't get in. "How do you mean?"

"If we have a baby."

"Why?"

"I mean, how else are they going to have a connection to where they come from?"

A puff of vapour escaped from Bryan's reddened lips, and I looked at his blue eyes and white skin, and wondered what it be would like for all of this to be easy. All he had to do was put up a Christmas tree and the rest of the world would do everything else for him.

We got into the car and buckled up. Bryan started the car and backed out. "You never wanted to do any of that before."

"I still don't." The thoughts lay heavily. How much more would I have to participate in, to give my own children access to their heritage? I didn't speak any of the languages, or go to temple, or even cook any of the food. Shruti did all of that, but Amit and I never had. "It's important, though."

"You don't even like Indian food. I eat it more often than you do."

"Butter chicken is not the totality of Indian food."

We were nearly home before I brought up the subject again. "Anyway, if we do look into clinics in India, it's probably a lot cheaper." I watched the street as Bryan gently slowed down and signalled to enter our parking garage. "That leaves us with extra money for the house. Maybe we could buy a big barbecue."

His eyes lit up. "I do love a good barbecue."

He did, I didn't. There was so little worth barbecuing that was vegetarian. The last time we were at Bryan's parents' for a barbecue, Lindsey had raved over how much she loved grilled vegetables, but they were hardly a treat for me when that was my only choice.

I kept talking, kept painting a picture of a normal, happy life with kids running around on the lawn and playing, a life that was simple and easy. I'd bring up the necessity of going to the wedding and checking out fertility clinics while we were there later, but right now I'd keep everything focused on the positives for the life we were building together. I'd keep all my worries of how to orchestrate this, how to bring this life into being, to myself. And Bryan would come around.

CHAPTER SIX

December 2010, Toronto

ON THE DAY OF THE FLIGHT, Bryan hadn't even packed. I opened a suitcase and started throwing his clothes in without looking at them. Shirts, underwear, pants. It didn't really matter. We could buy whatever was missing in India.

Bryan walked in while I was rummaging through his drawers. "What are you doing?"

"You've made your point, okay?" I added a handful of socks. "My mom is terrible for giving us a free trip to India because she gave it the wrong way."

"That's not the issue."

"Whatever. We need to get going."

"I'm not going." He crossed his arms.

I grabbed his toothbrush and razor from the bathroom and tossed it in the bag. If he wouldn't pack, he could make do with what I picked. "You have to go. Everyone's expecting you. They'll all be so upset if you don't go."

"Nobody asked me. Like, boom, some relative has a wedding and we drop everything and fly halfway around the world?"

"Yes."

He blinked. "That's nuts."

I started zipping up his suitcase. "That's how it works."

"No, that's how your mom works. She shows up with tickets like we don't have lives of our own, like we have nothing better to do—at Christmas—than go to some wedding."

There was no time for this. I took his suitcase off the bed. "We've got to get going to the airport."

He pulled the suitcase out of my hand.

"I've been saying all along that I'm not going. Haven't you been listening?"

I picked up my own suitcase. My mind was racing, searching for the magic words to make him see. "But what about checking out fertility clinics? It's the perfect opportunity. We'll be there anyway."

"We said we were keeping our options open."

"We have no options. There's nothing to keep open." I kept my eyes on his hands, white fingers wrapped around the black handle.

"We don't have to have kids."

I didn't want to have this conversation. "The flight is leaving. We need to call a cab."

He dropped his suitcase and took his keys off the dresser. "I'll drive you."

I slung my purse over my shoulder. I gripped his suitcase and mine and tried to drag both of them, but ended up having to waddle through the door.

"Pi, I'm not going."

"Bryan, please." As long as he came to the airport, as long as he brought his suitcase, there was a chance. Things would somehow be okay. "Please. We can talk about this in the car."

A long second passed. My mind began raising worries and addressing them. Mom might make comments about Bryan's packing, but no matter. He could work off my laptop if he needed to, and in any case, everything was slow around the holidays. We could call Barb from Mumbai, make it sound like a spontaneous trip, soothe her feelings about Bryan not being around for Christmas. Get her an extra-special souvenir from India. We could make this all work.

His shoulders sank with a slight sigh. "Fine."

The traffic to the airport was heavy, and I was edgy with anxiety. Bryan started talking as we inched along, his eyes never leaving the road. "I think it's all getting too complicated. All of a sudden, you're ready to go to some clinic halfway around the world. And I don't get it. You've never been baby crazy, like my sister." He checked over his shoulder and took his foot off the gas for a moment to make a tricky lane change. "Maybe we need to take a breather on all these fertility appointments."

I looked out the window instead of responding, watching the grey highway shoulder covered in dirty slush go by in a long, endless line. What was the point of taking a breather? Time would not suddenly make my body produce viable eggs, nor would it fill up all those rooms in our new house. Time wouldn't change our lives, or my parents, or the fact that our best chance at having children involved going to India.

I tried for a softer tone. "Will you at least come to the wedding? I know it's Christmas and your mom will be upset, but there will be another Christmas. Malika's only going to have one wedding."

He tapped the steering wheel with his ring. "If weddings are so important that we're supposed to fly around the world on a moment's notice, how come none of them came for our wedding?"

"They'd have come if they could."

Bryan didn't reply. We were entering the airport and he was concentrating on the mess of construction bollards and finding the turn off to the right terminal. The ashy light reflected off the industrial buildings, and dimmed his face.

I tried another approach. "This could be our one big adventure before we have kids. We could do a photo wall, something to help them understand where they came from."

Bryan kept looking around, navigating the complicated airport mess without speaking until he could park. Then he went around to the trunk and pulled out my suitcase alone. "Maybe this trip is coming at a good time," he said. "We could use a break. And not just a fertility one. A break-break."

I could feel my heart sinking through my shoes to the dirty wet parking lot pavement. "You could still come," I said. "We could skip the fertility clinics. Just come with me."

He shook his head, leaned in and kissed the top of my forehead. I hesitated before reaching up to give him a hug. But he pulled away quickly and got into the car. He really wasn't going.

"Wait." I opened the passenger door.

He leaned toward me. "What is it?"

I pulled out his passport from the side pocket of my purse. Surely he'd go home and realize he'd made a terrible mistake. "You can still change your mind. Even if you miss this flight. You can get another one."

A long second passed before he plucked the passport from my hand. "Have fun with your mom." He reached over and shut the passenger door and then drove off, leaving me standing by an empty space.

I didn't want to go into the terminal. What if he came back? Even if he left the drop-off zone he could still turn around and drive back in. But I had to get on the flight.

The airport itself was busy with people travelling for the holidays. I stood behind a couple wearing wide-brimmed straw hats with their winter coats. Wherever they were going, it was probably more fun than India.

I finished checking in, but stayed near the check-in desk and scanned the line for Bryan. He could have gotten off the highway and turned around. I sent him a text.

If you change your mind, it's not too late

Then another. *I'm heading to the gate*

Don't send another, I told myself. Don't be a crazy person. The grey light filtering through the glass windows in the terminal and the voices of people jumbling together gave me the feeling of being in an aquarium.

I sent another text. *Talk to the counter people, maybe they'll expedite you through.*

When I arrived at the gate the flight had not yet been called, so I wandered around, passing the airport shops and the Tim Hortons. A dandelion yellow tote caught my eye at the store. I stopped and ran my fingers over its smooth skin. This was a bag that stood out. I could never carry a purse like this. From my greying sneakers to my jeans to my old black winter coat, there was nothing about me that stood out.

Who are these people, I wondered, who stumbled upon an expensive airport bag and bought it. Did they just toss out the old one? I adjusted my own purse, a noisy black nylon over a knife-resistant material that was supposedly theft-proof. I hated it. Mom had given it to me for this trip, so I had to bring it. "You don't know how to act in India," she'd said. "Someone could rob you in a crowd and you won't even notice. This will keep you from getting into too much trouble." I had no idea what trouble I could get into since I'd be spending the entire time at my uncle's flat, or the wedding, or possibly the mall. The only time I'd be alone was on the plane.

I called again. Voicemail. I left a message this time. "Bryan, I'm sorry. I don't know what I've done wrong, but I think you could still make the flight. Or maybe the connecting flight. Please?"

The waiting areas held a large contingent of Indian people. Some older women were in crumpled soft saris, but most were like me, in jeans or comfortable pants. Some sat in groups chatting and eating. Others quietly checked their phones or stared off into space. I recognized no one. But someone might still recognize me, because who knew who my mom knew? What would they think of me travelling alone?

I couldn't think of an Indian kid who'd gone backpacking through Europe solo like some of our white friends had. I wondered what it would be like to be able to go places and do things instead of feeling like my nose was always pressed to the glass.

The airport attendant started calling the flight. People began lining up even though they were only on business class. I headed to the line to make sure make sure I could get on first when my row came up. Bryan wasn't dashing up breathless and apologetic. He really wasn't coming.

I started rapid-firing text messages.

You are being selfish.

My mom is going to freak out. My whole family is going to freak out. And I'll have to deal with all of that alone.

I hope you're happy now that you've made your point.

How dare he just refuse to come because no one gave him an engraved invitation. Don't call him, I told myself and then I speed-dialled his number and hung up before the voicemail kicked in. He'd have seen the missed calls and the text messages, but hadn't even acknowledged me.

I phoned Shruti. She wasn't flying until tomorrow. "Bryan's not coming. He was mad about Mom," I explained as I shuffled around in line as people began to board the plane.

Shruti sounded incredulous. "That's ridiculous. It's just Mom being Mom. Shouldn't he be used to it by now?"

"He's not answering. I don't know what to do."

"Mom is going to kill you." I could picture her pacing. "You can't tell her he refused to go."

I nodded to myself. She'd want to know what I'd done to Bryan to drive him away, and how could I marry a person who would do such a thing, and what was wrong with his family that they would raise such a terrible person, and underneath it all, I'd hear her saying, *I told you so. You should have let me find a husband for you.*

"Talk to Amit."

"What? Why?" I rarely called Amit.

"He's good at getting around Mom and Dad. He'll know what to tell them."

I got off the phone and fumbled for my own passport to show the flight attendant and then raced down the long tunnel to get on the plane. There was no room in the overhead compartment. I couldn't waste time looking—who knew when the flight attendant would make us shut off our phones?—so I shoved both my backpack and my purse under the seat in front of me and hoped it would be enough to not be chastised.

Amit picked up after one ring. I quickly explained the situation.

"Why are you on the plane?"

"What kind of an asinine question is that?"

"Bryan just walked off," said Amit. "Go home and talk to him."

For a moment, I said nothing and watched the plane fill up, people finding seats and stowing luggage, getting themselves comfortable for the long flight. "Mom will murder me."

"Is Mom really more important than your marriage? Come on." He exhaled. I could hear the exasperation. "Just get off the plane."

"I've already boarded."

"What are you, five? Explain it to the flight attendant."

For a second, I pictured it. Leaving the plane, going home to the condo and having it out with Bryan. Staying home for Christmas. Maybe we could even avoid his family by letting them think we were in India, and do something special by ourselves. But then I pictured my mother, in India, expecting me and then having to explain to the whole family that I had not shown up, ballooning with rage as they questioned her the same way she would question me. "Nothing is as easy as you think, Amit."

"It's not that hard. Just go."

"You don't understand." People glanced in my direction, probably appalled at my bad cell phone etiquette and worried that I would be a problem on the plane. One of those passengers that makes the flight miserable. I lowered my voice. "You never do." Life was simple for him because other people picked up the pieces, took over his obligations, and he was totally oblivious.

"I understand you're being a dumbass right now."

I hung up on him. The seats around me were filled, save for the one Bryan should have been on. The flight attendants were starting to close the storage bins. I sent Shruti a text. *Amit not helpful*

She replied immediately. *I'll talk to him*

I dropped my phone into my purse and attempted to settle into the airplane seat. There was nowhere to stretch out my legs with both bags under my seat. I looked down the aisle, but there was no Bryan trying to make his way toward me. It was just empty. I could see little beyond the tops of heads, or parts of arms on armrests of the people waiting for the plane to take off. I reached under the seat and pulled out my purse and backpack and put them under Bryan's seat. At least I could worry in comfort.

CHAPTER SEVEN

October 1997, Toronto

ALONG THE LONG CORRIDOR OF THE OLDER WING of my high school were bay windows. They didn't seal properly, and sometimes the ivy grew inside, suckering on stone frames. In winter, cold air blew in, but that was balanced by the rads under the windows that were turned up so hot they would melt the rubber soles of our shoes if we lounged at the study tables set up in each bay instead of sitting properly in the hard wooden chairs. Most girls lolled, showing the contraband boxer shorts they wore under their kilts. I sat decorously, pretending to study, not wanting to reveal that I didn't have any cool boxers to wear underneath my kilt, since I wouldn't know how to explain to my mom why I had men's underwear in my room.

I had a spare, and normally I would spend it walking around the hallways of the school for a while, as if I were on my way somewhere, and then through the small, wooded ravine that divided the grounds of the Upper School from the Lower School. This was to disguise the fact that I had no one to hang out with during the spare. But today was too cold to stay outside in my knee socks and kilt.

I knew I didn't fit in from the first day of school. Mom's version of a pep talk was to remind me for the millionth time that Radha Aunty's daughter went to the school. "You two will be good friends," she'd said when she dropped me off, as if saying this would make it so. I'd stood and stared at the ivy-covered, church-like building while other girls—athletic, white, freckled—shrieked hello and hugged and clomped through the arched doors. We all wore the same uniform but they wore theirs like a long-standing in-joke, hip-cocked, shirts untucked, ties askew, while I felt like a doll perfectly and primly dressed in the wrong clothes.

I met Radha Aunty's daughter at lunch that day, when a brown hand tapped my white-shirted shoulder. I twisted around from my sandwich to see a short-haired Indian girl. "I'm Lilly," she said. "Mom said I should say hi."

She led me over to some of her friends. "Hey everyone. This is Payal." She said my name slowly and carefully.

"Pile?" asked one girl.

Lilly corrected her before I could tell them all to just use the anglicized version of my name, the one I'd been using all through school so far to avoid having to correct teachers. "Two syllables," she said, repeating it slowly and guiding the other girls through it several times. It was strange hearing my name said the right way, and I wondered how often I'd have to correct people now that Lilly made saying my name the right way important.

I fielded a few polite exchanges about which classes I was taking and who my teachers were before the conversation rolled around to sports.

"Lils, when are the field hockey tryouts?"

"Next week." Lilly drummed on the table confidently. "Payal, do you play?"

I had just taken a bite of my sandwich and chewed frantically while everyone stared and waited for me. "We didn't have field hockey at my old school."

"Oh, you can pick it up. What sports did you play?"

The peanut butter felt dry in my mouth. "I don't really play anything." No one spoke, but I could feel a sense of surprise.

"That's okay," said one of them. Her eyebrows were nearly as pale as her skin. "You'll find your sport soon."

I continued to sit with Lilly and her friends for a while but eventually drifted away. They were nice enough, but we had nothing in common. I tried joining some clubs, but I felt phony being there. I didn't really care about photography or the school newspaper or anything. All these girls had hobbies and passions and dreams.

For the most part, the hallway I sat in was empty, but I'd carefully arranged paper all over the table so that anyone who walked by would think the other chair was unoccupied because I was busy, and not because I was some sort of friendless loser. I slid the papers aside and revealed a neon orange flyer for the school semi-formal dance. Despite it being an all-girls school, everyone had a date. Boyfriends, boys they knew from the cottage, boys who lived in their neighbourhood, boys who were friends of their friend's boyfriend. Everyone was talking about what they were going to wear, and who was having the before party, or the after-party. I kept finding ways to leave the room so that no one would feel like they ought to include me in the conversation. I wasn't going. There was some small comfort in knowing that no one was going to notice that I wasn't there.

There was a semi-formal dance every year, but this year, the fact that I wasn't going hit harder. I was seventeen, peak teenage years, and I wasn't allowed to do anything a normal teenager did. No concerts, no parties, no dates. Not that the opportunity to ask my parents if I could go ever came up. I knew the answer was no. Even Amit had to lie to go out.

But what was worse was that they didn't understand why it mattered. They didn't know about being a teenager in North America. They had no fond memories of high school dances and dates. Even just complaining about having to study all the time brought on a long lecture about how I should respect my elders because they knew better, except they didn't know better.

"Once you get married, we can die happy," my parents would say. "But until then, study."

Once, when I was in a crabby mood, I asked, "If that's all you need, why don't you just marry me off now?"

My mom smacked me. "Don't talk nonsense. What will people think? Without education and hard work, how will people know what kind of good family we are? And then why would another good family want to join their son with a worthless girl from a worthless family?" She dropped a plate of food in front of me and wandered off, muttering about how selfish I was, and what had she done in her past life to deserve a daughter like me.

I folded the flyer corner to edge, lining it up carefully to make everything as precise as possible, and then detached the bottom strip to leave a square. From memory, I went through the steps of making a crane. Then I divided the bottom strip into smaller squares and made smaller cranes. The clean sharp edges of the folds soothed me. Later, I would stash it in my locker with the other paper cranes.

A teacher once told me that if you folded a thousand cranes, you'd be granted a wish. I had nowhere near enough cranes. I had no idea where I would put them once they overflowed the bag in my locker. I wasn't even sure specifically what I'd wish for, except a vague sense of wanting life to be different. To have different parents: ones who were more like the parents I saw on TV, who wanted their teenagers to go out on dates and go to dances and be popular. The ones who said that these were the best years of my life.

I ran my fingernail down a crease in the paper to crisp it. My future was a box, defined and enclosed on all sides, constructed by my family and my community and probably the whole world, and all I knew was that staying inside was supposed to make me happy. What if they were right? Why couldn't I accept this? Looking outside, where all the other girls in schools seemed to live, certainly wasn't working. But maybe their boundaries were only a little further away. Why was I struggling so much for so little? What was wrong with me?

"Whatcha doing?"

I looked up to see a tall girl. Jennifer M. She was one of the seven Jennifers in our year.

"Oh, just homework."

She picked up one of my two cranes. "How do you know origami? Isn't that Japanese?"

"I guess so."

"How do you know it? You're not Japanese."

I shrugged. "I learned some when I was a kid. This is all I remember."

"What is it?"

"A crane."

"Neat."

This was the longest conversation I'd had with Jennifer M in my entire time at school. I'd never encountered her without her usual crowd of mostly blond girls. Maybe if I kept talking, she'd see that I was okay. She might hang out with me during our spares now and then. We could never be friends. I wasn't remotely cool enough. But perhaps we could talk once in a while. "Do you want to learn how to fold one?"

"Sure."

I pulled my bookbag off the empty chair and started tearing some of my carefully arranged papers into squares to lead her through all the folds.

I heard footsteps in the corridor and then a chorus of squealing "Hi!"s to Jennifer M and some perfunctory nods and soft "hey"s to me. The other girls, other Jennifers, Sarahs, and

Megans joined us and soon I was guiding them all through folding cranes.

The other girls started talking amongst themselves, but also to me, asking where I'd learned this and how I knew how to do it so well. Asking me to slow down and show them again and again. We laughed over each other's mistakes, and gently, I corrected them. I had talked to some of these girls before, bland conversations about homework and math class, but I had never sat with them like this, all in a group, laughing and joking. Other people could walk down the same hallway and mistake us for a group of friends.

If only there were an origami club. I wished I knew more about origami, something beyond making these boring cranes.

The girls continued to sit and chat after the cranes were folded. Megan R started decorating hers with eyes and flowers using markers from her book bag. But I noticed now that the cranes were done, I was saying less and less. They would soon move on.

There was a brief lull in the conversation. I spoke up. "According to an ancient Japanese legend, if you fold a thousand cranes, you will be granted a wish."

The other girls came alive with questions. Do you have to personally fold a thousand cranes? How many cranes had I folded? Who makes the wish? I answered as authoritatively as I could for a person who knew nothing.

Megan R spoke up. "I would totally wish for a BMW."

"Oh my God, Megan, you can't be serious."

"What?"

"You're going to fold a thousand cranes and waste the wish on a BMW? Think bigger."

"Like what, a Porsche?"

"You are so dumb."

I thought hard. The conversation was turning to a discussion on wishes. They would ask me mine, and I had to have an answer.

I closed my eyes for a second and tried to picture it, what would I want most in the world?

I pictured myself in a small, sunlit apartment. I was alone. The apartment was mine alone. There was no box. There was no one there telling me who I had to be, or what I had to do. There was just me on the balcony, looking out on a world of possibilities, able to do whatever I wanted and decide everything on my own.

Jennifer M spoke to me. "Payal? What started all this? What do you wish for?"

I couldn't tell the truth. My wish was ridiculous. Who wishes to be alone? I grasped for an answer. "Oh. World hunger to end."

"That is so great!" said Jennifer M. "That's a great wish. We should all fold cranes for you."

The other girls nodded and exclaimed enthusiastically. My hasty answer was good. Maybe we could still do this, hang out in our spare periods, folding cranes together.

"In fact," said Jennifer M. "Maybe we could make it a school-wide project. Like a charity thing. If everyone contributed a dollar and folded a crane?"

The girls chimed in about how great it would be, and my vision of folding cranes with potential friends fell apart under the crushing math. If everyone in school participated, we would have a thousand cranes in less than a day.

Jennifer M smiled, satisfied. "It's going to look so good on my college applications, organizing an origami charity drive."

"Do you know what would be awesome?" chimed Megan R. "If we went to that Japanese Paper Place on Queen? You know, the one with all the cool handmade papers?"

I had no idea what store they were talking about, but apparently everyone else did. The other girls began making arrangements about who would drive, when they would go, whose house they would meet at to plan the charity crane folding. I knew it wouldn't be my house. I didn't live anywhere near where they did.

And wherever they went, I'd have to leave early and explain that my parents would want me home to study and it was a long bus ride home. It was the semi-formal all over again, and I had no part in it. I gathered up my things. "I have to get going."

The girls broke off conversation for a second to say "Bye Payal!" and then immediately picked up chatting again. I left my cranes folded on the table, nondescript among the rest.

CHAPTER EIGHT

December 2010, Mumbai

THE PLANE LANDED IN MUMBAI AT NIGHT. The heat blanketed me as soon as I stepped on the metal staircase to disembark. I followed the crowd onto a tram. Most of the plane had been filled with Indian faces: people going back home for a visit and glad to be here. There were only one or two white faces, tourists probably unfamiliar with the landscape, but ready to embark on a grand adventure. I was already counting the minutes until I could go back home.

I'd checked my messages in Frankfurt. There had been only one text from Bryan saying, *Do you even hear yourself?* and a voicemail from Shruti with a suggestion for handling Mom. I didn't know how long I could pull this off. But hopefully Bryan would come to his senses before then.

Shruti had also suggested that Naresh could have a man-to-man talk with Bryan, but I texted her to say that there was no need, hoping he hadn't already been to see him yet. I liked Naresh, but how well did I really know him? How much could I trust him?

The tram took us a short distance to the terminal, where we walked down a long corridor to the customs and baggage claim. Every few feet stood a tall, yellowing air conditioning unit blasting out cold air, so that the walk alternated between quick chill and moist heat. I dragged my feet along the carpet, striped red and orange like thin, worn corduroy. The air smelled like disinfectant and underneath that was a faint, sweetly rancid smell that I've always associated with cockroaches.

I stepped out of the line of people to turn on my phone and wait for messages to load. Nothing from Bryan or Shruti. I sent Mom a message to let her know that I had landed. A few moments later, there was a barrage of texted instructions. *Don't forget to claim your bags. Hang on to your immigration form. They will give you a piece of paper at Customs, give it to the man in the security uniform after you leave the baggage claim.* I half-expected a text with instructions on tying my shoes and a warning not to talk to strangers.

I stood under a sign that said Foreigners. There were other people with Indian faces in that line, people who like me were returning to a homeland that wasn't home. The customs agent nodded at me to hand him my stiff, blue passport and immigration form. I waited for questions but he handed them back and waved me along. One hurdle down.

Next, baggage claim. I took up a defensive stance, my backpack between my legs and the theft-proof purse my mother told me to bring under my arm. My black roller bag was nearly identical to all the other bags on the carousel. I'd meant to tie a ribbon on it before I left, but I had forgotten while I was dealing with Bryan. What if the bag was lost? How would I describe it to the lost baggage people? I couldn't even remember the brand name on it. It had been some no-name bag my mom got on sale and told me to bring. Would they think that I was a nitwit who couldn't remember the details of her own bag? Someone too irresponsible to manage their own suitcase?

Trying to keep all my belongings in close physical contact with my body, I started checking address tags on every bag. Not mine. Not mine. Not mine.

Mom would worry if I didn't show up soon. But if I showed up without my bag, that would somehow be more proof that she needed to run my life for me. Not only was I incapable of bringing my husband with me, I couldn't even manage luggage.

Around me, women stood wearing everything from jeans to saris, though men were mostly in pants and Western-style shirts. Almost everyone wore sandals. Hands from everywhere would shoot between people and grasp a suitcase handle, yanking it off the baggage carousel with remarkable speed.

Beside me stood an older woman in a soft purple sari, the pleats muddled instead of crisply ironed in. She was on her cell phone, her ordinary black handbag hanging wide open off her thin shoulders. Anyone could have gotten anything from it. Her voice was loud and sharp, and utterly unconcerned. I watched as she tapped a young man on the arm and pointed to a blue suitcase making its way down the carousel. The man said a few words and she held her head away from her cell phone for a moment to briefly confirm. A moment later, her bag came around and the young man pulled it off the carousel, and placed it in front of her. She nodded at him as a thank you, and he waggled his head as if to say *it's nothing*. And then she left. They hadn't known each other at all.

I unlocked the zipper on my theft-proof purse, feeling foolish for wearing it.

The address tag on the next bag showed that it was mine, but it was starting to sail beyond me before I was sure. I tried to grab it before it got away, stumbling over my backpack, but I missed it. A man with a moustache grabbed it and brought it to me. I nodded a thank you.

I'd have to face my mom soon, and explain Bryan's absence. Shruti had suggested a sudden work emergency, but Bryan worked in IT. What kind of emergency could possibly force him to miss a flight? I pulled my suitcase along the hallway to the green uniformed security guard, gave him my immigration slip, and a moment later I was outdoors. The sky was black, but outside the airport was bustling like a street festival. People were massed along a low fence, looking and waiting for relatives to arrive, and behind them were food stalls and people sitting at tables, eating and talking. Except for the tall palm trees, it could have been any food court at any mall in Toronto. The air smelled hot and moist and faintly like diesel and cooking.

My mother stood out in front of the fence wearing a Kelly green salwaar kameez. She looked around, confused. "Where's Bryan?"

I shrugged expansively. "There was a huge problem at work. They called the whole IT department back in." I started walking away. *Please no follow-up questions.*

She grabbed the handle of my roller bag and stopped me. "What kind of problem needs the whole department?"

Fuck. "I don't know, he was in a big rush. He didn't have time to tell me much."

"And you're only telling me now? Everyone is expecting him. How am I going to explain that he's not here?"

"I'm sorry. I just..." I trailed off. I had been hoping Bryan would come to his senses and tell me he'd rebooked his flight, that he was still going to make the connecting flight to Mumbai, or maybe get onto a flight arriving a little later. "I'm sorry."

Mom looked at me suspiciously and then her expression softened. "But he's coming soon?"

"I think so," I said. She was buying the story. "It really depends on his work."

We continued to walk for a moment, before she peered critically at me. "You look very tired."

"I just got off a plane."

My uncle, Chandu Mama, was waiting near his car. "Payal!" He was oval-shaped and dressed in a white short-sleeved shirt with grey pants, and smiled easily.

"Chandu Mama!" I went to hug him, but he gave me an awkward one-armed half-hug half-pat on the back. Neither my mom nor I were huggers, but we'd adapted to Canadian norms of casual hugs. I'd have to adapt back.

Chandu Mama stood back, confusion all over his face, glancing at Mom and then me and then back to Mom. "Where is Bryan?"

"Work problem. It's a long story," I answered. "How come you're driving us? Don't you have wedding preparations to attend to?"

He held mom's gaze for a second and then casually brushed off my questions. "Most important preparation is bringing guests to the wedding." He loaded my bag into the back of a shiny white SUV.

Mom opened the car door. "Once we get back to the flat, you should sleep right away. The more sleep you have now, the easier it will be to get past jet lag."

I buckled up, but no one else did. "New car?"

"All cars in India are new," said Chandu Mama.

"No more Ambassadors?" I asked remembering the square boxy cars from visits to India in my childhood.

He laughed slightly. "No, no. Now, all cars come from Japan, from Korea."

"Very nice," I said. It was a bigger and nicer car than what Bryan and I drove. We'd been sharing a car since Mom decided to give my car away to Shruti. We'd need another when we moved into the house and I knew Bryan was thinking about an SUV. He'd admire Chandu Mama's car if he were here.

India had changed and yet it hadn't. It was two in the morning, but the roads swarmed with shiny new cars, motorcycles, and black-and-yellow auto-rickshaws darting through, and the noise of horns honking and engines revving nearly drowned out the Bollywood music Chandu Mama had put on the stereo. Drivers used their horns constantly in Mumbai—as turn signals, as an addendum to their brake lights, and as far as I could tell, as random amusement.

The car dipped and bounced over the streets. "If you want to drive on the moon," said Chandu Mama, "come to Mumbai." He glanced at me in the rearview mirror, jerking his eyebrows up as if waiting for a response. I chuckled dutifully and he continued. "It happens in the rainy season. After so much rain, the roads are full of holes. Then people complain. It goes in the newspaper. Government says yes, yes, yes, we are fixing the roads. We are spending so much money fixing the roads. And then by the time they're ready to fix, oh-oh, raining again, cannot do the work." He laughed a little bit as though he found all of this very clever.

Mom snorted. "Government is the same everywhere. They say, they never do."

Chandu Mama shrugged. "What can you do?"

I calculated the time in Toronto. It was early evening there: not too late to call. I sent Bryan a text message to let him know that I had arrived safely. That was the right thing to do, despite his snotty message from before. There was no immediate reply, which shouldn't have surprised me, but somehow it still did.

I looked out the windows. There were small structures lining the roads, little shops made of corrugated metal, each up next to its neighbour without an inch of space in between. The outside walls were covered in sooty grime, but the signs were lettered in bright English. They came in series: car repair shops, then cell phone shops, then satellite dish shops. Most of them were closed, but people still lingered in front, mostly men with stray dogs. Occasionally, we passed a cow lying as placidly on the packed dirt beside the asphalt road filled with honking cars as she might lie in a silent grassy field.

I turned my phone off. I couldn't keep checking it without my mom wondering what I was doing.

Eventually, we turned into a smaller street, passing a storefront on the corner ablaze with light and filled with people. "Very popular restaurant," explained Chandu Mama. It was the middle of the night. How could so many people still be out at a restaurant in the suburbs so late? Back home, the downtown streets were mostly quiet after last call.

We pulled up to a gate, and two turbaned men in uniform came out to open it. Chandu Mama drove in and stopped the car. We'd arrived.

Mom and I got out and walked around to the back of the building. I hadn't been here in years, but I still knew where to go. We climbed a short flight of red marble steps to the elevator. Mom slid open the metal lattice door and a shrill electronic version of Vivaldi's "Autumn" began playing, sounding like a cell phone ringtone except far louder. I'd forgotten about the musical elevator. The music was to prevent people from leaving the elevator door open, since you could hear it through all the flats in the building. Despite the piercing song, I could still hear the honk of car horns from the street.

There was hardly room for my mother and me and my backpack. Just above the panel of buttons was a small sign: "Max Capacity: 6 People."

"Do they really think they could fit six people in here?"

"Six Indian people," smiled Mom. "We would make everyone fit." She shut the elevator door and the music stopped.

I pressed the button for the fourth floor, surprised that I still remembered. "How?"

She laughed. "The same way we used to fit ten people in one car."

We triggered the music again getting out, and I quickly shut the door, and added my sneakers to the shoes littering the front hall. Everyone had already gathered by the door. I hugged my aunts and my female cousins and a few women whom I didn't recognize but were probably related to me. I shook hands with all the men.

Standing near the edge was Ammaji. My grandmother. She looked smaller than I remembered, like a slight, wrinkled bird.

Mom elbowed me. "Page lagavum. Touch her feet."

"I know," I hissed, before bending to do it. Ammaji put her warm hand on my back, and I stood up, folded my hands, and bowed slightly.

She smiled broadly and spoke in Gujarati. My mother translated. "She's so happy you're here."

I smiled back, hoping my expression would communicate my words for me. "I'm happy to see her."

Ammaji spoke again, this time with less smile in her eyes. "She wants to know, how come you haven't come to India sooner?"

My smile felt strained on my face. "Well, you know," I began lamely. "It's hard to get away. It's not easy to find the time…." I trailed off, the gaze of my grandmother's greying eyes unwavering. She spoke again. My mother answered back. They went back and forth a few times, glaring at me.

"What?" I said.

They kept talking, but eventually Mom answered. "She wants to know why your husband isn't here."

"I told you. They suddenly called the whole IT department in."

Mom nodded. "But what kind of problem?"

"Hackers," I blurted out. "There was a big problem with hackers, that's why they needed the entire department." My stomach flip-flopped. I shouldn't have said hackers. I'd had the whole flight from Frankfurt to Mumbai to think this through, and instead I'd been replaying our argument we'd had before I left. As if that would change anything.

"Why didn't he say he had to go to a wedding?" said Chandu

Mama. He'd come up the stairs with my suitcase. "Malika is your cousin-sister. He should explain this to his boss."

Mom looked annoyed for a second. "It doesn't work that way over there."

"Here, no problem," said Chandu Mama.

"What if they're out of vacation days?" I asked.

He shrugged expansively. "What can you do? It's a wedding."

Around me, everyone was starting to set up charpoys, a woven rope bed that doubled as seating during the day, for sleeping and rolling out mats to make places to sleep on the floor. I looked around for Malika, but it turned out that she was at someone else's house. We normally all had beds when we stayed at Chandu Mama's flat, but with extra family in Mumbai for the wedding, they were doing things old-style. I had a vague memory of having to roll out mats to sleep on in Ammaji's flat when I was very young. I'd only ever been there once. Chandu Mama had bought a bigger apartment shortly thereafter, and Ammaji had moved with him.

I was led into a room at the end of the hall. Mom flipped the tube light on. "We're in here."

There was one bed in the room. "All of us?"

"You and me. We'll move when other people arrive." It was often how we split up: my Mom sharing with my sister and me, my Dad with Amit. Everything would be different now that there were spouses coming.

If Bryan didn't come, would I have to keep sharing with my mother?

Mom took soft sheets out of the kabad, a large metal cabinet that was the only storage in the room, and paused holding them. "Shannon and Amit are staying at the Taj hotel."

"I heard," I said sourly.

"You need to do me one favor," said Mom. "We introduce her as your friend. Then, after everyone meets her, Amit can stay here and Shannon can stay at the Taj. It's a very westernized hotel, so she should be fine there."

My uncle's flat was fairly modern, with a Western-style toilet, although we still had to take bucket showers. The Taj was downtown in the heart of tourist India, where there were services for foreigners and English-speaking people. Amit would be in the centre of Mumbai instead of being isolated in the suburbs. He could walk out the door, find a restaurant, and order a meal. It wouldn't have to be all Indian food. He could hire a driver to take him anywhere he wanted to go. He could probably go to Starbucks.

"If Shannon's supposed to be my friend, shouldn't I stay at the Taj Hotel?"

Mom spread open a sheet like she was cracking a whip. "Don't be ridiculous. Everyone is here."

"How come Amit gets to stay at the hotel?"

She gestured, a movement between a shrug and throwing her hands in the air. "You can't stay alone. It's not right."

I rummaged through my suitcase for pyjamas. "But Shannon can stay there alone?"

She snapped the sheets open. "It's better for her to stay in a hotel. India will be difficult for her."

I suspected staying at a luxe hotel that catered to wealthy Western travellers, with a private bathroom, was miles easier than sharing a bed with my mother in a flat filled with relatives. "Why don't we all just stay in a hotel?"

"You want to break Ammaji's heart?"

"Amit gets to break Ammaji's heart." I didn't look up at her.

Her forehead wrinkled in irritation. "Don't be selfish. Besides, what would you do in a hotel all day when all the fun will be here?"

None of the fun would be here. But what would I do in a hotel by myself in the middle of Mumbai? I had no idea where anything was. Still, just the idea of being able to come and go when I chose was appealing. I wondered if the idea of visiting India would be bearable if I had some choices about it.

I dug out the power converter for my phone and set it up to charge, turning it on in case there was a message from Bryan. Still nothing. I sent him a text letting him know I was at my uncle's flat just to have an excuse to send a message. I didn't know how I would convince him to come. I wondered about looking up flight info for him, removing as many obstacles as I could from his decision, but I told myself not to suggest it. Not yet, anyway.

My phone vibrated and for a moment I hoped it would be an apology. But Bryan had only texted *ok*.

It was still daytime in Toronto. *Everyone is asking where you are.*

I told you I wasn't going. If everyone is expecting me, whose fault is that?

I glanced over at my mom, who was under the soft sheets because despite the chilly blast from the air conditioner, everyone thought Mumbai was too hot for blankets. She was not yet asleep. I couldn't let her see that I was angry. I undressed and got into pyjamas. Whose fault was it that Bryan didn't understand that his absurd point of pride—that my family would never understand—was going to cause huge problems for me? Whose fault was it that he refused to listen? Whose fault was it that he was expecting the impossible out of my mom?

I threw the clothes into my suitcase as hard as I could, then guiltily jerked my head around to see if my mother had noticed. She hadn't. She was drifting off to sleep.

I sat heavily on the edge of the bed.

It had to be my fault. Maybe I wasn't clear enough. Maybe I should have demanded instead of hoping he'd come around. Maybe I'd spent so long running down my family and India that he didn't realize that all of this mattered.

I texted Bryan: *You don't understand. This is humiliating for me.*

I grabbed a fistful of my hair and twisted it around my hand and pulled, forcing my neck the other way until I could feel the painful tug and sharp pinpricks of the individual hairs. I stopped before I yanked any of it out. I let my eyes fill with tears.

Mom began to snore softly, but between jet lag and travel and Bryan, I was wired and awake. The room was too noisy for sleep. The dull roar of the air conditioner didn't quite drown out the sound of honking horns and revving engines, or barking dogs. The entire flat was dark by now. No one else was up or awake. I closed my eyes and hoped sleep would come. It occurred to me that this was the first time I'd shared a bed with anyone but Bryan in a long time. I lay as still as possible, trying not to disturb Mom.

I kept the phone on all night, hoping to hear an apology. Words that would show me that he understood the impact of his choices. But the phone never made a sound.

* * *

The darkness in the room seemed to be lightening. Dawn. My mom's snores had gone on all night, although the roar of engines and honking horns had had lessened in frequency. The street dogs barking had occasionally changed to howling, and at one point, the howls had overlapped and harmonized, creating waves of eerie, inhuman sound. I'd risen slightly to see if my mother had woken up at all, but she was undisturbed.

I was restless from lying down too long, and got up to go to the bathroom. Thankfully, the water was working. The last time I'd been in India, the water hadn't run consistently. Chandu Mama explained that it got siphoned off by illegal taps on the municipal supply; they had been trying to work with the other residents in the building to arrange for private delivery into the building's storage tanks. If Bryan were here, I wouldn't know how to explain any of this without him pitying Mumbai like some kind of undeveloped backwater. Even though I'd spent every moment of my last trip wanting to be back in a city where I could take turning on a faucet for granted.

I carefully opened the door and tiptoed into the living room. The charpoys were filled with sleeping people, and there were more on mats on the ground. I edged my way to the dining table and sat down. I couldn't imagine having so many people in our condo.

If we found a donor, and it worked, would we still have to do this all over again for a second child? If it didn't work the first time, would we have to come back to Mumbai over and over again? If nothing worked, what then? We'd move and try to fill the empty, useless rooms. Bryan had talked about a games room, even though we'd lost touch with the friends we used to play games with; a home office, even though neither of us worked from home; a guest room, even though no one visited us.

From the corner of my eye, I saw Ammaji was up. I hadn't noticed her in the dim room, but she'd rolled up her mat and was dressed in her usual homespun white sari. She sat cross-legged on the floor, holding a worn copy of the Bhagavad Gita with a small LED reading light clipped to it, chanting quietly to herself. I remember she did this every morning. The car noises, the engines and honks, were starting to increase, but the gentle sound of Ammaji's voice was soothing.

As she finished chanting, the rest of the household awoke one by one. The elevator began to sing, cutting off mid-song and restarting again as people arrived and left. My aunt, Geeta Mami, who was Chandu Mama's wife, came out of her room, and as the servants came to the flat, she began to organize them into making breakfast while simultaneously twisting her salt-and-pepper hair into a bun. The milkman arrived carrying a large brass pot of milk on his head, and poured out the household's milk from a small spigot at the bottom; most of it would be boiled for chai, or made into yogurt. I thought of the cows we passed lying by the side of the road. Was that where the milk came from?

Ammaji rose in one smooth motion, despite her age, and after gripping my shoulders in greeting, began to help Geeta Mami and the kitchen servant. Chai was made, more people woke up and their sleeping mats were rolled away, cushions were replaced on the charpoy to make them more comfortable to sit on during the day. Someone came to pick up clothes for laundry. Gradually, people in their pyjamas began to gather around the table, and as they sat down, food was set out for the grabbing: small metal bowls of homemade yogurt, crumbly yellow gathiya, sugar-soaked swirls of orange jalebi, round flat theplas left over from the night before, pickled chilies.

My mother, her face still puffy with sleep, came out and sat next to me. "Sleep well?"

"No."

Geeta Mami put out white plates of orange slices, melon, and some dark brown fruit.

"What's this?" I asked.

"Chiku," she said.

"What's that in English?"

She looked confused and spoke to my mother quickly in Gujarati. My mom turned to me: "What's this called in English?"

Mom hadn't been paying attention. "I was the one asking Geeta Mami."

"Try it and tell me," said Mom.

I took one bite. It was sweet and slightly grainy, a bit like a sandy pear but totally unfamiliar. "I don't think we have these in Canada."

"Maybe not," said Mom. "You only get good fruit in India. Try these oranges." She pulled the plate over and popped a segment in her mouth. "So sweet," she said. "Not a trace of sour at all. Food here is the best."

Ammaji and Geeta Mami brought out chai in mismatched mugs, steaming hot with a brown skin forming on top. Breakfast at home was usually nothing more than a coffee, but I felt hungry. Maybe it was the travel. I put some thepla on my plate. I couldn't remember the last time I'd eaten thepla. With one hand, I tore off a piece and scooped up some yogurt. Ginger and chili and methi leaves all blended together in my mouth. The yogurt was plain, but it didn't have the sour tang of supermarket yogurt at home, and it was softer and looser. I picked up a chili pickle and took a cautious bite, expecting a searing heat, but instead it was only lightly spicy. I tore off another piece of thepla and scooped up more yogurt. Why didn't I make this at home? It couldn't be that hard. Shruti cooked Indian food all the time. If she could learn, couldn't I?

Ammaji smiled at my appetite, bringing out more thepla and fruit, and pointing to the gathiya and jalebi with the question, "Do you want some?" in her eyes.

Nodding, I took some more. "How do you make thepla?"

Mom turned in surprise. "Since when are you interested in Indian cooking?"

I felt embarrassed. "I don't know. I was just wondering."

Mom turned back to the table. "Do you know who makes excellent thepla? Shruti. She learned from me. Each one, perfectly round-round."

I took a sip of chai as Mom raved on and on about my sister. Our next topic would probably be Amit. At least with him dragging Shannon to India, some of the shine might have come off his golden child position.

I felt a warm hand on my shoulder. Malika. I sprang from the table to give her a hug. "Congratulations."

Chatter bubbled up from both of us. To me, in her kurti and jeans, she hardly looked old enough to be married. It felt strange to have missed her, even though I didn't know her well. But she was the only one of my relatives that I felt comfortable around.

"You must be busy with the wedding," I said.

She sipped her chai. "Not really."

I thought back to planning my wedding with Bryan, all of the details I was trying to get right so that both our families would approve, but also that there would be something unique to ourselves in it. All of the bridal magazines talked about the importance of making this our day. But no one in those magazines had to contend with my mother, who would simply call up the vendors and change things on us. And none of them questioned the bride's mother calling up and taking charge. I couldn't very well call them up and explain, and make our family sound crazy. So instead, I had to explain to Bryan and Barb that the menu had changed, the flowers had changed, the wedding size had changed. By the end, so much had changed, that it was clearly my mother's wedding.

"You must be having a big wedding," I said. "How many people?"

She shrugged. "Not so big. One thousand, one thousand five hundred people."

"That's huge."

A voice from behind me replied. "Not for India." It was Reshma Masi, my aunt and Malika's mother. She sat down beside me.

"But that still must take a lot of planning."

"No, no." She shook her head. "In India, it's very easy. You have someone to do everything. All Malika had to do was pick out her wedding sari. And we did that together, so it was not so difficult."

Malika enlivened slightly, "My sari is so pretty. And my reception dress."

"What does your fiancé think about it?"

Before Malika could answer, her mother spoke up. "Raj is a very nice boy. Very good family. Father has an IT company. Raj works there." She nodded approvingly at her own words, and then suddenly grabbed her daughter in a backwards hug and started sobbing. "My dearest daughter, leaving us forever."

Malika tried to pat her mother's arm, but her own arm was trapped in her mother's grip.

Mom got up from the table, and awkwardly patted Reshma Masi's back. Mom spoke lightly. "The girl is only getting married. He lives in Mumbai?"

Malika nodded. Reshma Masi wiped her tears on Malika's hair.

Behind her back, Mom rolled her eyes, but continued to try and comfort her sister. "She's not moving far."

"She's leaving us forever." Reshma let go of Malika and grabbed my mother, who looked startled. "We will never see her again."

Around us, everyone else continued to chat as normal. Evidently, they were used to scenes like this.

"Reshma," said Mom, slowly disentangling herself from Reshma Masi's grip. "You see your own mother every day. I have two daughters married and I see them all the time. Shruti comes to dinner every week, and she drops her own cooking for me, and I visit her. And Payal, we see at work. We tell her to stay for dinner every day, but she runs away from home. I don't know why. Food is cooked. She could stay, take some home for Bryan. But Malika is a good girl."

"What's that supposed to mean?" I asked. But no one paid any attention to me.

We moved from the table and settled on the charpoy. Ammaji sat on the floor, pulling a string that rocked a small cloth cradle where her great-granddaughter, Saanvi, was curled up, sleeping. She was my cousin Kaushik and his wife Kajal's daughter, Chandu Mama's son and daughter-in-law. She looked soft and puffy, like sweet, underbaked dough: warm and soft and too delicate to be moved. Ammaji looked on fondly. I looked away, not wanting to think about my body's inability to grow such a tiny, perfect thing.

Mom nudged me and gestured her head towards the baby. "She's very sweet."

I nodded.

"Don't worry," she said, speaking softly. "I can fix this for you."

"Payal," called Reshma Masi. "I keep telling Malika that daughter-in-law is the heart of the family. She must show her future mother-in-law that she has enough love for her to be the heart. Like you do."

Malika was playing with her phone, not looking up once while her mother spoke. My mind was twisting over my mother's words. Fix what? How? "Bryan's mom and I get along fine."

Mom shook her head. "I keep telling Payal this. But she does things the Canadian way. So stubborn. Shruti is coming tonight. Malika should take advice from her."

Reshma Masi continued as if she hadn't heard, directing her words at her daughter. "You must charm your mother-in-law, Malika. Learn to make her favorite food. Learn to keep the kitchen exactly the way she does. Learn to give her massage." She blotted her eyes with a corner of her dupatta. Malika changed positions, but still didn't look up. "Mother-in-law is the key to a happy marriage. Payal, tell her how you and your mother-in-law are close. How you dote on her like your own mother." Her voice broke for a second, but she composed herself. "Tell her how she cares for you like her own daughter."

My mom spoke under her breath. "Are we on a new serial?" No one heard but me, but seeing Reshma Masi's dramatics, we clearly only needed some TV cameras and dramatic music and we could have our own show. I thought about Barb. She was nice enough, but we had no common ground beyond Bryan. And what could I say to her about him? We weren't close, but then, Barb never expected me to be close.

Malika put her phone down. "Mummy, it's not like that anymore. India is a modern country."

"Modern or not. Some things don't change."

"Shruti and her mother-in-law are very close," said Mom.

"Didn't Naresh's mom drive her crazy at first?" I asked.

Mom waved her hand to brush this off. "Everyone needs some adjustment period. It's nothing."

Ammaji turned away from baby Saanvi and spoke in rapid, complaining tones.

Malika translated. "She wants to know why your in-laws could not come to India too. She wants to be able to meet them."

The window air conditioner was blasting directly at me. It was strange to be in a hot country and still feel cold. "Tell her," I began lamely. "It's too difficult for them to travel here." I couldn't picture my in-laws in Mumbai. Barb thought downtown Toronto was too busy and noisy, and compared to Mumbai, Toronto was a barren wasteland.

Ammaji shook her head sorrowfully and spoke again. Malika translated. "She says, she is missing a part of her family because she's never met them."

I gestured helplessly, trying to convey that there was nothing I could do about that. My in-laws would never come here, would never understand why it was important to my grandmother, and would be miserable the entire time they were here. I hadn't even been able to convince Bryan to come here. I excused myself under the pretence of getting dressed and headed to the room my mother and I had slept in. I checked my phone. I would have to get a local SIM soon, the roaming charges would be killer.

There was a series of text messages from Bryan. I scrolled back to read them in order. *You keep complaining about your mom, but you are just like her. You don't listen to anything I say. You just expect me to jump through hoops.*

Then another message: *We can't keep doing this.*

And then finally: *I'm sorry if I made things difficult for you.*

When on Earth was anything my way? What about anything

in this situation was what I wanted? I started angrily stripping off my pyjamas and tossing them back in my suitcase. I didn't want to be in India, or go to a wedding, much less be incapable of having a baby, and having so few options either. Who asked me what I thought about any of it? Who was sitting at home doing whatever the hell he wanted while I was stuck here?

I texted back *Fuck you* and then threw the phone on the bed and began rummaging for clothes in my suitcase. But I regretted sending the message before I'd even pulled any clothes out. I picked up the phone again and started writing. *I'm sorry, but you have to understand—*

I stopped writing. How could I explain?

It was evening in Canada. Bryan would have seen the *fuck you*. I had to text back before I ruined everything. I deleted back to the words *I'm sorry*.

What was I sorry for?

I reached into suitcase and found a t-shirt and a pair of jeans. I wasn't the one who created this mess. If he had come along to India like he was supposed to, things would have been fine. Why should I be sorry when I wasn't the one having a temper tantrum? I turned off my phone and put it in my bag before I could change my mind.

I got dressed and opened the door to find Reshma Masi standing by the doorway. She nearly pushed me right back into the bedroom. "So will you talk to Malika?"

I tried to think of a way to tell her without having to explain myself. "You don't want Shruti to talk to her?"

"You're the elder sister."

I didn't know how to back out without making myself look like some kind of a failure. "I guess I could."

"Good," said Reshma Masi. "I have been very worried about her. The closer the wedding comes, the less excited she seems. He's a nice boy. Good family. We looked into them carefully.

They are modern people. She's very lucky."

"It's probably just nerves. It's a big change."

"I hope you're right." After a moment, she said, "When I got married, I cried for two full days before."

"Really?"

She laughed a little and then said, "It's funny now. They were doing my mehndi and wiping my tears all at the same time. Now, I think, maybe I knew. Foresaw my future."

I had no idea what she was talking about. "Why were you crying?"

She glanced back at the closed door. "I didn't want to leave my mother," she said. "I didn't want to leave my home."

"Malika isn't leaving. She'll be right here in Mumbai."

"Yes, but who knows?" said Reshma. "Your mother, she got married and wanted to stay in Kolkata. But then your father ended up in Canada. And so there she went, and so could Malika." She began crying again. "Or she could end up like me." She dabbed at the corners of her eyes with a small hankie that was tucked in her blouse. "Mother's heartache is never included in the wedding. Only daughter's happiness, and…" Her words muffled into her sniffles.

"I'm sure it's just nerves." I felt silly for repeating myself, but I didn't know what else to say.

"Tell me, beta," said Reshma Masi, composing herself. "You've been married some time now, everything is good? Both of you happy together?"

"Yes." I hoped it would be enough to stop her from crying. Before this trip, I'd wouldn't have hesitated to say yes, because I didn't think we had any reason to be unhappy. We never fought. "Of course, both of us are happy together." I hoped she wouldn't have follow-up questions about where Bryan was.

She seemed to calm down slightly. "In India, they say arranged marriage is best. So few divorces. But I think the American system is better. When something is wrong, you talk. Communication. And no shame when it doesn't work. Everyone marries, divorces, marries. So easy." She began to sniffle. "Malika is very lucky Raj's family doesn't hold her parents' marriage against her."

I wondered what she meant, but didn't ask, lest it brought on more tears. I knew Ashok Masa, Reshma Masi's husband, often worked in Dubai. Was it the distance that was so hard? Malika was grown and in any case, they lived near Chandu Mama's flat. Surely they could go back and forth between Dubai and Mumbai without much trouble?

Later, when Shruti arrived, I asked her about Reshma Masi. We were both awake late at night from the time change, whispering at the dining table while around us people slept.

"Didn't you know?" asked Shruti. "She and Ashok Masa separated."

"For how long?"

"Years?" said Shruti. "Remember when Malika visited?"

I did remember that her parents had been arguing then; I hadn't realized what it meant. "Is that why he's working in Dubai?"

"He lives there. And they live here."

"Lots of people work abroad, though."

"Payal," started Shruti. I hated that know-it-all voice she used. "It's his only daughter's wedding, and he's not here. Everyone is coming but the father of the bride isn't here?" She began to enumerate on her fingers. "Mom and Dad are here. Naresh and I are here. Amit is here, and you're here…" She drifted off, not wanting to say the obvious.

"Bryan will be here soon," I said. I twisted my fingers together under the table.

"You talked to him?"

I nodded. He hadn't replied. And there was nothing I could say to fix it now. I should have apologized. I shouldn't have sent the message to begin with.

"Has he booked a flight?"

"No," I swallowed. "It's complicated."

"He better come soon," said Shruti. "Everyone is going to be asking questions."

CHAPTER NINE

September 1998, Mississauga

NEENA AND I WERE IN HER ROOM, getting ready to go out with a bunch of her friends for Navratri. I'd learned to do raas and garba dances as a child, and every September we gathered en masse night after night, but I had no understanding of what Navratri meant beyond this. My parents apparently assumed I knew, and asking them now felt embarrassing. I had school tomorrow, but my parents didn't care that I'd be yawning all day tomorrow because I was out with Indian people, at an Indian community event.

Neena lived way on the other side of town from us, but it seemed like all the raas-garbas for Navratri were held in huge Mississauga school gymnasiums. Neena and I had put on our chaniya cholis, two-piece Indian dresses that mimicked a sari, and Neena was experimenting with how to arrange her chunni, a long diaphanous scarf, while I tried her Dark Mulberry lipstick and waited for her curling iron to heat up. We had large Indian costume jewellery scattered around the room, and our jeans and shirts lay in crumpled piles on the beige carpet.

Neena finally found an arrangement to suit her and safety-pinned the coloured cloth in place. "So, is your brother coming?" she asked casually. Too casually.

I tested the curling iron with my finger and jumped at the searing heat. "No." I glanced around the room, even though I knew Neena's parents were downstairs and couldn't hear us. "He has a date."

She paused over an open safety pin. "Oh. Well, she could have come with us. Like as our friend."

"She's not Indian." I didn't know much about her, but Amit had dated a lot of girls, and none of them were Indian.

"What did he tell your parents?"

I carefully gathered the lock of hair I'd left loose and attempted to curl it, holding the iron steady until I could feel the heat radiating on my forehead. One wrong shake of the head and I could have a burn mark on my forehead instead of what I hoped would be a perfect, springy ringlet of hair. "I think the usual. Studying at a friends'."

"Does he date a lot?"

"I guess." I pressed the lever and pulled the curling iron away from my face, hoping it would smoothly release the curl. It did not. I began to quickly unwind it with my other hand, and once it was free, let it go. "What do you think?"

Neena pursed her lips. "The top is really flat."

"I can never get this to curl right."

"You have to hold it horizontally."

I brushed out the curl and tried again while Neena smiled big into the mirror to sweep blush on the apples of her cheeks. Then she pulled out a thin, dark pencil and began drawing a careful line around her lips.

"What's that?"

"Lipliner," said Neena. "It helps your lipstick stay on."

I wished she had told me about that before I'd put on the Dark Mulberry. I pulled my hair free. Still flat on top. I never knew how to do these things. Shruti would have known, but she was home with my parents, getting ready to go to a different raas-garba with her friends in Mississauga.

"He's kind of cute." Neena smiled at her reflection in the mirror and struck a pose, Bollywood style, with a finger under her chin.

"Amit? Gross."

"He's not my brother." She took up the curling iron and began to attend to her bangs. "Wouldn't it be fun to be sisters? Our parents would totally approve of the match."

I hairsprayed my front curl and hoped it would hold, even if it was flat on top. "One sister is enough."

"Better a friend for a sister-in-law than a stranger."

"You could do way better than Amit."

I never quite knew how to describe my relationship with Neena, or any of the other girls we'd see tonight, but we weren't friends. We'd hang out at Indian parties, which happened practically every weekend at different people's houses across Scarborough or Mississauga or Markham. We'd eat our giant Indian meal together, and the kids would eventually gather in one room, maybe a wood-panelled family room that hadn't been redone, and watch a movie. Our parents, naturally segregating into men and women, would chat late into the night, and so would we. It was like we were friends. Except one day, all the other kids started talking or hanging out in between these gatherings with our parents, and I did not. Many of them went to the same schools and went shopping or to the movies together. Suddenly, Hindi movies weren't boring films our parents watched, but something they all saw and had opinions on. They argued over who was the best-looking Bollywood actor, and laughed at T-shirts they saw, like "We're the Brown Sheep" or "Hanging With My Om-Boys." Shruti was starting to get into it too; there were Bollywood movie magazines in her room, and she spent half the day on the phone with other Indian girls.

No one had given me the memo that being Indian was cool now. I didn't really want to go out with Neena, except that I could pretend to have friends, even if my mom had arranged it.

"You should have more Indian friends," Mom had said. "Spend more time with them. Be more like Shruti."

"That's racist." I was kidding, trying to get a rise out of her. "Why Indian and not anyone else?"

"It's not racist." She sucked her teeth but didn't take the bait. "You need friends from where you come from. Who have your background. Other people who aren't like you won't understand you."

"Amit doesn't have any Indian friends."

She rolled her eyes. "Amit is Amit. And Shruti does."

I didn't quite know why I couldn't just be like everyone else. It was as if they had some secret rule book, while I floundered.

Once we were ready, Neena's parents drove us to the high school where they were holding the raas. As usual, it was packed. We took off our sandals and left them by the jumbled heap of shoes outside the gym doors. The many colours and styles of the women's shoes would make it easier for us to find ours later. I didn't know how the men managed the sea of black dress shoes. Neena's parents found friends on the bleachers and settled in with them, while we wandered around the edges of the gym, looking for people we knew.

Little kids ran around the gym, some making a game of following the coloured lines from various sports painted on the floor. I remembered doing the same, and that our parents would have to find friends for us, and re-introduce us, and we would stand around shyly until we fell into playing.

I recognized most of the girls Neena and I found by face, but I didn't always remember names or who their parents were. I stood on the periphery of the group while they compared notes on which events were better, who was going where, which had better musicians. To me, the gyms and the music always seemed the same.

"Neena, Arvind is looking at you," said one girl, who I thought was named Rupal.

"He is not," said Neena, although she was smiling happily. "Oh my God, he's just my math class friend."

The other girls protested and began to tease Neena. I joined in where I could, although I had no idea who Arvind was.

"Payal, I like your dress," said one girl. I couldn't remember her name.

"Thanks, I like yours too."

She rolled her eyes. "Really? It's so out of style, but I've already worn all my other clothes. I need to go shopping in India."

Rupal interrupted. "Are you going to India? I'm going in December."

"Lucky!"

They began talking about Fashion Street and clubs their elder cousins had taken them to in downtown Mumbai. My cousins were all younger than me, and seemed to do nothing but study.

There was too little of this conversation for me to hang on to, too few ways for me to interpret a remark and pretend to be a part of things. My mind wandered to the bottle of Sleep-Eze I had snuck out of the medicine cabinet and into my nightstand. Very few of the pills had been used and sometimes I wondered if I could sneak downstairs to the liquor cabinet and get something to wash down all the rest, so I could go to sleep and not wake up. Except I didn't know if it would work, and I'd have felt completely useless if it didn't. Nothing that terrible had happened to me; my reasons weren't good enough and the whole world would think I was a bigger loser if they knew. But still, holding onto that bottle and thinking that maybe there was a way out; sometimes, that was the only thought that could calm my mind enough to sleep.

The music began. A slow, steady tripartite beat, and then a pause. Garba music. One-two-three, hold. One-two-three, hold. The general chaos of the people in the gym started to slowly organize, as a space cleared in the centre, and some women began to gather in a circle to begin. We joined in; the circle grew to include us. Later, new circles would form inside and around this first one.

The melody from the harmonium was familiar to me from childhood. I knew it even though I didn't know the name or the words. I began to hum along, my head swaying a little to the melody. There was only one line of the song I could translate. *I don't want to do garba, but my mother makes me.*

Around us, little kids in miniature Indian outfits were watching us and copying the movements. It was a simple dance. Step forward, step back, step back. One big leap forward, and two tiny steps back. Clap your hands with every step. I could feel the dance, a rhythm as familiar as walking, fill my legs. We would dance like this for hours, the beat slow for a long time, and then speeding up near the end.

Ahead of me, some of the girls pulled out of the circle. Neena followed them, so I did to. The gap we left soon filled in with other people.

I tapped Neena on the shoulder. "What's going on?"

"We're going to do the twelve-step one." She joined in with the other girls, who were forming a small line to encircle the concentric circles of women dancing.

"I don't know it." Garba was a three-step dance, and as far as I knew it always had been. What was this new variation?

"You'll pick it up, it's easy." And they started, almost all at once, as if they shared a mind. The beat was the same as the other dancers, but the moves were more complicated. They swayed and turned, moving forward and back and forward again. I tried to follow, but couldn't. My legs tripped over themselves, and the best I could do was to try and move away quickly so that none of the other girls would crash into me when they, unexpectedly to me, danced backwards.

Some of the boys joined in our line, easily following the dance moves. Where had they learned this? And since when did boys do garba? When did everything change and why didn't I know about it?

No one had ever called me a coconut, but I wondered if they thought that about me. If they thought about me.

I shambled along as best I could. I knew already that I wouldn't be able to keep up once the music went faster. But the alternative was to sit alone on the bleachers while everyone else was on the floor, so I kept trying to keep up, and hoped no one noticed me failing.

CHAPTER TEN

December 2010, Mumbai

I SAT ON THE CHARPOY NEXT TO my father; everyone else was sitting in a circle on the floor except for Ammaji, who was off to the side, pulling the string that rocked the cloth cradle where her great-granddaughter Saanvi slept.

The jet lag had nearly worn off, but I was exhausted. Mom had dragged Shruti, Naresh and me out for another long day of visiting one relative, then the next, then the next. Mom was trying to get all the visits in before Amit showed up with Shannon. At every house, we would be offered food, which we had to eat whether we were hungry or not. Then, came the questions.

"Do you remember me?" I almost never did, but skated by saying their face was familiar. Shruti usually remembered; had she studied in advance?

"How come you haven't been to India in so long? You should visit every year." And I would paste a fake smile on my face and try to answer, while Shruti managed to sound enthusiastic. As she had predicted, everyone asked where Bryan was, and I'd have to repeat my lie about hackers. Meanwhile, Shruti sat next to Naresh, who would chat with all of our relatives in Gujarati. Even if Bryan had been here, Shruti would still have one up on me.

Mom would make excuses for Amit, claiming he was tidying up loose ends at our business and coming later. The conversation would carry on, mostly in Gujarati, as not all of my relatives spoke fluent English, and those that did would forget to include me. I would sit there, bored but pretending to understand and be interested. Then we'd leave for another relative's house and do it all over again.

Kajal, my cousin Kaushik's wife, had given me a local phone to use, and I'd sent Bryan the number, but still hadn't sent an apology. He hadn't replied to my last angry message. For the first time in years, I had no idea what he was doing. I couldn't picture him hanging around our empty condo, but maybe he'd gone to see his mom or his sister. Maybe he'd gotten in touch with our old friends; they'd all been his friends before I came along.

Still, I'd need find a way to smooth things over and get him here before the wedding.

The window air conditioner was blasting away, but the honking horns and revving engines from outside still came through clearly. I was chilly, but no one else seemed bothered, so I said nothing.

Kaushik, my cousin and Chandu Mama's son, started dealing out a double deck of cards, three cards per person. He looked up at me, his eyes bright despite the dark circles underneath. "You can still join."

"No, that's okay."

"Okay to join too," he teased, giving a head waggle.

"I'll watch." I suppressed a sigh.

"You can watch while you play," he persisted.

No one ever listened when I said no.

He turned to my father. "Fua?" Father's sister's husband. There was a different word for every kind of relation and I could never keep it straight. If the Inuit had a hundred different words for snow, we had a hundred different words for family.

Dad put his hand up peaceably in refusal. "I'm not a gambler."

They were playing teen patti, sort of an Indian poker, and betting with almonds. I'd played before at Indian parties back home, but had to be retaught the rules each time. Bryan would have enjoyed it. He used to love playing Texas hold'em with friends.

On the floor, Shruti was chatting quietly with Kajal, hardly paying any attention to her cards. My eyes were drawn to the cradle holding Saanvi. I was glad I couldn't see her, but also couldn't quite look away. She didn't look like Kajal, Kaushik's wife, at all. The baby was all pudgy folds and tiny wisps of hair, and didn't have Kajal's thin face and thick tresses. Would anyone have noticed or cared if she'd had a genetically different mother? The brief idea of Kajal being our egg donor flitted through; she wasn't any more related to me genetically than a stranger, though. How much did that matter? I glanced at Malika, flipping listlessly through her cards, and then shook my head. There was no point in thinking about this without Bryan.

Dad tapped my shoulder. "You should help Amit more in training. He'd do better if you were more involved."

I sighed. "He's doing fine. This is a big change for him."

Dad harrumphed.

I glanced at the card game in progress. They'd hardly started, but already there was a small pile of almonds in front of Kaushik, and Naresh was frantically arranging and rearranging his cards.

"Where is Amit, anyway?" I asked. "Didn't his flight arrive yesterday?"

"He'll be here tonight," said Dad. "We sent the driver to bring him."

Amit had enjoyed a full day to himself at a fancy hotel. I regretted defending him to Dad.

"Has Bryan finished with his work?" asked Dad.

I froze. "He hasn't said," I ventured cautiously. *Think of something fast.*

"Surely the hacking issue must be sorted out by now."

I shrugged expansively and hoped it looked natural. "Didn't I tell you? There was a flood."

Kaushik looked up from the game. "A flood?" The game paused while all the players looked at me.

"Yes, they were solving the hacking problem and then some pipes froze? It was a terrible mess, the whole company had to come in to help clean up."

No one spoke for a second.

"Terrible luck," said Shruti. She was staring at a spot on the floor, and I knew she was avoiding looking my way so that she wouldn't laugh.

"Isn't it?" I replied, grateful that Shruti had supported me with this ridiculous story. "I guess everyone was so distracted by the hacking issue, they let the pipes freeze." *Please let them believe me.*

Shruti began to cough loudly, and Kajal thumped her back. Gameplay resumed.

I pulled out my India phone and started to write a message. *When are you coming?* And then I deleted it and stared and the blank screen. I should apologize. He wasn't going to come with things as I'd left them. But I also wasn't sorry. And even though his absence was embarrassing for me, it relieved me of the pressure of making India palatable for him. I didn't have to explain food that I couldn't always translate, or customs that I didn't understand, or conversations I was being left out of anyway. There was some relief in that.

Kajal spoke up. "Something wrong with the phone?"

I realized I'd been frowning at it. "No." For a second, I wondered if this was some sort of a hint. "Do you need it back?"

She shook her head. "No, no. You keep it."

"Are you sure you can spare it?"

"This is India," Kaushik broke in. "Everyone has a cell phone. In Mumbai, there are more cell phones than people. Even the rickshaw driver has a cellphone." The group around the pile of almonds chuckled and volunteered their favourite unlikely cell phone owners; landlines had never been a given for everyone here.

"Even the sweeper has a cell phone."

"Even the rag picker."

"Even the beggars."

The musical elevator blared, and cut off upon the metallic *swish* of the doors being pulled open on our floor. Mom handed off her cards to Dad and went to the door, but stopped short at the entrance and beckoned me over. As soon as I stepped in the vestibule, she shut the door behind me. I immediately saw why; Amit had arrived, flashing his movie star smile. Standing next to him, looking uncomfortable, was Shannon.

Mom kept her voice low. "Amit, how can you bring her here? She's supposed to be Payal's friend, coming to the reception only."

He dropped the smile. "If they don't like it, we may as well find out now."

"What will people think, Amit? This is Malika's wedding. How can you spoil everything for her?"

Shannon's face was reddening. She glanced back at Amit, and then to my mom. "If this is going to be a problem, I can go back to the hotel."

"It takes two hours to get back to Colaba," said Amit. "You're here. Let's meet everyone." He took her hand and gave it a reassuring squeeze.

Mom refused to move from the doorway.

"What were you thinking, Amit?" I said. It felt good to call him out with Mom's support for a change. At last, he couldn't charm his way out of the situation.

From behind the door, Chandu Mama called out a question in Gujarati. Mom answered back in pleasant-sounding Gujarati and then spoke English again in an angry whisper. "Amit, please. You're putting everyone in a terrible situation."

Amit stood tall. "I'm only putting me in the situation."

She tried to cuff him on the head, but he leaned back to avoid the strike. "How can you be so stupid? You think everything is about you? The whole family is in this situation."

The door opened from behind Mom, and Kaushik stood, holding his cards close. "The game is waiting." He stopped short, noticing Amit and Shannon. Mom said nothing. I waited for shock to register on Kaushik's face, but instead, he grinned. "Amitbhai, this is your girlfriend?" Amit made introductions. "I see your photo on Amit's Facebook all the time. Come, come." He gestured them both inside. "This is Amit's 'friend' Shannon."

Shannon stepped giraffe-like inside. The room broke into "*Welcome*!"s followed by fast conversations in a mix of languages, competing with the *beep-beep-BEEEEEEEP*s, from outside, and above all this Ammaji's stringy voice with questions that no one answered because they were all too busy asking their own. Mom followed them in, trying to explain, but no one was paying attention.

I stood alone outside the flat, surrounded by scattered shoes. Shannon had slipped off her wedge sandals before going in, the heels decorated with pastel flowers. They were two inches high, as if she needed to be any taller. I sat down on the stairs leading up to the next floor, the cold, hard red steps doing nothing too cool my frustration. He was going to get away with it again.

After a few minutes, I went back inside. No one had noticed I'd been gone. Chandu Mama was now trying to calm Mom down. "But how come you kept this a surprise?"

"I specifically told him not to bring her."

Kaushik broke in. "But we all know her from Facebook."

Ammaji began to shout, and the room hushed. Incredibly, Saanvi was still asleep. Mom went to Ammaji and began explaining in rapid Gujarati, and then Ammaji spoke again, this time at her usual volume. Everyone chuckled warmly. Amit, Shannon and I were confused, so Kaushik translated. "She said she thought Amit was going to die unmarried because he waited too long. But now that he has someone, she can be at peace."

Amit guided Shannon to Ammaji and directed her to touch her feet. Ammaji greeted her warmly, and then Amit began introducing everyone else. Before I knew it, Shannon was sitting cozily beside Reshma Masi on the loveseat, chitchatting.

"I'm so excited to be in India!" said Shannon. "It's always been a dream of mine. After the wedding, Amit and I are going to Delhi, and then to Agra to see the Taj Mahal."

"Taj is beautiful," agreed Chandu Mama. "But next time you come to India, you must go to Goa. Most beautiful beaches in the world." The others began to agree and disagree, giving their own recommendations for future trips to India.

Amit drifted over to Shruti and me. "That went well."

I punched him in the arm.

"Ow!"

"If everyone knew about Shannon, why did you make a big drama out of it?"

"Is it my fault they think I'm an old maid?" said Amit. "No wonder I never landed any high school movie roles."

"You should know better," said Shruti.

I wasn't ready to let Shruti off the hook, even if she was on my side. "And you. You spend half the day on Facebook, you couldn't have told Mom that everyone already knew?"

"Ammaji isn't on Facebook," said Shruti.

"Kaushik is."

Amit snorted. "Yeah, Mom was really worried about Kaushik's opinion."

As if summoned, Kaushik joined us. "How come you didn't tell us Shannon was coming?"

Amit nodded towards Mom, who was quietly talking to Ammaji. "I didn't think the not-married thing would go over well."

Kaushik grinned. “No problem. We have a wedding set up already. You can get married here.” Amit blanched and fumbled for words. Shruti laughed. I smirked. “Two weddings, one price. Whole family is already here.”

“We weren’t actually, uhhh…”

Kaushik clapped Amit on the back. “Relax, huh? If you get married now, how can we have the fun of your wedding too?”

“Dude, you scared me for a second there.”

Conversations around the room went back to a normal level. I pulled out my phone and sent Bryan a text. *Everyone just met Shannon. They seem really happy about it. They want to meet you too. It’s important to them.*

Mom came over to us. “How does that baby sleep through all this?” She smoothed Shruti’s head. “Go talk to Kajal. Find out how she has such a good sleeping baby.” Shruti skipped away, leaving Mom and I standing together.

“I wonder if Shannon has a tea to give babies for sleep?” I mused aloud. “Bed TEA bye-time, maybe?” The name I’d come up with was even lamer than Shannon’s.

Mom didn’t crack a smirk. “At least she tries.” She gestured at Shannon, engaged in conversation with all the relatives. “*She* wants to be here.”

“So everything is fine? Amit gets away with it again?” My face felt hot.

Mom looked pained. “When I left India, this would have been impossible. But Ammaji wants to get to know her. She’s been very worried that Amit wasn’t settled.” A pause. “Besides, it’s better for you. With Shannon here, maybe people will stop asking where Bryan is. You should thank your brother.”

I mumbled something about getting a snack but sat down at the table without anything to eat or drink. I wrote Bryan another message.

I’m sorry I got mad. Can’t we talk about this?

The words looked so bare, but I didn't know what else to say. I didn't know how we'd talk with so little privacy, but surely it had to be better than texting.

Kaushik rounded up everyone to restart the card game. "It's like poker," he said to Shannon. "But much easier. I'll show you." They began re-forming the circle.

Bryan texted back. *What's the point?*

"Deal me in," I said. The cards and almonds were passed out. I hoarded my almonds during the practice rounds, counting them over and over again. But when we began to play for real, I bet all my almonds on the first hand and lost.

I sat out the rest of the game.

* * *

Mom and I were at the dress shop counter, perched on red plastic stools, while salesmen pulled dress after dress out from the stacks lining the walls and held them out for us to see, to approve or disapprove, and then laid them out in an ever-increasing pile in front of us. I had already lost track of what we had bought, and what we still needed to buy. But it didn't matter, since the salesman only looked at my mom's face for signs of assent.

Everyone was shopping today. Shruti wanted new clothes and was being a big show-off about needing to have tailored them around her belly, and how she'd have to tailor it back again. I'd bit my tongue to tell her not to worry, because she'd probably end up pear-shaped anyway. But at this store, it was just Mom and me. Shruti and Kajal were with Shannon, who was so thrilled with all the colours and embroidery and beadwork, and similarly, the salesmen were caught up by the novelty of a white woman shopping for Indian clothes. Mom had lost patience over the amount of time Shannon spent examining each dress, and as much as I didn't want to go shopping alone with my mom, sticking with her meant it would be over a lot faster.

I'd attempted to argue against going shopping at all. "I have so many clothes I haven't worn yet."

Mom looked through what I'd brought. "You can't wear any of this. It's out of style."

"You picked it."

"I bought all of this before your wedding." She started pulling it all out of my suitcase. "I'll find someone to give it to."

I could tell her she was annoyed over the waste. She had bought so many things for me and most of it was still folded in the original bags. I hadn't wanted so much. Mom had expected that Bryan and I would be attending more Indian community events once we were married, but I came up with excuse after excuse to avoid it all. If Bryan thought my mom controlled too much of our lives, he didn't appreciate how much I did to shield him from what she really wanted us to do.

Of course, Shruti and Naresh were always at Indian community events, and now it seemed like Shannon might start going too, dragging Amit along with her.

I squirmed on the stool, straightening out my back and then slumping again. My grey cotton T-shirt wrinkled thickly around me. "How much more do we need?"

Mom felt the fabric on the yellow chaniya choli held out in front of her, endorsing it with a brief tilt of her head. "Most girls like shopping."

"You mean Shruti likes shopping."

"Always negative about Shruti. But look at her life: good husband, good house, baby. And she's always happy. Not miserable like you." She pointed at me with her nose, her hands still busy examining clothes.

I didn't want to get caught up in another conversation about why my sister was better than me. "Shannon seems to like shopping too."

She sucked her teeth. "Shannon doesn't know how to shop

in India. She gets too excited by every little thing."

"I know. She was taking forever in that last shop."

"At least she takes an interest."

A peon came with a tea tray and two small tumblers, offering them to us. Mom nodded and we both took a tumbler of chai. I sipped the sweet, milky drink and let it coat my tongue. I didn't really want it but drinking it gave me something to do; plus, the hot chai warmed me against the chilly air conditioning. Was every air conditioning unit in India permanently set on max?

The salesman began clearing the pile of clothes in front of us, swiftly removing and refolding the rejected outfits and setting aside the ones Mom had selected so that I could try them on. Another salesman began climbing the shelves, his bare feet nimble as he brought down a new stack of clothes from the top shelf. The ordeal wasn't over yet.

"What's really going on with you and Bryan?" She continued to examine the outfits in front of her, not looking at me at all.

I coughed on chai, covering my mouth so I didn't spray the clothes. "We're shopping for clothes!"

Mom thumped my back. Was she really going to make me discuss my marriage in public? I scanned the store. Women were in small groups along the counters, each being attended to by multiple salesmen and tailors. Aside from a few outfits displayed on cheap pink mannequins, all the clothes were tightly packed into shelves, handled only by the salesmen who knew the art of squeezing everything back into place. People were cheaper than space in Mumbai.

I reached out to touch one of the dresses in front of me. It was peacock blue and looked like silk, but the fabric felt plastic. I could tell already that it would catch on every rough patch of real skin.

Mom turned to me. "This is a family wedding. Bryan should be here."

I stayed silent and watched the salesman flick more clothes in front of us. Blue, green, gold, copper, silver, orange, red. Flashes of metallic embroidery, sequins and coloured beads. All things I normally never wore. The last time Mom was in India, she had come back with several kurtis for me, Indian-style tops that I could wear over my usual jeans. She told me they were fashionable among Canadians and encouraged me to wear them, but I never did. They made me look too Indian. I tried wearing one once and the number of times I was asked where I was from and when I had last been back noticeably increased.

Mom went back to looking at clothes. "Ammaji is disappointed she hasn't met him yet. And how does it look? That my own son-in-law isn't here? People are talking."

"He has to work."

She rolled her eyes. "Don't give me this hacking-flooding business."

"It's also Christmas. You know what Christmas is like in his family."

She swivelled towards me, one hand on her hip. "You always say his family. Never my in-laws."

"What's the difference?"

"There's a difference." She pointed at me for emphasis.

"In-laws aren't the same kind of positive thing that they are in India."

She waved this away. "They're your family. They're my family."

"It's just a habit."

She nodded. When I didn't say anything else, she continued. "Are you having some problems?"

The salesman had stopped showing dresses; they saw my mother was no longer looking at clothes, but looking at me and so they were also looking at me. The busy store was oddly quiet for a moment. I looked at the reflection of fluorescent tube lights against the glass countertops that housed displays of many-coloured bangles. The room was so full of colour and sparkle, and yet the attention was on me, a drab lump.

I looked down slowly, my head like a flower too big for the stem. Could I admit it to her? That my marriage was in trouble but I didn't understand why? Or rather, I understood but didn't know what to do about it. Bryan didn't have the same sense of family obligation that I did. And I wanted to tell Mom so that she would release some of her control over my life, and maybe she'd understand a little bit about what peace with her was costing me. But if I told her, would she understand, or would she tell me that I had been wrong to marry a white guy in the first place? Or that I'd entirely failed as a wife and daughter and that I was breaking Ammaji's heart by not having my husband here, and that if I had listened to my mother more, I wouldn't be having these problems? The weight of the words I knew she would say held me in place and kept me silent.

After a while one salesman spoke to my mother in Hindi, and a moment or two of conversation later, the salesman stepped away. "You need to try everything on," said Mom. "So they can fit it all properly." I nodded and started to stand, but she put her hand on my arm. "I told them we'd be a minute."

I sat back down. "Things are okay, Mom."

"No, they aren't."

Even if I said something, where else could I say it? We were usually surrounded by relatives. "Shouldn't I be trying on clothes?"

Mom waved this away. "It can wait five minutes."

I didn't know where to start. My parents had seemed okay with me marrying Bryan instead of an Indian boy like Shruti did later, but were they secretly disappointed? "I don't know what went wrong."

"This is about children, isn't it, beta?"

"It's about everything." Something fundamental had collapsed. I wasn't like Amit; I couldn't not care what my parents thought.

I imagined the pity, the uncles and aunties who would no longer have anything to say to me once they couldn't reach for their well-worn bag of jokes about getting married or having children. I'd be too old and too divorced to start over with anyone in the Indian community, and I knew nothing about dating, and so what was all of this with Bryan except watching my only shot at ever being happy slip away.

"I knew it at that party. I could see it on your face."

"Oh, Mom." I was ready to hug her, to tell her that the donor eggs were just the beginning when she spoke again.

"If you both came to dinner every week, Bryan would understand why he should be here." She thumped the counter for emphasis. The salesman stepped back toward the counter and then disappeared again.

"That's not it," I said miserably.

"Isn't it? He doesn't understand where you come from. Who you are. That's not his fault. He's a nice boy. But he never made the effort. He should be more like Shannon." After all the drama Amit caused, now Bryan was being compared to Shannon.

"That's not it either." But part of me wondered if maybe it was. Had I shielded Bryan too much? I hadn't wanted to go to all those Indian community events; should we have gone so he could learn when it truly mattered to show up? But would that mean being more like Shruti? Squeezing tighter into the mould?

Mom beckoned to the tailor, who led me to a niche with a sheet stretched over part of it, and handed me an outfit. Mom followed to make final decisions on each outfit and discuss adjustments with a tailor. He deliberately pulled and pinched the cloth around my body, handling the fabric with the tips of his fingers while standing as far away from me as possible. Both his pinkie nails were grown long, and he held these fingers upright as if he were having high tea. I could have been another mannequin.

After making her selections for me, Mom arranged with the tailor to deliver the clothes to Chandu Mama's flat later that evening.

We hailed a motor rickshaw to take us back to the last store to check in on Shruti, Shannon, and Kajal. The rickshaw dodged through the traffic, accelerating and braking hard, the engine chainsaw-loud and the horn sharp and frequent. I had a white-knuckle grip on the bar between the driver and the passenger though my mom sat back comfortably, swaying along with each turn. She raised her voice over the roaring engine.

"If you are having problems," she said, "maybe you should come home."

"What?"

"After we get back. Come home for some time. Let us take care of you, beta. Think about what you want to do."

In some ways, it was the ultimate failure to move back in with Mom and Dad, as if I'd never made it on my own. And yet I was touched. The idea that I could always go back, start over, had some appeal.

"He was never going to come," I said. "I kept thinking he would come around, change his mind. He's always been easy-going. I don't know why this time it's different."

The wind blowing through the motor rickshaw felt cold on my cheeks; tears had started to flow without my realizing it. Mom put her hand on my back, creating a small warm spot. "Whatever you do," said Mom, "don't be like Reshma."

I wasn't sure what she meant. "Don't separate?"

"No," said Mom. "Maybe you stay or maybe you go. But don't do things halfway like Reshma, married but not married."

I turned back towards her, still gripping the bar in front of us tightly. "But won't that look bad? If I left him?"

Mom snorted. "You think Reshma looks good?"

I smiled a little.

The rickshaw abruptly turned and stopped. We were at the store. Mom dug through her purse for some rupees to pay the fare. I climbed out and wiped my face with my wrists. I touched my mother's arm. "Maybe coming home would be a good idea."

"Good," she said. "As soon as we get back. I'll set it up."

CHAPTER ELEVEN

June 1999, Toronto

"WHY CAN'T I GET A NORMAL JOB?" I wanted a job like other teenagers had, somewhere that other people my age worked. "Canada's Wonderland is hiring. Or maybe I can find a job at the mall?"

"Accounting is a better job," said Dad. "Plus, we can help you learn."

This was supposed to be my last summer of freedom, the one between finishing high school and starting university, even though I never had freedom the way the rest of my classmates did. "But I don't want to do accounting."

"Why do you want to do a dirty job when we can give you a good one at the office?" said Mom. "Who is going to be a better boss than your own parents?"

I thought about secretly applying for jobs on my own, maybe going to the mall going from store to store, but then what if they called my parents? I had no experience except for working at the office. They'd have to call them for a reference, wouldn't they? And then what if my parents said no? Then I'd be in trouble and still have to do accounting all summer.

I probably wouldn't get a job like that anyway. I was too quiet. People never got me. "How come Amit never has to work at the office?" This summer, he'd finagled his way into some drama program at Stratford.

Dad only shook his head. "These teachers, I don't know. When the father has a business the son can step into, how come they don't take that into account?" He made no mention of my future plans at all.

Shruti spoke up from the kitchen table where she was studying. "I want to work at the office."

"You are such a suck."

Mom cuffed my shoulder. "Shruti has enthusiasm, some interest. Not always complaining like you."

"Then Shruti can work at the office." I knew it wasn't possible. Shruti was doing extra-credit summer school classes.

"How come younger sister is teaching elder sister?" said Mom. "You should be setting an example, Payal."

Not that I really wanted a job. But maybe if I had one with other people my age, I could find a way to spend the summer like I saw teenagers on TV doing—going to parties, dating, hanging out at the beach. Not that anyone went to the beach in Toronto. I'd never done any of that, and it would be my last chance to try before I went to university, having done nothing like some sort of freak.

A few weeks later, things got worse. I was filing papers—the least interesting job ever—when my mom announced that Malika was coming to visit. "You'll have to stay home to take care of her."

"Can't Shruti do that?" I tried to remember how old Malika was. She'd been a cute little girl the last time I'd been in India, but that was five years ago.

"Why? You don't want to do accounting anyway."

She had a point, but I wasn't about to admit that. "That doesn't mean I want to babysit all summer."

"You should be grateful to spend more time with Malika."

"Shruti can't be grateful?" I looked off to the side as if Shruti were standing right there, even though I knew she was at home.

"Shruti needs to study."

I sighed and started filing again; then another thought occurred to me. "Wait, where will Ashok Masa and Reshma Masi be?"

"In India."

"Malika is coming alone? Why?"

Mom only pointed to the stack of unfiled papers. "Finish this, then you need to come home and clean your room so Malika can share with you."

"Can't she use Amit's room? He's in Stratford."

"Don't talk nonsense. She can't sleep on his bed."

"Why?"

Mom looked uncomfortable and sputtered out, "It's not right." So I knew it must be some ridiculous Indian reason relating to Amit being a boy.

I jammed papers into files. "What am I supposed to do with a kid all summer?"

"Play with her."

"I'm a bit old for play."

Mom smoothed my hair. "Just spend time with her. You're her didi, her older sister. She needs a sister right now."

"Why?"

"Never mind," she said, and left the room.

In the end, staying home versus working with my parents seemed like a better deal. Malika arrived, and after fussing over her for a while, Mom left her in my room to get acquainted.

With the red-striped foam mattress on the floor, there was little space in my room. I sat on the edge of the bed and Malika sat hunched up on the mattress, chin on her knees, arms wrapped around her legs, like she was a much smaller girl. Her eyes were large and cautious. I hadn't remembered her as cautious. An image of Malika from a past visit to India came to my mind. We were all packed in a car, with her singing the alphabet song over and over again, only with a different ending. "X, Y, Zed, sugar on the bread. If you don't like then better go to bed. Next Monday morning come to me. I will teach you A, B, C!" and then she'd start the song all over again.

"Did you have a good flight?" I asked.

She nodded. Then she put her forehead on her knee, so I couldn't see her face anymore.

I didn't know what to say to her. "Are you missing school to come to Canada?" I asked. "Or is this your holiday?"

She mumbled a word into her into her chest that sounded like school. I didn't press further to find out more, but instead lay back on my bed and stared up at the ceiling. Neither of us wanted to spend the summer with each other.

Early the next morning, I tiptoed around Malika's mattress to get out of the room and away from her as fast as possible. My hand was on the doorknob when I realized that my parents were talking quietly in the hallway on their way to breakfast.

"What is Reshma saying?" I could hear Dad asking. I glanced back and saw Malika was still sound asleep.

"She's not saying anything," said Mom. "Only crying."

"Is Ashok coming home?"

I couldn't hear my mother's reply. I looked at Malika, curled up on the mattress, her long black hair covering her face.

* * *

By the time Amit came home for the weekend, Malika seemed happier. She had found my clothes, the ones I was hiding from Mom, and I told her she could try them on if she promised she wouldn't tell. Shruti sat with us after school, and I made her swear on her life she wouldn't say a word to Mom either.

Malika particularly loved a top I bought for clubbing. The

silky, slinky fabric hung loose on her skinny frame and we had to safety pin the deep V-neck together, but she enthusiastically tried practically all my clothes on with it to make an outfit. Even Shruti got into it, digging through her jeans and skirts to find things closer to Malika's size. We went through my makeup and jewelry, trying to accessorize with whatever we could find.

"Where do you wear all this?" Malika was sitting at my desk, where I'd propped a mirror against the wall, smoothing rainbows of colour-combinations on her eyelids from an assortment of mostly-unopened drugstore eyeshadows scattered across the table.

Shruti was trying on my lipsticks. "You are going to be in so much trouble if Mom sees all of that." She pointed a lipstick at the small pile of clothes.

I ignored her. "I'm saving it."

"For what?" asked Malika.

"University," I said. "For going out when I get out of here. When I'm free."

Malika looked away from the makeup mirror. "But what about when you get married?"

"I'm not getting married."

"Really?" Malika put down the makeup and spun the chair around to look at me. "You can do that?"

"Sure," I said. "Once I'm in university, I can do whatever I want. Who's gonna stop me?" It felt like something a streetwise older sister would say to her younger sister. Saying it made me feel like this could possibly be true.

"Mom and Dad," said Shruti. She held up a bright pink lipstick and studied it. "You'll be living at home for university. You can't do anything."

"I could move out," I said.

"Sure," said Shruti. "When you get married." She put the

pink lipstick down and picked up a darker shade. "Don't tease Malika with a silly story."

"Amit does whatever he wants—look at his degree." Amit was doing his undergrad in drama of all things. Indian kids did not study drama, ever. Doctor, engineer, commerce, accounting, or IT: those were the five fields of study that were safe from scrutiny. My parents had been shocked when the university would not allow them to register him in a different program.

"That's Amit," said Shruti. "Not you."

"It could be me."

Malika's face clouded with worry. "But what if your parents say no?"

"It won't be her," said Shruti.

"I'm eighteen," I said. "Legally an adult. I can do what I want."

Shruti snorted. "So why are you hiding your clothes?"

I began picking up the makeup so I could stash it away. Mom would be home soon. "Because our parents still think this is India and they have a say." Malika had put on eyeshadow in every colour, just to see what they were like on her face. I sent both of them to wash all the makeup off.

Shruti wasn't wrong, but I hadn't let go of the hope that university would mean a new kind of freedom. If it had worked for Amit, why couldn't it work for me?

At dinner, Amit began talking about himself, telling us stories about the other actors in his drama class, and even imitating them. I had to admit he was pretty good. We were all laughing, even Malika. He chatted with her easily, asking about her friends and her hobbies and school.

"Are you finished with school, Amitbhai?" asked Malika.

"I am," said Amit. "But I'm not."

I looked up from the table. Amit's face was calm, but the air around him felt tense.

"You're going back to school?" said Dad.

"See?" said Mom, looking at Dad. "Accounting is in his blood. He only needed a little time."

Amit dished himself more aloo. "Some of the other actors were telling me about this program. Very prestigious. You have to audition for it. But if you are accepted, all kinds of opportunities open up."

"Sounds very exciting," said Mom. "But this is for actors, beta."

"Amitbhai is as an actor," said Malika.

Shruti and I exchanged eyerolls.

Mom smiled indulgently. "This is just a hobby."

"He could be a film star. Hindi films," insisted Malika.

I smiled. "Except he doesn't speak Hindi."

"He could learn."

Mom put more food on Malika's still-full plate. "Don't be silly. Bollywood is for Bollywood families, not accounting families."

Amit was very quiet, almost as if he was gathering energy. "I auditioned last month. I got in."

There was commotion around the table as we all babbled in shock. Amit spoke loudly and broke through. "I'm leaving for LA in two weeks."

"LA?" said Mom. "You were going to acting school in Stratford."

"This is an amazing opportunity," said Amit. "Hollywood. I'll have so much more access to better roles than I would here." Amit's face was still, and his voice stayed even, but I had a feeling he was waiting for us to congratulate him. But one look at my mom's face told me that it was safer to not say a word.

"No," said Mom. "It's too far."

"Mom," said Amit.

"You can't take care of yourself. In Stratford, I can send you home-cooked food. In LA…" Mom shook her head. "You can't go."

"Playacting in school is one thing, but you cannot play your life away." said Dad. "What will people think? Already we feel so embarrassed by this we have to tell people you're studying accounting."

"Have you even thought, what girl would want to marry you?" added Mom. "Abandoned your father's business to be some unemployed actor? The answer is no."

Amit spoke very quietly. "I'm not asking you."

I caught Shruti's eye across the table. Both of us were frozen in place, waiting for the explosion.

My parents began shouting, telling him he was ungrateful and spoiled, that he was throwing his life away. I sat there, tearing my roti into small pieces without eating it. Part of me was amazed at Amit's nerve. But I was also angry with him. How could he hurt Mom and Dad like this?

The arguing at the table got louder and louder, and in front of me, Malika had stopped eating. She covered her ears and was rocking back and forth slightly. I got up from the table and led her away. She was shaking.

"What's wrong?" I said.

"I don't like fighting," she said. "It always makes me feel shaky."

I brought her up the stairs to my room. We sat on my bed. "When do you hear fighting?"

"Mummy and Papa," she said. "When I left, they were fighting a lot."

My purse was sitting on the floor at the foot of the bed. I picked it up and rummaged through it, finding half a Bounty bar, slightly squashed. I offered it to Malika, who took it and just held it.

"What do they fight about?"

"I'm not supposed to say."

We sat together without talking, listening to the argument downstairs.

"Is Amitbhai going away?"

I pulled myself back to lean against the wall. Mostly, I could hear Mom and Dad; Amit was inaudible. I wondered if Shruti was still sitting there. "Probably he is. For a while."

"Papa had to go away," said Malika.

"Is he coming back?" I asked.

She teared up. "I don't know."

I pulled her against me as she cried, her small, bony body shaking and her tears hot. I stroked her hair.

Later, I woke up in the middle of the night. Malika was curled up on the mattress, hugging the folds of the blanket. I got out of bed and tiptoed around her, and down the stairs to the kitchen.

Dad was sitting where he had sat at dinner. Had he even moved?

"Payal? It's late."

"I'm just getting a glass of water." I ran the tap, waiting for it to go from lukewarm to cool, and then sat at the table with Dad.

He spoke first. "Amit is going to LA."

I sipped at the cold water and we sat silently. The refrigerator began to hum.

"What is so wrong with accounting?" said Dad. "It's a good profession. You can go anywhere, work in so many different fields." His voice was distant, as if he was talking to someone who wasn't there. As if I wasn't there.

"I know, Dad," I said.

He kept talking as though he hadn't heard me. "I wanted to be an engineer. But my father said no, do accounting. That was the right decision. I built up this business. It was hard work. I came here with nothing. I knew no one. And now the hard part is done." He stared at the wall, still lost in his thoughts. "What was it all for?"

I wondered about switching majors from business to accounting, if that would fill the empty space in my father's dreams. If he would be as proud of me as he wanted to be of Amit.

I pulled in my chair in closer, making a quiet scraping sound, and he jumped, startled that I was there. Then he patted my head and stood up to leave.

"You should go to bed," said Dad. "It's very late."

CHAPTER TWELVE

December 2010, Mumbai

AFTER NEARLY TWO HOURS IN STOP-AND-GO traffic, the driver let me out at the circular driveway of the Taj Hotel. Amit and Shannon had wanted to do some sightseeing, and they convinced Mom to let me come too. Not that I wanted to spend more time with Amit and Shannon, but Mom dragging me from one store to another? No thank you. But even shopping with Mom beat another round of relatives. I'd refrained from gloating about my day of freedom to Shruti, who had Naresh's family to visit.

Plus, I could call Bryan. I felt a little less pressure after talking to Mom, but I still needed to do something about the situation. The texting back and forth led to frustration. Amit and Shannon would leave me alone long enough for a private phone call, if only I could get him to pick up the phone.

The Taj was a large Art Deco-style brick building, decorated in varying shades of light and dark taupe, unlike the dusty blocks of buildings near my uncle's flat. It reminded me a little of Old City Hall in Toronto, except much more ornate, and evoked an oddly comforting familiarity in its being a remnant of the British empire.

People crowded around the entrance, and it took me a moment to realize the metal detectors and green-uniformed guards checking through people's bags. There had been a terrorist attack at the Taj two years ago.

I pressed forward, following the crowd, but a guard stopped me and pointed to the line on the other side of the table, saying something I didn't understand.

"I don't speak Hindi." I hoped I'd guessed the language correctly.

The guard spoke again in English. "Ladies line." He gestured to the other side with his head. In the second line, a female guard in the same green uniform checked women's bags and directed them through the metal detector.

After passing through security, I entered the front doors of the Taj. A marble corridor led off to the left, and most people were streaming down that side. Other tourists kept stopping to goggle at things, while I blundered through the expansive lobby. It was less congested than it had been outside, but the cyclone of other people's conversations swirled arounds us despite the thick carpets and plush furniture.

Amit waited for me near the edge of the central carpet. "We're meeting Shannon by the Christmas tree." He pointed to the centre of the room, where an all-white and obviously fake tree stood at least ten feet high and beautifully decorated with what looked like large, silvered feathers and red bows. The front desk was festooned with tinsel swoops, and the fake topiaries by each window were adorned with big red bows.

"I think these are the first Christmas decorations I've seen," I said. At home every store had something—lights, bows, trees—but I'd seen nothing at all in Mumbai.

"Huh," said Amit. "I never noticed how much of that was missing."

Bryan would be home with our sad tabletop Christmas tree, although he'd undoubtedly be going to his mom's or sister's a few times over the holidays. Both of their houses would be covered with lights and plastic greenery and shiny, sparkly decorations. They'd play cheesy Christmas music and make their terrible Christmas dinners of boiled vegetables and turkey. Even Mom's place in Toronto had some lights up, although they'd be on timers right now.

I tried calling Bryan while we waited. No answer. His voicemail chimed in and then beeped, and then my words tumbled out. "Hey, it's me. I'm out with Amit and Shannon today, so it's probably a good time to talk. Well, a better time to talk. The texting isn't great. You can call me..." I tried to do the time-zone math in my head but failed. "...well, I guess up until you have to go to bed should be safe. Hope you're doing okay."

Amit rocked on his toes, hands in his pockets. I mirrored his stance. Eventually, he spoke. "So you didn't get off the plane."

"Obviously." I wished I hadn't called Amit from the plane.

"What went wrong with you guys?"

"Nothing's wrong."

He tilted his head and stared at me.

"It's complicated."

"Ah," he said. "'Complicated' is what people say when they don't want to talk about it."

"Fine," I said. "I don't want to talk about it." I crossed my arms and stared at the Christmas tree.

There was a tap on my shoulder, and I turned to see Shannon, who was beaming with excitement. "Are you ready to do some sightseeing? I've been exploring. This place is so amazing."

The sour expression on Amit's face was replaced with his usual grin. He kissed Shannon hello, which he couldn't do at Chandu Mama's flat, but who would see him here?

Shannon continued to rave. "The colours, the smells, the sounds—there's always so much happening. It's fantastic. Oh, and the food. The food is beyond delicious."

"You need to be careful about food."

Shannon shrugged. "It's no worse than travelling anywhere. Egypt. Mexico. Peru. Everywhere I've gone, it's the same. You can't let that stop you." She gathered up a cloth bag with no clasp and pulled out a large yellow sun hat. "Let's go."

"Are you sure about that bag?" I tugged at my theft-proof purse. An old Indian lady at the airport was one thing, but a foreign woman in downtown Mumbai? I imagined people reaching into Shannon's bag and taking things from it. Or putting things into it and turning Shannon into some kind of unwitting mule, or worse.

"Isn't it great?" She showed off the design. "Batik work."

"They do that kind of work in our village," said Amit. "The one our family originally came from."

"Since when do you pay attention to our village?" Not that Shruti or I knew any more than Amit did. But what was he trying to play at?

He shrugged; the wall was up again. "I'm a man of culture."

"Staying in a hotel instead of with your own uncle. Real authentic experience, dude."

Shannon laughed. "I know, this place is crazy expensive, right? But one of my suppliers got me a deal. Who could pass that up? Maybe next time, you and Bryan could stay here too."

For a moment I imagined coming to India and staying in a comfortable hotel with a normal bathroom. Real coffee with breakfast. Being able to leave and do things without clearing it with someone else first. I wondered if Amit was getting any blowback from this; or did the Shannon of it all change things?

I followed Shannon back outside and stood on the steps. The hotel was on a busy street, but beyond that was the ocean. I pictured Bryan and myself in a hotel room, maybe with a sea view. From inside, perhaps we wouldn't hear the car horns and traffic and people. Perhaps it was possible to go to India and find it peaceful.

We hurried down the stairs, dodging people as we went. Shannon's face was already reddening from the heat. "It's this way."

I looked at her curiously. "How do you know?"

She pulled a blue book slightly out of her bag and let it drop back down again. "Lonely Planet India. Don't leave home without it." She gestured forward. "We're going to cross the street here."

There was a long line of black, yellow-roofed taxis parked immediately in front of the hotel, but beyond that there were swarms of cars and bicycles and flower-festooned horse-drawn carriages, all dodging each other. Horns were honking constantly. There were no lights or crosswalks, not that one would have made a difference. Mumbai drivers tended to treat the rules of the road like suggestions.

"How do people not get killed?" I spoke before realizing I'd said it out loud.

We stood at the edge of the road and walked between the taxis to stand just outside the moving traffic. Cars, cyclists, and even other people walking along the side of the road passed us by inches. Horns continued blaring, and all around us, Indian people and foreign tourists stood in small groups waiting for a moment of clear space in the traffic.

The road in front of the Taj was unusual because the two directions of traffic were separated by a slight median not even a person wide. Shannon held up her hand to signal Amit and me, and as the space cleared, she dropped her hand and said "Go!" She scurried across the street to the black-and-yellow striped median, Amit and I just a half-step behind, with him hauling me by the arm to get across quickly.

"Mumbai is one big game of chicken," said Shannon.

Amit laughed a little. "Guess that makes us the chickens."

"Yeah, well this chicken is amazed anyone can cross the road." I grumbled. I pulled my arm away and followed Amit and Shannon down the street, squeezing through tight spaces between people. It was almost better that Bryan wasn't here. I'd have to guide him through, even though I wasn't comfortable either.

"Look," said Shannon, pointing forward. They were at a railing with the ocean in front of them. There were no waves; the water was calm and grey-blue like twilight.

We walked along the footpath leading to the Gateway of India, an enormous triple-arched monument overlooking the harbour, like a massive gothic castle entrance without the rest of the castle. It had been built less than a hundred years ago to commemorate the first visit by the British monarch, who was Emperor of India. But this first visit, occurring before the Gateway was built, turned out to be the only visit. Less than twenty-five years later, it was the place the last British troops left from after Indian Independence, ceremoniously ending British rule. A Gateway to welcome the West, that was instead used to send the colonial rulers away, allowing the country the British had created from numerous princely states and arbitrary borders to figure out how to rule itself at last.

We stood in a cluster near the Gateway. I felt confined and invisible as people kept pushing by me with little space between us, the body heat radiating from them more suffocating than the heavy heat of the sun. I kept trying to step away to leave more room, but no one would give more space.

"You're going to walk into the road," said Amit. "Just stay still and let people go around you."

I kept a tight arm over my purse and stopped trying to step away. Amit and Shannon stood at ease, snapping pictures and talking with each other as if there were no one else there. Had Bryan and I ever been so wrapped up in each other?

Touts kept approaching us, selling beaded necklaces, bracelets, postcards, cotton candy, snacks, decorated pens, even puppets and toys. "Souvenir, souvenir, very good price, only two hundred rupees." Shannon smiled distantly, but they kept approaching her, showing her more goods.

Amit stepped even closer to her. "Don't worry about them. They're just trying to make a buck."

Shannon nodded. "All part of the local colour." She pointed to the left. "Let's get a group photo over there." She arranged us and held up the digital camera, all of us leaning back together. "Smile!" I stretched out my mouth and hoped I looked okay.

Shannon wandered around taking photos. "Shouldn't you keep an eye on her?" I said.

"She's fine," said Amit. "Besides, she's easy to spot."

It was true. There weren't many white people. It was Amit and I who blended in, which was disconcerting. I seldom stood out in Toronto, even if dinners with Bryan's family were quiet reminders that I didn't fully fit in either. But I wasn't used to being so indistinguishable. "Strange being around so many brown people."

Amit nodded. "It's like the reverse of Hollywood." He paused, his eyes still on Shannon. "It's too bad I don't speak Hindi. Maybe I'd have a better shot in Bollywood."

"Is that why you came back?"

He nodded again. "There are only so many roles for doctors and terrorists. Doesn't matter how good you are, that's what you get, at best." Seagulls screamed overhead and we both ducked. "I got sick of waiting tables and selling cars."

"So you came back to be an accountant."

"Yes. Don't fire me." He smiled. "It's a good thing Dad has you to be the real accountant."

I teared up and blinked hard to keep all the feelings in so that I wouldn't have to explain to Amit what I wasn't sure I could explain to myself: that Amit of all people saw what Dad never did. "Do people really tell you to be more like me?"

He snorted. "Dad still thinks I'm going to take over the business."

"I mean, you did come back from LA and like, joined the business."

He laughed. "I can see why that's confusing."

More seagulls began screaming. They were gathering on the pavement, fighting over some dropped food. They were taking up so much room that people tried shooing them away, but the seagulls ignored them.

Shannon skipped over, effortlessly weaving through the people. "Why the glum faces? We're on vacation."

"You're on vacation," I said. "I'm on family obligation."

"Not today, you aren't." She linked my arm with hers and started pulling me forward. "This way."

* * *

Shannon led us to Fashion Street, keeping her arm linked through mine as she led me through the throngs lining Mahatma Gandhi Road en route. Amit walked behind us, letting people flow around him. I felt like I was swimming upstream in a deluge of people.

Shannon kept chattering away. "It's almost like a mosh pit."

I was only half-listening, trying not to crash into anyone. I'd never been in a mosh pit but for a change I was glad I'd missed out. "There's a billion people in India."

"It feels like they're all right here."

I looked around as we walked through, and in my jeans and T-shirt I resembled just about everyone, except most of the women carried nicer purses than I did. Shannon was again one of the few white people and the only redhead. People were staring at her, but she didn't seem to notice.

We arrived at Fashion Street. I'd never been here before, despite hearing all about it from Indian friends who had shopped here with their cousins. It had sounded so glamorous, but it turned out to be a long section of a regular street market. One side of the walk was densely packed with narrow stalls covered by corrugated plastic roofs, as if they had been built for that day, even though they'd existed like this for years. Each stall was packed with both North American and Indian clothing, shoes, costume jewellery, watches, purses, sunglasses, and people. On the street side were trees and food vendors with carts, and other sellers seated on blankets or at small tables, selling more of the same, plus souvenirs. I saw rows of mini Taj Mahals, even though Agra was a thousand kilometres away.

Shannon perused a store that had every square inch of the wall and even the ceiling covered with watches. She examined one and then another. Beside her was a compact man with a neat moustache, looking to see what caught her interest and directing her attention to other watches that she might like. "Madam? Madam?" he said, over and over, as he pointed out watches in gold and steel and with colourful leather wristbands while she nodded in equal admiration of all of them.

I stood just outside the stall with Amit next to a long rope hung thickly with Crocs, a sort of chandelier of plastic shoes. The conversation at the Gateway was rattling around in my mind. "How did you do it?"

"Do what?" asked Amit.

For a second, it seemed like all the cars on the road blared their horns at once. "All the pressure not to disappoint Mom and Dad, to follow in their footsteps."

He nodded. "And I became an actor instead. Crazy, right?"

"But how? You know how it is." I didn't need to spell it out to him, the omnipresent pressure to go to university, study what was expected of us, work where we were expected to, get married, have kids, and then pressure our kids to do the exact same thing.

At least that's one thing they can't make me do.

I stood still for a moment, confused by the sudden thought. If I couldn't have children, all the pressure in the world wouldn't change that. Around me, the air smelled of diesel, and motorcycles roared like race cars amid the cars honking like a flock of geese; people talked and laughed and shopkeepers touted their wares, but for a moment, it was like I couldn't hear any of it.

If Bryan and I never had kids, we had freedom from the checklist of Life To-Dos. There would be nothing left that we had to do. We could tear up the list, reveal the blank pages underneath.

I shook myself, and caught up with Amit, who had meandered into the stall. The same vendor was still talking to Shannon. "Madam? Madam? I have very good price. Best price, Madam."

Shannon spotted me. "Isn't this great? You should look, too."

"Are you buying a watch?"

"I'm just browsing."

I was annoyed with her on the watch vendor's behalf. I wandered into the next stall, walls covered with suffocating layers of shirts on hangers, with more folded on narrow shelves or hanging from rods through the ceiling and on racks rigged up through the middle, all of them arranged so brand names like Gap or Zara were prominently displayed. Amit followed me. The shirt vendor smiled at him. "Best quality, sir. For you, I make special price."

We looked around for a moment, and then walked together from stall to stall, past ones filled with sneakers or children's clothes or women's dresses, every inch covered with clothes for sale, trying not to get too far ahead of Shannon, who was taking forever examining practically every item. Amit held up a black shirt with black embroidery. "What do you think?"

I raised my eyebrows. "It looks like a FOB shirt."

"What?" He held it out and stared at it more critically. "No, it doesn't."

"It totally does."

Amit dropped the shirt and picked up another. I looked at a few, checking the brand names. Hollister. A&F. Bryan would probably appreciate a few new shirts when I got back. If he was still around when I got back. I stepped out of the stall and looked back at Shannon, who was hopping up and down as she tried on sandals. Everywhere, vendors were hawking their wares over the sounds of cars, while people were strolling by in their jeans and T-shirts and kurtis and salwar kameez, oblivious to the chaos around them.

My phone rang. Bryan. "Hi."

"Hi."

Neither of us spoke for a moment. "It's good to hear your voice," I said.

"Yours too," he said. "How's India?"

I told him about visiting the Gateway and about Fashion Street. As I talked, I ambled into the next stall, picking up small items and putting them back down without really looking at them. We spoke politely, like we were distant acquaintances. Neither of us wanted to start the conversation we needed to have, as if we could hold this gossamer thread of pleasantries unbroken forever and everything would be okay.

But eventually, Bryan began. "So, I got your message."

"Yes," I said.

"I'm sorry," he said. "I know I put you in a tough spot. And I should meet your grandmother. I wasn't thinking about that."

"Thank you," I said.

He rushed on before I could say anything else. "But I really do think you were pushing ahead without listening to me. About India, about kids, about everything. I just want to, I don't know, take a minute. Why is it always about the next thing with you?"

"What else are we supposed to do?" I stepped out of the shop and tried to stay out of the current of people. "We can't just do nothing."

"Yes, we can," said Bryan. "We can do nothing. Enjoy the life we have. Have some fun for a change."

What was the life we had? Working for my father and never being recognized for holding the business together. Coming home to make dinner, do some chores, and go to bed, surrounded by other people in other houses doing almost the exact same thing, and to do this every day for the rest of my life, and never stop hearing from my mom about how I wasn't as good as my sister, and never stop hearing from my dad that I wasn't my brother, and never stop hearing from Bryan that I wasn't fun enough.

And not a single person would hear anything from me.

At that moment, I wanted to be left alone for a while, to think without the relentless pressure of doing the correct thing all the time.

"Pi?"

"I just want to be happy, Bryan.'"

"Happiness is a choice," he said. "And you keep choosing misery. You hate working for your dad? Quit. You don't want to go to India? Don't go. We can't have children?" His voice caught for a second. "Not everyone does. We can be the cool aunt and uncle."

We could have choices, but how did we know which choice was correct? "It's not that simple."

"Why do you make everything harder than it has to be?"

He was wrong and I didn't know how make him understand he that he was wrong. If I hadn't gone to India, I'd be showing my grandmother and all my relatives that I didn't care about them.

I attempted to pace on the busy path, and also not lose track of Amit and Shannon. If we didn't have kids, I didn't know what would happen, except it was the only thing left to do, and what if doing this one last thing was the key to making our lives fulfilling and worthwhile? What if we were steps from the finish line and talking about whether or not we should quit the race?

"You don't get it."

He exhaled, calming himself. "Look, it's late here. Let's just sleep on it and talk later."

"I can't talk later. There are people around all the time."

"You can't work things out with your husband when there are people around?"

"They don't know we're having problems."

"You didn't tell them? Where do they think I am?"

A particularly loud horn blared for what felt like a year. "I told them you had a work emergency."

"All this time? What kind of IT emergency takes that long?"

My stomach sank from the embarrassment. "Hackers," I admitted. "And then flooding."

"Seriously? What were you going to say next, an earthquake?" He understood the problem, and now that he could see it, he would solve it. Wouldn't he?

"I thought you would come around," I admitted.

"And I'm supposed to go along with this?"

Hope surged and words tumbled out of my mouth. "I can help you find a flight, and don't worry about what to pack. We can get anything you need for you here."

"You're unbelievable." He hung up.

The air was blurry with dust being kicked up off the street. There were tall neem trees, frothy-leaved with spreading branches along the road, but they seemed almost tired, as if they were worn down by the busy city.

"Hey!" Shannon. I hadn't seen her approach. "You okay?" She fished a lacy handkerchief out of her bag. I hadn't realized there were tears in my eyes. She waited quietly while I dabbed at them, the thin white cloth soaking up the tears before they could spill over.

Amit joined us "What's with Payal?" Shannon swatted at his arm.

"I'm fine."

"You're not," said Shannon. "But it's okay."

For a moment, I wondered if she was going to offer me one

of her bullshit teas. It was an unkind thought. I was a shitty person for thinking it.

People streamed around us and for a moment even the street vendors stopped asking us if we wanted to buy things. We were a small island of calm. I took a deep breath. "We should get moving," I said. I went to the next stall and paged through jeans without really looking.

Shannon went back to trying on shoes, but Amit stayed close. We checked out a few other stalls in silence, and then he spoke. "You were asking me how I became an actor?"

I picked up an orange box containing a bottle of perfume. *Clinique Happy*. I put it down again. "How did you get away with it?"

He spoke quietly but still his words carried over the traffic and the people. "I guess I was lucky. I found acting. And it just meant more to me than anything else."

"More than Mom and Dad?"

He was thoughtful for a moment. "When I'm acting, I'm just alive in a different way. I feel more myself. And yeah, being myself means more to me than being whatever Mom and Dad want me to be."

"But how do you do that and still hurt Mom and Dad like that?"

"Do you know what it's like to really feel like you're doing what you're meant to be doing? I know that sounds hokey."

"I mean, you failed at that." I poked him lightly.

He gave me a wry half-grin. "It's tough when you fall in love with a racist industry."

I smirked and started picking up perfume boxes, sorting them. The shop vendor asked if I wanted to buy anything, but I waved him off without speaking.

I didn't know quite what Amit meant by that feeling of doing what he was meant to do, of feeling more himself. I couldn't think of a time I'd ever felt like myself.

"Anyway," started Amit. "I'd rather have Mom and Dad on my side about acting, but that's asking a lot of Indian parents." He picked up a small box of CK1. He tossed the box in the air and caught it behind his back with his other hand. The shop vendor chastised him in Hindi, and he held his hands up in apology and backed out of the stall.

I followed him out. "I don't know if I could do that. Stress Mom and Dad like that, make them give up all their dreams, everything they've worked so hard for." My brain could only hear my mom's voice saying *what will people think* over and over.

"You don't know if you could fail at your dreams and then slink home to work for Dad?" said Amit.

"To be fair, nothing you do at the office is actual work."

He laughed, but without bitterness. "At least Dad has you for that."

"Lucky me."

He put his arm around my shoulder. "Come. Let's see if Shannon actually bought anything yet."

"Are we going to spend all our time shopping? We did that yesterday with Mom."

"Yes, but this time, Mom's not here." He pulled me along to see what Shannon had found.

I waved him ahead. "You go ahead. I'll catch up."

He let go. "Suit yourself."

I called Bryan back, hoping he would pick up. He did. "I'm sorry," I said. "You're not coming. I get it."

"And you're going to tell your family?"

"Mom already knows." I thought of our conversation in the dress shop. I didn't have to go home to Bryan. There was another choice.

"You told your mom?" He sounded surprised.

"She worked it out. But yeah, we talked a bit. It was kind of okay."

"That's new." A pause. "Why are you calling back, Pi?"

"I know you're not coming," I said. "And I know you said you wanted to take a minute on the donor eggs. But I'm here anyway, so maybe I can check out some clinics?" I wasn't sure how I'd pull that off. But perhaps Amit and Shannon could help me. "Just to get a feel for how it works here."

I could hear Bryan rearranging himself under the sheets and blanket. He'd evidently gone to bed. "I don't know that you should. The idea of going to some other country and taking some stranger's DNA. I'm not comfortable with it."

I spotted Amit and Shannon leaving the shoe place. Amit caught my eye and we nodded at each other as he and Shannon went to check out another store. "Okay," I said. "So if we don't, what then?"

"We live our lives," said Bryan. "Work, hang out with our families. We'll have a backyard soon, we can have a barbecue with our old friends."

It was exactly the same life we planned on, but the thought I'd had earlier was still vibrating in my brain. "But if we don't have kids, we have other choices."

"Like what?"

I didn't have an answer yet. "I'm just exploring the idea. We wouldn't have to restrict ourselves in the same way."

"Yeah, but who's restricting us? We have an awesome house in a great area. Maybe down the road we could get a sports car since we wouldn't need a minivan. I guess that would be cool. Or maybe we could afford a cottage."

I didn't know quite what to think. Bryan was describing all the markers of a successful life, the kind my parents had always wanted for me, and here I was with a vague idea of a life that I'd be criticized for living. I looked up, spotted Amit leaning in close to Shannon while she looked at clothes, and then they both burst out laughing. I couldn't see Amit and Shannon in a bland house on a bland street. Was that part of what Amit meant by feeling the most like himself?

"Pi?"

"I've got to go, Bry."

CHAPTER THIRTEEN

December 2010, Mumbai

RESHMA MASI ARRANGED FOR SHRUTI AND ME to go with Malika to get a manicure and pedicure before the pre-wedding parties began. "This way, you girls can talk," she said, looking directly at me.

"Shouldn't Shannon come?" asked Shruti.

Reshma Masi shook her head. "Better for you married ladies to talk." She giggled, but it rang false. Before we left, she pulled me aside. "Remember. Tell her how to be happy in marriage."

The salon was neat and clean, with pure, plain white walls and clinical florescent light. It smelled of nail polish and tropical fruit, with a hint of a cleaning agent behind it. We sat in our chairs, our feet in pans of warm water, and a pedicurist sitting beside them. I noticed they used faded, mismatched towels, a small crack in the impression they were trying to make.

I had no idea what to say to Malika. "What's Raj like?"

She shrugged and gave a half-smile. "He's a good person." She had her phone in front of her, tapping out replies to messages as they came in.

"That sounds like something your mother would say," said Shruti, smiling as she glanced at a pamphlet of services. "Oh look, they have facials here. And massages."

"It is what my mother says."

"What do you say?"

Malika looked bewildered. "What more is there to say?"

I gave her a sharp look. "Was this arranged?"

"Payal," said Shruti.

"It still happens."

"Not in our family," said Shruti. Our grandparents had been betrothed as children, growing up always knowing who they would marry. Ammaji had practically lived with her future in-laws as a girl, so that she could get used to her future home. Our parents had been more semi-arranged, with introductions set up by the families, but with the bride and groom given a few weeks to get to know each other and make a choice.

"I've known Raj some time," said Malika. "We came to know each other and decided it would be a good match."

"We'll meet him soon," said Shruti. "Right Malika?"

She nodded and turned to me. "When can I meet Bryan?"

"Soon," I said. I pretended not to notice Shruti's expression, one that both said *Yeah right* and *I'm not saying a word* all at the same time.

"What's he like?" asked Malika.

I smiled. "He's a good person. We came to know each other for some time, and decided it would be a good match." They laughed, but it struck me that I didn't have much more to say about Bryan than Malika did about Raj. "Actually, we've been having some problems."

Malika's eyes flicked up from her phone. "Are you fighting?"

I remembered her visiting as a little girl, scared and sad from her parents' arguing. What had it been like when she went back? Had her parents even told her what was happening, or was Ashok Masa simply gone, working in Dubai, never to return, and Malika left to piece things together over time?

I owed her the truth, but also the gentlest version of the

truth. "We're just discussing," I said. "But we can't quite agree yet."

"What can't you agree on?" asked Malika.

I thought about what to say. The most recent was the house, which I'd only realized was a problem because of the infertility. Which was also a problem because of the donor eggs. Which was something we could investigate here, except Bryan didn't come because of Mom. Which wasn't exactly a problem I thought Malika would understand. "We just can't agree on what our life is supposed to look like."

"What do you mean?"

I squirmed a little in my chair, trying not to twist my foot out of the pedicurist's hands. "Like, he wants to move to a big house, and I think we could do something else."

"Your new house?" asked Shruti. "You don't want it anymore?"

"I don't think we need it," I said. "It's too much space."

"Who complains about too much space?" asked Shruti.

I glowered at her and was ready to tell her off, but Malika interrupted us. "Did you live by yourself before you got married, Didi?"

"No," I said. "I lived at home when I was at university, and then when Bryan and I got engaged there was no reason to leave until after the wedding." I remembered our friends thinking it was strange that we didn't live together before getting married, like I was part of some horribly restrictive culture. Even Bryan thought it was strange. But it hadn't seemed worth fighting with my parents over. "I always wanted to live on my own," I admitted.

"My single friends say it's lonely," said Shruti. "They're all looking for a guy to marry and have a family with."

Malika sighed. "In India, they don't let you try."

I smiled, ruefully. "In Canada, they don't want you to try either. Not if you're Indian."

"Did Amitbhai live alone?"

"He did in LA," said Shruti. "Sometimes, anyway."

"If he was housesitting," I added. "Other times, he had roommates."

"And now he lives at home?"

Shruti and I exchanged glances. I spoke first. "No. He lives with Shannon."

"Our parents try to pretend it's not happening."

Malika giggled, the first smile I'd seen from her in a while. "I thought everything was different in Canada, but this is just the same."

I remembered thinking that in marrying Bryan, I'd be out of my parents' house with the least amount of fighting for permission. Now I wondered if it would have been the same for me as it was for Amit, that they would pretend like it wasn't happening.

"Are you and Raj moving to your own flat after you get married?" asked Shruti.

Malika resettled in her seat. "We'll be staying with my in-laws." The brief spark of joy had faded from her face.

"Are you going to look for your own place after?"

She shook her head. "I don't think Raj's parents would agree. And my mother would worry that I wasn't pleasing my mother-in-law. This way is better for everyone." She critically examined the shelf of nail polish colours while the pedicurist carried on in silence.

I decided to try doling out some big sisterly advice. "You should talk to Raj about this."

"But what if he wants to stay living with his parents?"

"Is that what he wants?"

"This is India," said Malika. "You get married, you live with the boy's family."

"Not always," said Shruti. "You know that India is changing. Talk to him."

"But what if we end up fighting like Payal Didi and Bryan?"

"We aren't fighting." I took a deep breath. "It's just a discussion."

Malika looked at me carefully. "And everything will be okay between you?"

"Of course," I said brightly, and then hoped it didn't sound too fake. "You have to talk to Raj. Tell him what's important to you."

Shruti took up the narrative with an increasingly reassured-looking Malika. I thought of my conversations with Bryan. He'd told me repeatedly that he wasn't coming to India, but I hadn't believed him. I'd assumed he'd go along because of his easy-going nature. It hadn't occurred to me that there were limits to that nature, and that I'd gone too far.

Was there any coming back from this?

Did I want to come back from this?

We moved on to the manicure station. I walked across the spotless pink floor on my bare heels, trying to make sure I didn't smudge my toes. Malika had never talked to Raj about what she wanted, but had I ever talked to Bryan about what I wanted, or just what I thought was expected of me?

What if Malika could postpone the wedding and find a place of her own? Spend time really talking to Raj about their life together? It would be near-impossible for her to do it, but it had only been uncomfortable for me, and I hadn't tried. What might have been different if I had?

While our manicures were drying, Malika suggested we get a coffee. "There's a good place near here."

Shruti shook her head. "I want a facial. Pregnancy is making my face break out."

"Please," said Malika. "We must go. It's a very good coffee shop."

"I'd rather stay."

Malika sat up in her chair, and looked at me pleadingly. The idea of a facial was appealing, but it was unlike Malika to insist. On the other hand, it was also unlike Shruti to say no. "Shru, why don't you stay? Malika and I can meet you back here afterward."

Shruti agreed and Malika and I pushed our way out of the

cold salon and into the hot, dusty sunshine. The streets still made me uneasy, the people dressed in a mix of Western and Indian clothes walking by, as if oblivious to other people in rags holding out their grimy hands and asking for money, the cars packed in the streets as if the line markings were widely-ignored suggestions, the smell of diesel and smoke, and the sense of being swallowed up in a slew of others who moved at a confident pace while I picked a hesitant path, trying to keep an eye on Malika, who kept getting ahead of me.

The coffee shop was small, with white tile floors and large purple and red signs that read "Café Coffee Day. A lot can happen over coffee." The bright, printed sign stood out amid the hand-lettered signs at the stores around it.

We waited in line to order, the conversations in the café echoing and blending together. "I need you to help me, Payal Didi. But you have to keep it a secret."

My heart sank. Was Malika going to call off the wedding? How could I help her without my mom, Reshma Masi, and Ammaji coming down on me for ruining everything? How could I not help her if she didn't want to go through with it?

She shifted her weight from one foot to the next, as if she couldn't yet get comfortable with standing. "My father wants to meet me."

Outside, I could hear car horns and the screech of brakes, followed by the sound of several people all trying to shout each other down. Had there been an accident? I couldn't understand the words. But inside the café, no one appeared to react. "Your father is in Dubai."

She shook her head. "He wanted to see me before the wedding, but he didn't want my mom to know. I didn't want to meet him alone."

"Is that why we're here?" I could have been having a relaxing facial with Shruti.

"He never wanted to see me before. Why does he want to meet me now?"

I tried to think, but the constant clatter of dishes and scraping of chairs under the echoing rattle of conversation in the café made it hard to focus. Was this why Reshma Masi thought Malika wasn't herself? "Maybe because you're getting married? It seems only natural."

"Do you think so?"

I had no idea. In a Hallmark movie, this would be some sort of a special father-daughter moment, some bonding time before giving the bride away at the wedding, but we were hardly in small-town America. I was out of my depth here. "Did you talk to anyone about it? Kajal? Kaushik?"

She shook her head. "My mom might hear and she would be so mad. He's only coming to the wedding ceremony because she thinks it won't look good if he's not there."

Reshma Masi would be upset that I'd enabled this visit, but I couldn't leave Malika to deal with this on her own. But I still needed a moment to clear my head. I told Malika I'd save a table for us, and miraculously, one cleared just as I got to it.

I didn't remember what Ashok Masa looked like, but I scanned the room for anyone who looked familiar. I brushed the crumbs off the white plastic table. Had Ashok Masa found a way out of the system? Living on his own in Dubai, but still giving the outward appearance of not letting anyone down? Except, of course, for Reshma Masi and Malika.

I imagined Bryan moving to the house while I stayed in our condo, never letting my parents know that we'd split up. It was a futile thought; I knew he wouldn't agree, and what would be the point, anyway?

What if I'd had the guts to live on my own? To not get married? To ignore all the pressure, like Amit had? There were a few big decisions that had put me here, but they'd been made up of so many tiny choices, ones made in the hopes of it all being easier, or less confrontational, or simply more normal. The hard part wasn't deciding to do something different, but deciding in myriad ways over and over and over again.

At the next table sat a pale-faced little girl. She sighed heavily and lay her head sideways on the table, as if she were carrying the problems of the world on her back. She looked the way I felt. But then a man sat in front of her, and set a tall glass of ice cream and chocolate syrup down. She perked up and dove in. For a moment, I pictured Bryan at a similar table with a similar girl, and smiled to myself.

"Papa?"

I twisted around and saw Malika standing behind me, holding two coffees.

The man at the table turned. "Malika!" The little girl, now swinging her feet, kept spooning up ice cream, a smear of chocolate on her lip. The man—was it really Ashok Masa?—glanced away from Malika and, using his thumb, carefully wiped the smear off the child's face. He turned back to Malika. "This is your younger sister, Dipika."

"Mummy never told me..." Malika's whisper trailed off and then she started shouting. "You never told me!"

"Malika." He half-stood, but didn't go to her. Dipika dropped her spoon and was looking up at her father.

Ashok Masa began speaking in Gujarati in a cajoling tone, but Malika's voice only got more frantic and choked with angry tears. Ashok Masa began to sound defensive, gesturing at Malika to calm herself, which made her more upset. I sat at the edge of my seat, not knowing when or how to intervene, watching the argument grow. Should I get Malika out of here? Or was she saying something she needed to say? Around us, everyone in the coffee shop had gone silent, watching the argument unfold.

Dipika had forgotten about her ice cream, her small head

swivelling between Malika and her father, her eyes growing bigger and rounder, an echo of Malika as a child. She burst into tears, and Ashok Masa turned from Malika mid-sentence to attend to her, giving her a hug and speaking soothingly to her, and then pointing a chastising finger at Malika and berating her in a sharp voice.

Malika stood still a moment, her eyes flared with anger and her face wet with tears, before turning and pushing her way outside. The people in the café began to mumble disapprovingly in her direction. I went after her, glancing back before leaving to see her father look towards the door, hesitate for a moment, and then turn away to soothe his younger daughter.

I shouldered my way through the chaos of the street back to the nail salon, where I hoped Malika was heading. I found her a few stores away, crying.

I gave her a hug and she sniffled into my shoulder. "Raj would never do this."

"No," I told her. "He's a good person."

She nodded but didn't look up. "Everyone says so. Everyone can't be wrong. Can they?"

I patted the long, dark hair that fell over her back. "No. Everyone can't be wrong."

* * *

Mom had commandeered the driver for the morning, and brought me to a low grey office building. The uniformed guard nodded at us as he stepped aside, answering my mom's brief questions. They weren't speaking in English and she hadn't told me where we were going, and nothing about the blandly modern building gave me any clues. We entered through a frosted glass door to a reception area when I realized we were in a doctor's office. A fertility doctor's office.

"Why are we here?"

"I told you I'd fix everything." She accepted a cup of chai from the office peon, and gestured to me to take one. I waved it away, but she took a second cup and gave it to me.

Bryan would be angry that I was here. I lowered my voice. "You know Bryan and I are having problems."

"I already made the appointment." She picked up a magazine and began flipping through it.

"Without telling me?" I put down the cup of chai on a side table.

"I told you. How did you think I would fix it?"

"You should have talked to me."

She kept flipping pages. "Well, we're here."

Eventually, we were led into a smaller, private office. The doctor was a man with a soft face and a soft voice. He began running through the clinic's success rates before asking me where my husband was.

My mom answered. "He's still in Canada. He'll come next time."

The doctor turned to her. "What is the issue?"

Mom gestured at me. The numbers jumbled in my head: hormone levels, follicle count and sizes, medication dosages, the number of cycles we'd tried.

I took a deep breath and organized my thoughts, then ran through the timelines: Two years of trying before we'd seen the reproductive endocrinologist. Three years with the reproductive endocrinologist. What we'd been told, what we tried, what happened. The doctor only nodded and took notes, but as I spoke I could only feel the weight of the time and effort of trying for so long.

I summarized the entire story. The doctor nodded in confirmation, and asked my mom about medical records.

I caught the words 'Canada' and 'shaadi'—wedding—in her reply. They began a rapid back and forth, the doctor at first seeming annoyed and then relenting, and I wondered why I even needed to be in the room at all.

We were led to another room and waited at a conference table. "What's going on?"

"The doctor wanted to start trying today."

"Mom!"

She ignored me. "I told him we wanted to choose the donor first. Make sure he has good ones."

"We can't pick a donor today." I could feel the blood pulsing at my temples, felt the constriction as pressure built up.

"Don't worry, I'll make sure we pick the right donor, right family."

The moment of understanding we'd had at the dress shop now felt like a sham. I was foolish for thinking Mom could change. "Bryan's not here." Surely, she knew we couldn't proceed without him. I was horrified at the possibility of having to say the word 'sperm' to my mother.

"We can still look." She started rummaging in her purse for her reading glasses.

"This is totally crossing the line!"

Her face twisted in annoyance and disgust. "What kind of a daughter are you? How can you make a decision like this for yourself? If I were dead, would you be grateful for me then?" I tried to interrupt but she plowed on. "What did I do in my past life to deserve a daughter like you? You should be happy I'm here to pick a child for you who won't turn out like you."

"Mom—"

"Do you think I don't have your best interests at heart? I have been on this earth much longer than you, you think I know nothing?"

"You can't pick someone's child for them."

"Why not? If I'd picked your husband for you, it would be the same."

"It's not the same."

"How?"

She was right and she was wrong and I was too angry to find the words to explain it to her. "Well, you didn't pick my husband."

She sniffed and turned back to her purse. "Maybe I should have." She plucked out her glasses and then leaned back in her chair, not looking at me. I slouched, angry with myself for speaking up, but also wondering if she saw something I hadn't seen about Bryan. Were we a mismatch? Was it obvious?

A woman in a trim grey skirt suit came in with a thick folder. "Today, I cannot show you all the donors. You must become a patient first. But here is an idea."

I expected Mom to argue, but she only nodded, and the woman placed the folder in front of her and opened it. Mom began paging through, passing me papers after she scanned them. I was reminded of matrimonial ads I used to see in my parents' copies of *India Abroad*: fair skin, good family, well-educated, homely. *Homely* always sounded odd to me until I realized that in India it meant good at housekeeping. I half-smiled, remembering myself as a teenager telling Shruti she was homely.

"No pictures?" asked Mom.

The woman shook her head.

"In Canada, we can see pictures," I added.

"In India, this is not allowed. Donation is completely anonymous. No one will ever know."

"How do we know if the skin is fair?" asked Mom. "Or the family is good?" She tapped the papers. "I want to see for myself."

The woman began explaining in a mixture of English and what was probably Hindi. I caught the words *highest standards* and *best quality*. "Husband is white, hm?" Mom nodded. "Then there is no problem. Husband's skin will balance out any issues with the donor, nothing to worry."

"What about the family?" asked Mom.

"Your family will be the family," she said, deliberately misinterpreting the question.

A spider of worry crawled up my spine. "Is this a closed donation?"

"If you have questions about the donor, we can tell you the answers. But this is the law in India. No contact between the donor and any child arising from donation. No information to identify the donor can be given."

"But how will the child know their heritage?"

"Your heritage will be their heritage, Madam. They will be your child."

I wondered if that would be enough. My own sense of my own heritage was so thinly grasped. We could be building the next generation of our family, and all of its expectations, on a blank slate, a lie of omission because we were not permitted the truth.

I started to speak, but Mom put a quieting hand on mine, and then asked a few more questions in Hindi and nodded. She flipped through more papers without really looking, and then handed them back. The woman gave us some brochures, smiling pictures of pretend families, which my mom passed to me, and then the woman walked us out. I didn't catch what she said as we left, only the cheery tone of her voice.

Mom texted the driver, and we stood in the lobby for a moment, waiting. She looked at me, and as I gathered my thoughts to try and explain why we couldn't go ahead, she shook her head. "This is not a good idea."

I nodded, limbs softening in relief. Did she understand more than I had realized?

Mom pulled out her phone to play Sudoku while we waited. I pulled out my own and texted Bryan. *You were right. We should rethink donor eggs.*

CHAPTER FOURTEEN

October 2002, Toronto

"YOU'RE SO EXOTIC," HE SAID, and then leaned in to kiss me again. It was soggy, wet and sloppy, all lip and tongue and the taste of beer. This was my first time kissing anyone, but I hoped he couldn't tell. Was it always this wet? I kept kissing him, since that's what college girls were supposed to do at parties. Wasn't it? But at least if one of my classmates asked me about my weekend on Monday, I wouldn't have to say *Stayed home and studied.*

Stayed home and studied was what all the other Indian girls seemed to do, the ones who were like me and lived at home. Unless there was some kind of a South Asian Student Association event, in which case they all went out to look for suitable Indian husbands that their parents would approve of. I never went to those events because I didn't want to be like those girls. I mean, I lived at home like they did, and studied diligently like they did, and listened to my parents, and was even in accounting with a lot of them. But I wanted people to see that I was different. That I was my own unique person, unlike all those good Indian girls who looked like me, even if I wasn't exactly sure who that person was.

None of those girls were at this frat party. I'd lied my way out of the house to get here. It was my first real college party. There was only one more year of university left, but maybe there was still time to have a normal college life.

I opened my eyes, but all I could see was an extreme close-up of his face, nose, and closed eyes, and forehead framed by hair. There were people all around us when he started. Were they watching me? Could there possibly be someone who would report this back to my parents here? I'd told them I was sleeping over at Denise's house, where her parents also lived, although in fact, Denise's parents lived in Alberta, and Denise lived in a dorm.

"I guess you could crash with me," said Denise, when I'd asked her where I could stay the night. "Like, on the floor."

"What should I wear?" Denise and I weren't really friends, but she was borrowing my notes again, so I figured I could ask.

She shrugged. "You know, party stuff."

I didn't quite know, but I dug out a black satin tank top that I'd been hiding from my parents and wore it with my low rise jeans. Denise said I looked good when I got dressed at her place. I felt like the top was too low-cut, too much like lingerie instead of actual clothing, but a quick glance at the other women at the party told me that I was being too conservative. I would not let my parents' out-of-touch rules define me. I would be normal.

The guy I was kissing suddenly put a hand on my breast and began squeezing. It hurt. I grimaced slightly.

"Does this turn you on?" he breathed into my ear, but kept doing it, not waiting for an answer. He leaned his weight forward against me, crushing me and pushing me back against the couch with him on top of me. I glimpsed around the darkened room. No one was paying attention to us. Other people were sitting around, drinking and talking, hardly giving us a look.

"I've always wanted to do it with an Indian chick," he said. "Indian chicks are so hot."

I could feel panic starting to form in my stomach and spreading through my body. Was he going to try something right here? I couldn't do this, not with him, not in the middle of a party.

I didn't even know his name.

His bare fingers were making their way under my bra. I pushed him away and tried to struggle upright. He kept trying to keep me down. "Wait," I said. "Wait."

He pulled back and let me sit up. I tried pulling the top of my shirt up higher but it slid down again. It was too low cut. It didn't matter that other people my age dressed like this. I was lame.

"You want to go somewhere quiet?" he said.

"I have to go to the bathroom," I said quickly, and got up to leave the room.

He stood up too and blocked my path. "Come on," he said. "There's one upstairs."

"No, really. I have to find my friend."

He grabbed my wrist and tugged but I didn't move. People pushed passed us to get into the room. I glanced back. The couch we had been on was already occupied.

"Come on," he said.

"I really need to find my friend. And pee. But I need to find her first."

He rolled his eyes but let go of my wrist. "Whatever." His shoulder slammed against mine as he pushed passed me, making me stumble. "Bitch."

I was relieved and also ashamed. He thought I was a loser and he was right. A goody two-shoes like my sister, indistinguishable from every other good Indian girl. I couldn't be normal. I hadn't been raised normal. I wiped my mouth with the back of my hand and it came away wet. Gross.

Denise would make fun of me when she found out what happened. I just knew she would, because I wasn't cool and didn't know what to do when some guy drooled on me. But he did call me *exotic*. Should I have said thank you? It didn't feel like a compliment, even though I think he intended it that way. House plants are exotic.

I wandered from room to room, looking for Denise. I didn't see her. I saw the guy and ducked away before he saw me, and then I realized he was chatting up another girl. I felt pathetic for hiding from him; he'd forgotten me in a minute. I was just some ridiculous girl he'd tried to make out with, a lame-ass girl who was wandering around alone at a party because she sucked too much to have friends.

I recognized one of Denise's friends standing by a speaker and talking to some other people. Denise had disappeared with her and some others within minutes of getting to the party. I tapped her on the shoulder and yelled over the music. "Hey, have you seen Denise?"

"Uh, I think she might have left?" She turned back to the conversation. I tapped her shoulder again.

"Is she going home?"

"I don't know. She might have left with someone?"

"I'm supposed to crash at her place. What am I supposed to do?"

The girl shrugged. "Maybe she's outside? I don't know. I definitely saw her leave the house."

I thanked her and went out on the porch. A few people were standing around and smoking, but no Denise. Shit. What was I going to do? I couldn't go home—how could I explain why I wasn't at Denise's or what I was wearing? My regular clothes were at her place.

Not for the first time, I cursed my parents for not understanding what was normal in this country. They'd lived here long enough—why didn't they understand? Denise had been shocked when I told her I wasn't allowed to go to frat parties.

"You're twenty-one years old! What do you mean, you aren't allowed?" she'd asked when she was chatting about her weekend plans.

"It's just different with us."

Her eyes had widened. "What, like your father would beat you? For dishonouring the family?"

"God, no, nothing like that."

"Does he have a marriage arranged for you? Your future husband would reject you?"

"No," I said. "It's just different." I didn't know how to explain. You weren't an adult because you turned a certain age and could suddenly do whatever you wanted. Someone had to step aside and let you, had to believe it was fine and not argue with you about living on your own as if you were talking about arming yourself to rob a bank and buy heroin. It was that or being constantly reminded that you were a disappointment, and being called on to justify your choices daily. I'd seen them do that to Amit, although I guess he could ignore it better from LA.

Denise let it go, but she didn't understand. How could she? Her parents asked if she was seeing anyone.

I sat on the porch steps. It was a warm night, but my face felt cold from tears that had spilled over. I couldn't find Denise and even if I could, I didn't know if I'd be able to stay there—what if she had some guy over? I couldn't stay all night at the frat house, not with that guy I'd kissed and who knows who else living here. I couldn't go home because I'd constructed a huge web of lies about where I was and who I was with and what I was doing. I'd even made up an early morning study session at school so that my parents wouldn't try to pick me up from Denise's and meet her parents. I'd planned to tell them that it had wrapped up early to explain why no one else was there.

"You okay?" A guy with spiky blond hair stood in front of me. He looked familiar.

"I'm having a bad night," I said.

He sat down next to me. "You're in my calc class, right?"

"Am I?" But it turned out I was. I usually saw him amid a group of friends, but right now he was alone.

"I'm Bryan."

"Payal."

"Sorry, what?"

"Just call me Pi." I wasn't in the mood to go through the hassle.

He grinned. "Hey, we rhyme. Pi and Bry."

I stayed quiet. Had I made him believe we were a thing? I didn't think I had, but I hadn't consciously signalled to the guy from earlier that we were doing anything but talking, and then suddenly he was all over me. How could I know what I was telling people when no one had taught me the language? When I couldn't let anyone see that I didn't know? I hugged my knees close. Bryan didn't move any closer, keeping a clear gap between us.

"You're not in comp sci too, right?"

"Accounting."

He nodded. "I'd have remembered if you were in comp sci."

Another guy leaned out the front door. "You coming, Bryan?"

"I'm good."

The guy glanced over at me and went back in.

"You don't have to stay out here with me," I said, looking back at the door.

Bryan shrugged. "It's only a party."

We chatted a bit about class, about homework, about nothing in particular. The feeling of being a loser faded a little. People going in and out of the party would see me as a normal college girl talking to a normal college guy about normal college things. The porch light glowed around us like a campfire. Bryan's friends came out with their drinks or smokes and would chat with us. Eventually, more people came out than went in.

I hadn't intended to explain my dilemma, but he was easy to talk to. "It's embarrassing. But I can't go home."

He sat back, thoughtful for a second. I waited for that look, like the one Denise had when I told her about needing permission from my parents. I'd seen that look on people all my life. But instead, he said, "Don't take this the wrong way, but you could crash at my place."

"What?"

"I live at home with my folks. The couch pulls out into a bed. This is a totally platonic offer." He held his hands up in peace. "It's out in Scarborough, but I could drive you to your friend's place in the morning."

"Your parents won't mind?"

"No, they'll be fine. My sister used to have friends crash on the couch. My parents always say it's better for us to get home safe than worry about getting in trouble. Same goes for our friends."

I could get my clothes, go to my fake study session on campus, and my parents would be none the wiser. I studied Bryan for a second, and he smiled back. He hadn't so much as patted my shoulder, unlike the guy who'd slobbered on me earlier. "Why are you doing this for me?"

"Why not?"

"But why?"

He gestured around helplessly. "I don't know. So when I see you in calc, you don't think, *Oh, there's that asshole Bryan, he left me sitting outside a frat house all night.*"

I gave him a half-smile and could feel myself relax. "Okay."

He stood up. "Let's go."

"You're not mad you missed the party?"

He waved this off. "It's just a party. There'll be another party." He reached out his hand. I grabbed it and pulled myself up. The lie I'd told my parents would stay intact. I wouldn't have to face their disappointment nor would I lose what little freedom I had.

Bryan's mother, Barb, was sitting on the couch when we got in. I half-expected an interrogation about who I was and what I was doing here and why we were out so late—but there was none. "Nonsense," she'd said, when Bryan offered me the couch. "Lindsey's spending the night at Greg's. She won't mind if—"

she hesitated over my name "—your friend stays in her room."

Was this real life or television? "The couch is fine," I said.

Barb led me upstairs. "Do you need water? It'll help with the hangover." She stopped and looked at me. "You're not going to be sick, are you?"

I shook my head. I'd only drunk a few sips of beer from a red plastic cup I'd carried around so I wouldn't look out of place. It had been my first beer, and I hadn't liked it at all.

Barb nodded approvingly. "Smart girl. Know your limits." She bustled around, finding a T-shirt for me in one of the drawers. "I remember the first time Lindsey came home drunk." She began to chuckle. "She was so miserable and tried to hide it. I ran the vacuum cleaner right outside her door at seven in the morning—she'd come home at five. The look she gave me."

I laughed along with her, but I was still amazed. Did all white people have it this easy? Not even Amit would risk coming home drunk. My parents wouldn't have laughed over it. They'd have lectured us endlessly over what people would think, and how this reflected badly on them, and that we'd never find anyone good to marry us if people knew we were such worthless children, and what did they do in their past life to deserve this?

Bryan drove me to Denise's the next morning and went with me to her dorm. I knocked and waited. Then knocked again. Eventually, she opened the door; her hair was messy and her makeup smeared, as if she'd slept with it on.

"Sorry," I said. "I came to get my things."

She yawned and glanced behind me. "Who's the guy?"

Bryan introduced himself, and they chatted about the party and people they knew while I gathered up my belongings and changed in the bathroom.

I thanked him when I came out. "You totally saved my life."

He half-smiled. "It's no big deal." He said nothing, and for a second the air was both very still and full of sparks at the same time.

Is he going to kiss me?

"So, you okay from here?" he asked.

I nodded.

"I'll see you in class then."

Of course he wasn't going to kiss me. Why would he? "Yeah," I said. "See you." I wasn't sure if I was disappointed or relieved.

As soon as he was out of earshot, Denise started asking me about him. "He's cute," she said. She seemed impressed with me. I was strangely proud. "Are you going to see him again?"

I attempted a casual shrug and immediately wondered if it looked fake. "Maybe."

CHAPTER FIFTEEN

December 2010, Mumbai

WE HAD A QUIET EVENING WITH RAJ and his family, a moment of calm before all the wedding parties began, quiet and calm being relative terms in India. There must have been fifty people in and out of the flat, everyone considered a close relation. Ammaji, Geeta Mami, my mother and the cook, along with some of the other women, were busy putting freshly made food out on the table and insisting everyone take more. Reshma Masi was in and out of the kitchen too, trying to be helpful but mostly getting in other people's way.

It was the first time I'd met Raj, and nothing about my first impression distinguished him as anything more than a nice boy. He was taller than Malika but not tall, and had a thin mustache—like so many Indian men—and medium-toned skin. He sat slightly hunched, as if ready to shrink into the background.

Malika and Raj sat beside each other on the couch with a decorous space between them as people cycled in and out of conversation with them, each person asking them if they were excited about the wedding. Shruti was off to the side, getting pregnancy and baby advice from every aunty in the place. At least I would never go through that.

I sat with Amit and Shannon, which meant I didn't need to talk much, since when people came by to talk they'd be struck by Shannon's whiteness and red hair. They'd ask her what she thought of India and make the same joke about her and Amit getting married at Raj and Malika's wedding. I don't know how she managed to sound enthusiastic answering the same question over and over again, but it meant I could contemplate my babyless existence in peace.

Amit was also strangely quiet. He kept checking his phone for messages.

"Did you have a hot date?" I asked.

"Ha ha." But he didn't look up.

I'd left my phone in the bedroom so I couldn't keep looking at Bryan's last message. He'd been relieved to see my text from after the fertility clinic visit with my mom. But then he'd sent: *Maybe we should talk to a marriage counsellor?*

Did he think our marriage was that bad? And if it was, we should go to counselling, but the idea sounded tiring.

I overheard Raj talking about their honeymoon plans. "We're going to a hill station in Mahabaleshwar."

Shannon nudged Amit and asked: "What's a hill station?"

"Like a resort town," said Amit. "But up in the mountains where it's cooler. The British established them because they were wilting in the heat."

I'd been to Mahabaleshwar with Malika and the rest of the family. There was a long mountain drive to get there. Every day was the same. We'd stayed at the resort and mostly never left, spending the days sitting in our rooms or beside the clean, unused pool. We ate thali, a set meal served in stainless steel dishes, for breakfast, lunch and dinner every day at the resort restaurant.

The memory reminded me of my future life with Bryan. Was this why we needed counselling? Bryan hadn't seemed unhappy with our future when we talked about it, so why was he suggesting counselling?

I tried to stop thinking about it by focusing on the voices around me. Shannon was talking about their plans to visit the Taj Mahal after the wedding. “I can't wait,” she said. “I can't believe Amit's never been.”

“None of us have,” I said. “We're always busy visiting relatives.”

Naresh nodded his agreement from his seat beside Shruti. “Same story for everyone. We hardly get to see so much of our family for so many years. There's never enough time to spend with them.”

“I wish I could go,” said Malika. “Such a romantic place.”

“That would make a beautiful honeymoon,” said Shannon. “And there's a lot to do nearby in Delhi. I have all kinds of places highlighted in my Lonely Planet.”

“Oh yes,” said Raj. “Much to see. But Delhi is very dangerous. You could talk to a stranger, and the next thing you know, they have made you smuggle drugs.” He began advising Shannon to be careful.

I nudged Amit, who was still checking his phone. “Did you hear that?”

“Hmmm?”

“Did you have a job interview? We trained you and now you're off to KPMG?”

“Shut up.”

Seeing his irritation, I keep ribbing him. “Listen, if you can't make it at Dad's firm, I don't know if a Big Four firm is for you, but maybe you can act your way through the interview.”

He glanced around and lowered his voice. “If you must know, I'm waiting to hear from my agent.”

“I thought you failed at acting.”

“I failed at LA.” He popped a dahi puri in his mouth from a plate Mom had set in front of us earlier.

"Have you talked to Dad about this?"

"What for?"

I picked up a dahi puri of my own and crunched it. The dahi hadn't soaked into the puri yet so it had all the textures: crackly puri, creamy yogurt, crunchy sev, soft tomato and potato, sweet and hot chutneys. It was fresh and delicious and this annoyed me, because it didn't suit my mood.

Near us, Kajal sat on the floor, legs partly spread and baby Saanvi sprawled in the space between. She couldn't crawl yet, so she lay there, waving her arms and legs at her mother and trying to kick off her socks. Every few minutes, Kajal straightened out the baby's clothes and pulled her socks back on.

"Her dress is so cute," said Shruti. "I can't believe her socks are so tiny."

Kaushik smiled from the sofa. "Every time we leave the house, Saanvi has a new outfit. Everything matching. Matching dress, matching socks, matching hat."

I leaned over to look. For hanging out at home, Saanvi was wearing a green-and-pink dress, with green-and-pink bloomers over her diaper, green-and-pink socks on her feet, and tiny green-and-pink bows in her wisps of hair. Bryan's niece and nephew were never dressed this ridiculously.

"It's so hard," said Kajal. "But each time she goes out, I make sure she's properly dressed. This way, she grows up knowing she must be looking nice all the time. She must understand proper values."

"That's so smart," said Shruti. "I never would have thought of that."

I wondered how my sister had suddenly lost her brain. Since when was clothing a value? I looked around the room, but everyone who'd heard was smiling agreeably. Only Shannon's face showed a flicker of disapproval, but she quickly replaced her expression with a warm smile. "Mothers. Always making things so hard on themselves."

There was a small relief in this, that there wouldn't be yet another thing I'd get wrong all the time now that parenthood was off the table.

Raj moved on the couch to be closer to Amit and me. "So, you all work in your father's company?"

Amit nodded. "Yes, all three of us."

I smiled and looked past Raj at Malika, who was paging through Shannon's *Lonely Planet* guide, gushing over places to go and see in India. I hoped Raj would take her travelling, to go to places beyond a resort at a quiet hill station.

Raj smiled back. "I'm doing IT in my father's company."

He was clearly expecting praise. "Sounds great," I said.

"In Mumbai, you can have anything you want if you work hard." He laughed a little, to show he was about to make a joke. "But I am not working hard, I am hardly working."

Amit caught my eye, but kept his expression bland. "Sounds great," he said, imitating my unenthusiastic tone.

I picked up another dahi puri and ate it, scanning the room for an escape from this conversation. I saw my mom sitting next to Ammaji, in her usual simple white homespun sari. I looked back at Saanvi, then at Ammaji again. Proper values.

Raj was still talking. "Some men, they want very extraordinary life. But I only want an ordinary life." He looked over at Malika, who was now excitedly pointing things out to Shannon in the *Lonely Planet* guide. "Wife, job, family life. For me, this is enough."

I suppressed a sigh. Malika's life would be stuck with this boring man, but he wouldn't abandon her like her father. I hoped it would be enough for her. It seemed to satisfy so many people, Bryan included. Is that what marriage counselling would do? Help me realize that what I had was all I needed, even with no children but with a perfectly decent husband and a perfectly nice home?

And yet, when I thought about Malika, I hoped she'd have more than that. Because for me, following the beaten path felt like so much trudging over hardened ground.

"Tell me," Raj said. "In Canada, do you all live alone?"

"Not exactly," said Amit.

I spoke up before Amit could explain about living with Shannon and undoubtedly shock Raj. "My husband and I have our own place."

"Your husband is Canadian, yes?"

He meant white. "Yes."

Raj nodded as if that explained everything. "It seems very lonely, everyone by themselves. Not a joint family system like in India."

"Shruti and Naresh live separate from their parents," said Malika.

Malika had spoken up; I smiled at her a little before continuing with Raj. "You don't find this too much? Too much noise, too many people?" I gestured at the claustrophobic room full of the chatter of voices everywhere, the clanging of stainless steel and china plates from the kitchen, the random children I didn't know running around, the rumble-honk of traffic underneath it all.

He looked around, as if noticing the number of people for the first time. "It's best when everyone is here." He looked at me sharply. "Your husband is missing all the fun."

Kajal's voice cut through the clamour. She had gathered up Saanvi and was cooing at her. "Until God brought Saanvi into my life, I did not truly know love. I did not truly know my purpose in life." All the aunties looked on approvingly.

Did she really believe that, or was this what she was always told? And now, what was my purpose in life? Bryan had been right, there was always a next thing I was rushing to do. What did I do now that I was out of nexts?

Kaushik came over and grabbed a dahi puri off the plate in front of Amit and me, popping it in his mouth as he sat down. "I've been thinking."

"Always dangerous," said Amit.

He grinned and continued. "We are all grown now, all of us cousins. We should not wait for our parents to visit before we spend time together."

I thought back to past trips to India. Sitting around and playing Business—Indian Monopoly—with Kaushik and Malika. The time they took us all to an amusement park and Shruti threw up over Kaushik. The time I dared Kaushik to pour a full glass of Tang over Amit's head and was shocked and surprised when he did it. We had history. We were family. Would India be less interminable if we were less distant?

"It's a good idea," said Amit. "We really should start visiting more on our own. Right, Payal?"

"Sure." I had to admit it was nice to see everyone again, to feel that inexplicable bond that linked us, even though we scarcely saw each other. But for me, Mumbai was unbearable.

Kaushik seemed to understand my reluctance. "We don't have to come here. We can meet somewhere else, just all of us together."

"That would be great." My mind churned. Europe was the halfway point between Mumbai and Toronto. Renting a villa in Tuscany was far more palatable than returning to Mumbai. It would be like *Under the Tuscan Sun*: a movie, I immediately realized, about a woman post-divorce.

"Sounds good," confirmed Amit. "We could make a big trip out of it, for all of us."

"Think of the places we could travel," said Kaushik. "So many places in India we haven't seen yet." He began naming them.

My excitement waned. They would always be family, part of us, but with that came a level of discomfort, of differences we couldn't quite cross. I noticed Shruti leaning into the conversation with interest. Perhaps there would be more differences only I couldn't cross.

Malika was enthusiastic. "We could go to the Taj Mahal. Look!" She started flipping through the book. "We could plan and arrange it now."

Raj gently reached over and closed the book. "Someday, we will go."

I stood to stretch my legs and headed toward the bathroom, but instead detoured to a bedroom that was mercifully empty. So many people and most of them were unfamiliar. I could never talk to them about the questions on my mind, about Bryan and what to do with my life now.

I started at the sound of the door opening. Ammaji. She smiled broadly at me, and spoke to Malika, who came in behind her, followed by Shruti and Shannon. Ammaji gestured at everyone to sit on the bed with me, and then opened the metal cabinet, reached inside, and unlocked a box. She pulled out a little plastic box, and then sat on the edge of the bed and opened it. Inside were clear ziploc bags and padded red cloth envelopes. One by one, she opened them, setting out the contents on the bed: necklaces, bracelets, pendants, bangles, earrings. Shruti immediately began picking up pieces and looking at them.

Ammaji spoke and Malika translated. "She wants to give you some of her jewellery."

"Oh, I couldn't," said Shannon. "This is for family."

Ammaji turned her shrunken face to Shannon and spoke softly. She nodded at Malika to translate. "She says, you are all my daughters. And she wants to give away her belongings before she dies."

Shannon took Ammaji's hand and nodded sagely.

"Shouldn't Kajal be here?" I asked. It felt odd to me that Shannon was here and Kajal was not, and yet, Ammaji had called her one of her daughters.

Ammaji spoke, using Kajal's name, then mine and Shruti's, and then Malika's and Amit and Shannon's. The name 'Shannon' sounded odd and foreign coming from Ammaji's mouth. Malika translated: "Kajal picked a piece before her wedding. And Payal and Shruti haven't been here since before they were married. And now it's my turn. She doesn't know if she will be alive for Amit and Shannon's wedding, but she doesn't want to miss this chance."

Shannon hopped off the bed and gave Ammaji a hug. She towered over my grandmother, but Ammaji reached up to hug her back. It occurred to me that for a long time now I had been assuming Amit would tire of Shannon and move on.

On the faded blue sheets, Ammaji arranged her jewellery. Gold, dark yellow 18 karat and 22 karat gold, not the pale, faded 10 karat and 14 karat that people used in North America, was curled into filigrees and coiled around large stones of all different colours: blues and greens and yellows and purples and pinks. Silver too, though it was tarnished black in the intricate corners of the work.

Shruti ran her fingers through the pile. "Are these all real?"

"Some of it is costume jewellery," said Malika.

Ammaji started holding out pieces towards us, inviting us to pick one we liked, and after a few moments of shyness, we all pawed through the rings and pendants and earrings, holding them up and giggling like we were playing dress-up. Shruti lay necklaces over her belly, accessorizing the baby. I felt like a pirate going through loot in a treasure chest. I wondered if we were being overly avaricious, but Ammaji only smiled and pressed a ring into my hand before picking out some bracelets for Malika to try on. She looked the same as always, a plain, slightly worn white sari wrapped around her, her hair oiled into a thinning grey braid. She wore her usual modest gold and diamond wedding ring, small diamond studs in her nose and ears, and a thin gold chain around her neck—the barest minimum by Indian standards.

My aunts and mom habitually sported more and bigger pieces. For my part, I annoyed my mother by wearing nothing beyond a simple wedding band; for me, this was easy and practical, but for Mom, this was both too plain and too little. But where would I wear any of Ammaji's?

The ring she'd passed me was too big for each of my fingers. I passed it to Shannon, and it fit her perfectly. She held it out. The centre stone was a large, pale green citrine. "What do you think?"

Malika giggled. "It matches your eyes."

Ammaji examined Shannon's hand and waggled her head in approval. Shannon smiled and nodded as a thank you. I settled on a yellow pendant that wasn't too obtrusive, and Shruti picked out some gold earrings. Malika was having trouble choosing. Ammaji eventually went back out to the party, asking us to put the jewellery away when we were done. Shannon kept picking up and trying on pieces.

"You've picked yours," I said.

"I know," she said. "But it's fun to try on." She held up a silver necklace. "This would look beautiful against your skin."

I'd heard words like this all my life, but it felt strange at this moment, since Shannon was the only person in the room with different coloured skin. She would be the only one who would worry about which metals would look okay against her skin.

"Shannon, when are you and Amitbhai getting married?" asked Malika.

"We're not," she said, cheerfully.

Her tone surprised me. I'd assumed Amit was stringing her along.

Shruti was also surprised. "Why not?"

"I don't want to get married," said Shannon. "Amit does, but I don't."

"But everyone gets married," said Malika, frowning.

"Not everyone."

"In India, they do," said Malika. "What about your parents? How are they letting you stay unmarried?"

Shannon laughed, a sound like the jewellery jingling together as it ran through her fingers. "My parents don't run my life. I'm a grown adult."

Shannon didn't get it. She could be speaking Martian as far as our family was concerned. And watching Amit interact with our parents gave her no perspective on what it was like for the rest of us.

"It's different for you," I said as I readjusted my perch at the edge of the bed. I began fishing one piece after another out of the pile, delicately untangling it before packing it back in one of the small bags or cloth envelopes. "Your parents don't expect to be running your life. Your community doesn't expect that. They see you as your own independent person, not an extension of themselves. Not an extension of the entire family."

"Your parents have lived in Canada a long time," said Shannon. "They know it's different there."

"They know it's different for white people," I said. Shannon flushed slightly.

Malika spoke into the silence. "Payal Didi was telling me she wouldn't be allowed to live on her own, not even in Canada."

Shruti nodded. "If we suggested it, they would spend every day telling us we were worthless children for leaving and in the next breath, ask us why we would ever want to leave when they could take care of us."

Malika and I laughed. Then I added, "And then they ask if we don't love them, and tell us we might appreciate them when they're dead, which would be soon because we broke their hearts."

The three of us laughed while Shannon looked confused. "But Amit—"

"Amit gets away with everything." I paused, thinking of what Amit told me before. "Amit is lucky he had acting to fill the hole he had after Mom and Dad were done haranguing him."

Shannon sat pensively for a moment.

"They're relieved he's no longer trying to be an actor," said Shruti.

I kept quiet, wondering what it had cost Amit to join the business. Mom and Dad saw it as admitting that he'd been wrong and should have listened to them all along. Was Mom and Dad's praise enough of a balm?

Shannon spoke softly. "But your parents only want you to be happy." She didn't say it like a question, but I could hear the question in it. She was wondering about Amit too.

"Our parents think they get to decide what makes us happy." There was a bottle of Bisleri in the corner of the room. I wasn't sure whose it was, but I got up and cracked it open and took a sip of lukewarm water. Shannon loved Indian culture. She loved ayurveda and yoga and spicy food, and ornate buildings and beautiful clothes and intricate jewellery. But she didn't know what it was like to live it.

"Look, you love being independent," I continued. "Your run your own business, you don't want to get married. But you get to do that. You only represent yourself. And everyone around you sees you and only you..." I trailed off, wondering how my life would look if I had what Shannon took for granted.

Shruti filled in the space for me. "They see us as a small fraction of a whole family. So everything becomes about the family. So doing something else, it's like we're breaking the family."

"It's their dharma," added Malika. "Their duty in life is to see us settled."

"And if we haven't done that, they have failed," I added. "And they will stop at nothing to make sure they don't fail." I ran my fingers through the jewellery, clearing a space and then filling in again.

"It's not always that dire," said Shruti.

“Only because you want exactly what they want. The checklist.”

Shannon pulled Ammaji’s ring on and off her finger. “What checklist?” she asked softly.

“University, as long as it’s an acceptable degree, then marriage to someone from a good family in an acceptable career—”

“—preferably Indian,” said Shruti.

“Guju too,” added Malika.

I acknowledged these with a nod. “And then you move to a house near your parents and have kids and work in the family business, and repeat the cycle with your own kids.”

Shruti patted her belly. “It gets better every generation. Ammaji had a child marriage. Think of how much has changed.”

“Great,” I said. “Maybe I can be my own person in my next life.”

We sat quietly for a moment and listened to the barking street dogs amid the car horns.

Shruti came over and rubbed my back. “They want us to live a good life, and this is the kind of life they understand. You can’t blame them for wanting the same for us.”

I absently turned the yellow pendant over and over in my hand. Shruti wasn’t wrong.

“Except when you want to live your own life, and no one wants you to.” Shannon was looking straight at me.

I met her eyes, steady and really seeing me in a way I had never allowed myself to be looked at. “Yes. That’s it exactly.”

“Women everywhere get pressured about getting married and having kids,” said Shannon.

“It’s just more for us than for you,” I said.

Shannon nodded.

“I had a dreadful feeling before my wedding. Like everything had been decided for me, and I didn’t even need to be a part of it.”

I was speaking to Shannon, but I also noticed Malika listening as well. I searched for more words to dig into that feeling, hoping I might be able to voice a worry she might need to hear out loud.

"You get told all your life that this is what you're supposed to do," I said. "All the aunties are relentless about it. Every time they see you, they ask you about getting married. Every joke is about getting married. Every question is some detail they can add to your biodata so they can help you get married."

Shruti chuckled in recognition.

"They just overwhelm you, and you can't even tell if you want to get married or just accept it because no one will let you think about any other option."

Malika nodded. "And in India, they don't let you think at all. Your parents are always pushing the next thing. School and then marriage."

I thought of Reshma Masi and her sham marriage. Despite her histrionics about Ashok Masa and her despair over her daughter getting married, she still kept pushing Malika to live her life traditionally.

Shruti spoke softly, rubbing my back again. "And then have children." I knew she was thinking about my infertility. I'd been through school and then marrying Bryan and working for Dad and getting on the property ladder, always chasing the next step and the next and the next. And now we were at a dead stop. What did I have to lose anymore? What did Malika have to gain by seeing what could happen?

I took a deep breath. "I don't know if Bryan and I have a future. But it's like I've been running after everything I was supposed to do for so long, I don't even know what I want to do anymore."

"And Bryan was part of that," said Shannon. "All the supposed-tos."

I nodded.

"So you go to counselling," said Shruti. "Talk to each other. Relationships take work, but you stick together and work it out."

"That's what you're supposed to do." I was tired of the long list of things I was supposed to do.

"What do you want to do?" asked Shannon.

"I don't know," I said.

"You never had a dream of your own?" she pressed. "Something you wanted to do before you were so far down the path of what your parents wanted?"

I stayed where I was on the edge of the bed, arranging and re-arranging the cloth bags and plastic cases. I thought back, but it was all a blur.

"Payal was going to start a business," said Shruti.

I was surprised that she remembered, especially when I didn't. I'd wanted to major in business and be an entrepreneur. I didn't know what kind of business I wanted to start, only that taking over the family business with my father second-guessing my every decision wasn't the same thing. But my marriage was the more immediate problem.

"What do I do about Bryan?"

Shannon took the jewellery from my hands and set it aside, and then sat down beside me. "If what you want has changed, that's okay. You and Bryan started on the same page, and maybe you're on a different page now. It's okay." She handed me a handkerchief as the tears began to leak out, and put her hands on my shoulders as gently as a blanket.

CHAPTER SIXTEEN

December 2010, Mumbai

THE NEXT DAY, MY FATHER NEEDED my help with the computer. He handed me a device that looked like a long USB key and showed me the laptop. "Chandu Mama says that they use this to connect to the Internet here. There's a number on it."

Written on a piece of masking tape on the device was a series of numbers, which I guessed was a cell phone number for a cell phone modem. I plugged it in and set about trying to understand what to do with it.

"When you get online, can you check the bank?" asked Dad. "And my email?"

Glad I got a degree in accounting so I could be your assistant, Dad. But I did it anyway.

We worked away, my father asking questions and me checking the computer, making notes about things to check on when we got back and what we could go ahead and file electronically here.

Dad shook his head. "Unbelievable," he said. "When I started accounting, you couldn't do any of this so quickly. We wrote all the accounts by hand in ledger books. Everything we sent went in the mail." Dad said this every time we worked at a computer together. Shruti usually did all the computer entry for him, but he could work out all the numbers instantly in his head, and he had an instinct for finding errors or issues. I could never do that. I had to sit and calculate. I had to know what I was looking for before I found it.

He sighed. "I'm going to miss this when I retire."

"You don't have to retire."

"I know. But I do. It's time."

I couldn't imagine what he'd do with his time, with his life, if he truly retired. What would occupy his days?

He rested a hand on my shoulder. "Maybe one day it will be you and Amit sitting together, working like this."

The weight of this hand could have been a vise grip holding me in place. When I complained about work, Bryan would tell me I could quit, or that when it was my company, I could sell it. But how could I do that while my father was alive, when this was the one thing I'd done that might make him proud? What would he have left if I let it go? And then after Dad died, how could I sell his legacy? One day I'd run the business, but I'd never love it the way he did. I'd keep it from slipping away, but no more than that.

"You're typing very hard," said Dad. "Something wrong with the computer?"

I realized to my embarrassment that I was pounding on each key with the force of a hand clap. I consciously relaxed my fingers and eased up some. "The computer is fine. Everything is fine."

Dad read off some reports over my shoulder, asking me to zoom in every now and again so that he could see the numbers. "It's a good thing I have you to help me," he said. And my heart sank, because in the end, that's what I was to him. Computer help.

"No problem," I said. "That's what daughters are for."

After a while, Dad left with Chandu Mama to see his office while I kept working. When I was done, I discovered that I was alone. Everyone had gone to work or on visits or various errands. Almost everyone; Ammaji was napping in the next room, and the sweeper was there, cleaning dust off the floors with a small hand brush and then washing them down with a worn, wet rag. I felt rude sitting there with my feet up, worrying that my footprints on the floor might make him mad although he probably wouldn't say anything. But he carried on with his work as if I weren't there.

I started scrolling through Facebook to pass the time. There were so many pictures of families with kids—all our old friends, relatives, old school classmates. Everyone was smiling, going off on trips and small adventures. This wasn't going to be Bryan and me. But it looked like it wouldn't be Amit and Shannon either, and they were happy anyway. They always lit up in the other's presence.

Had I ever lit up for Bryan? I'd never been particularly unhappy to see him, but I'd never felt that light of joy just because he was around.

And Bryan never understood that my family mattered to me in a way that was different to how his mattered to him. Shannon didn't fully understand it all either, but she seemed to accept it and tried to understand better. Bryan didn't get why we had to be at this wedding whether we were directly invited or not. No one was here because of what they wanted to do individually; our presence was part of what we owed to each other as small pieces of a larger collective. I didn't like India, but not going wasn't worth hurting my family over. If we'd had kids, they'd be part of this collective too.

Would he have understood better if we'd had kids? If we were more than two individuals living under one roof?

I thought of the ways Shannon had reached out to me, ways that I'd rejected her so many times, but she kept trying anyway. Shannon had understood we were family long before I did.

The sweeper unrolled the rug and moved to another room. The floor had already dried. There was no one in the room, and yet I was expected to sit here, waiting for my mother or my aunt or my uncle to tell me what to do next. They'd all forgotten about me. I looked at the door, then around the room to reassure myself that I was alone, and then at the door again. I wanted to take a walk. I was restless with too many thoughts in my head and nowhere to go with them.

I'd never gone out anywhere on my own in India before. Mom didn't think I could manage, and in any case, none of my relatives understood why anyone would want to go out alone when they could have company. But surely there was no harm in taking a walk. If Amit and Shannon could stay in a hotel by themselves, couldn't I go outside the same four white walls of my uncle's flat?

My heart pounded but I felt curiously light. I left the flat and put on my shoes, and instead of summoning the musical elevator, I took the stairs.

Halfway down, I came across a man rolling up a bedroll on the landing. I stopped. He didn't look like a street beggar; he looked too clean and healthy. Maybe he was a neighbour's servant. Was I not supposed to take the stairs? Did I violate some sort of rule between domestic help and the middle class? "Sorry." I pointed through the stairwell. "Can I pass?"

He answered, but I couldn't understand the words. Was this a bad idea? Would he report me to my uncle? But eventually, he gestured down the stairs.

I half-tiptoed and half-ran. Did everyone know people slept here? I held my breath at every landing, hoping they would be empty, that anyone who might be sleeping had already packed up for the day. I made it out of the building with no further incidents.

The engine rumbles from the road were louder at ground level and there was a haze of dust in the air. A group of men were standing around near the base of the building, chatting. They ignored me entirely. I let out the breath I hadn't realized I was holding.

I went around to the front of the building and stood, trying to decide what to do. A dirty yellow dog dashed by, ignoring me. Even if I could think of an errand to run, I didn't know where to shop or how to haggle. I didn't have any money with me. Most of the street was lined with small shops—places where you had to ask the shopkeeper for everything—and here in suburban Mumbai, English was relatively rare. Amit and Shannon appeared to be getting around easily, but they were in a tourist area. No one came here for a vacation.

The street was full of swerving cars and rickshaws missing people crossing the street by inches. I had done this in Colaba, but I'd had Amit and Shannon with me. The small bubble of lightness that had propelled me this far flattened a little. *You're a grown woman. Walk up and down the street.* Why was I making such a big deal over something as simple as a walk? Surely other people could go for a stroll without having so much mental drama about it. I turned on my heel and started walking, promptly crashing into a hawk-faced old lady.

"Sorry, sorry." I clasped my hands together and bowed a little bit, feeling like I was imitating a bad movie about Indian etiquette. She had probably already realized that I was either a foreigner or a fool.

I strode along and hoped I looked like I knew where I was going. The streets were dusty, but not as crowded as I had pictured, no worse than the flow out of a subway station at rush hour at home. Around me, beggars crouched in corners, women in jeans and bright sleeveless tops chatted on cell phones, and blandly dressed men stared. Mom had never allowed me to bare my shoulders in India—Kajal and Malika were similarly not allowed. For some reason, this was too much within our family, although it clearly wasn't an issue in Mumbai as a whole. I felt frumpy in my wrinkled T-shirt. I wondered if people noticed. In the shop windows were mannequins dressed in salwar kameez—

long dresses over pants—and saris lined up on display. They had white skin, blue eyes, and auburn hair. Shouldn't they be brown mannequins? Or did no one really care?

I kept moving down the street in a straight line. Not a single person looked at me. I thought about exploring the small side streets, but what if I got lost? No one knew where I was. I had Kajal's old phone, but I'd mostly used it for Internet access and texting Bryan; I hadn't stored anyone's number in it because it hadn't been necessary when I was with family nearly all the time. There was surely a mapping app on the phone, but what was Chandu Mama's address? None of the buildings had street numbers on them, and I could see nothing that resembled a street sign.

This was a bad idea. What was even the point of going in a straight line to nowhere? The inanity of my little adventure made me feel ridiculous. I stopped and faked checking my pockets, and mimed smacking my head as if I'd forgotten something before turning around. No one had noticed my performance. *Of course they didn't notice. Everyone here is too busy to notice you.*

I hurried. What if my relatives noticed I was gone? What if they'd called my mom? Or told Ammaji? I could hear the lecture I'd be given when I got back: *Why didn't you wait for one of us to come with you? Why would you walk alone? Where were you going? Why were you going to nowhere?*

I continued for a little while, but nothing looked familiar. The store windows and signs seemed different. Had I not noticed them before? I stopped, this time not pantomiming a reason, and looked both ways up and down the street, looking for some kind of a landmark. Should I keep going forward? Head back to see if I'd been missed the flat? Ask for help? But would standing around looking lost in the middle of Mumbai make me more susceptible to some kind of harm?

No one knew where I was.

I pulled out Kajal's phone and texted Bryan. *Went for a walk on my own. Everything is confusing.* It was the middle of the night at home, and it wasn't like he'd be able to help me, but at least I felt less alone. If I got in real trouble, maybe they'd be able to trace my whereabouts from the cell phone records.

I texted again. *I'm sorry.* Because I was. If it wasn't worth it to anger my parents over a trip I didn't even want to go on, why was it worth it to anger Bryan over the same thing? *I took you for granted.* If Bryan and I had come to the end of the road, I wanted to part as friends. Because we were friends, if nothing else. I wanted to remember how kind he'd been. *We should have talked a lot more before I left.* And then I sent: *I shouldn't have left at all.*

The phone rang, startling me. Bryan. I answered. "It's the middle of the night there, what are you doing up?"

"I couldn't sleep. I got your messages."

"I'm sorry," I said again. "I got caught up in everything with my mom, and I didn't listen to you. We should have talked more."

"We should have." Bryan's voice was soft. "I'm sorry too."

I took a few steps forward, looking around a familiar sight. "I'm glad you called."

There was a pause. "What are you doing right now?"

"Just taking a walk."

"It sounds really loud where you are."

I laughed. "That's just India. It's always loud here."

"What have you been doing?"

"Visiting family. Wedding stuff. It's pretty boring." The magenta salwar on a blue-eyed mannequin caught my eye. Had I seen this before? "My mom did one thing that was kind of nuts."

"What?"

"She took me to a fertility clinic."

"Without me?"

"That's what I told her."

A soft chuckle. "What did she think was going to happen without me being there?"

"I don't know." I kept going, feeling a little more confident. I was not lost. I had not gone too far. "She wanted to look at egg donors. We didn't pick one. They told her I had to become a patient first. But she wanted to look anyway."

"She's unbelievable."

I felt better talking to Bryan, having one person who could see how ridiculous my mom had been. I could see my uncle's building up ahead and started walking faster. I didn't know when anyone would be home, if they hadn't already discovered I was gone and started to worry.

"Were there donors?" asked Bryan.

"Oh yeah, lots. They only let us look at a sample, but even that was a huge pile."

"Huh," said Bryan. "The whole thing still kind of weirds me out. Still…"

Two women hurried towards me. I squinted. Reshma Masi and my mom. Shit. Bryan was starting to speak but I interrupted. "Bry, I have to go."

"Can we talk more about this?"

I shook my head even though he couldn't see me. "We're on different pages on so many things. What's the point?"

"We could go to counselling?"

"Payal!" My mom was pissed.

"Gotta go." I hung up on him while he was mid-sentence.

"How could you worry us like this?" said Mom.

"I was taking a walk." I'd hoped to sound confident, but my voice came out small. "I was just coming back."

"You should have waited," said Mom.

"Malika could have gone with you," added Reshma Masi. "Shown you some dress shops."

They ushered me back home and into the musical elevator.

"What were you thinking?" said Mom. "Wandering the streets alone? What would people think?"

"It was just a walk," I protested. She didn't need to know that I had thought I might be lost.

She carried on as if I hadn't spoken. "You should have asked someone to come with you. Why would you go alone?"

She reacted entirely as I'd predicted. But nothing had happened to me. I'd left a building and come back. I was nearly thirty, not a toddler. "Mom," I said firmly. "I'm fine." I pulled the elevator door open and headed into the flat, away from her.

CHAPTER SEVENTEEN

May 2004, Toronto

I WAS TWENTY MINUTES INTO THE COFFEE date when I realized that I couldn't remember his name. Vinay? Vikash? Did it even start with a V? I didn't really matter, since I had no intention of seeing him after this. I was only here because my parents—specifically my mom—forced me to go. "Just meet him," she'd insisted one night while we were tidying the kitchen. "What can it hurt?"

"I don't need to meet this guy to know he's not for me."

"Don't be ridiculous. You have to meet someone soon, before all the good ones are gone."

I shut the dishwasher. "People get married at all ages."

She pointed her J-cloth at me. "In a few years, everyone your age worth marrying will be gone. Do you want to cry about how you should have listened to me when it's too late?"

"Can't this wait?"

"Why? We went to so much trouble to find a good boy for you. What will people think if you don't meet him?"

I didn't answer because I couldn't answer. I hadn't told her about Bryan yet. I focused instead of sweeping the floor, and mercifully, my mom had to take a phone call.

I brought the dilemma up with Shruti that night when we

were alone in my room. She hadn't met Bryan, but she knew all about him. "You have to tell Mom and Dad sometime." I must have looked worried, because she started reassuring me that they wouldn't care that he was white and started naming friends of theirs whose kids married white people.

"It's not that." I twisted the edge of the comforter in my hands. "The moment I tell them, they're going to expect us to get married soon." My parents, who'd been introduced to each other a month before they agreed to get married, had no concept of why anyone would need to date for months, let alone years.

"So? Don't you want to marry Bryan?"

"It's too soon to think about that." Although we had talked about it. I'd explained that we'd have to present a different timeline of when we met and started dating to my parents, and he understood. I was checking things off the Grand To-Do list of Life and the moment I said yes to Bryan, I'd be trapped in an hourglass with all the space being filled by sand.

I couldn't understand why I felt this way when I wanted all of the sand. I'd been told every day of my life that this was the path to a good life, one that my parents had left their families and culture and everything they'd known in India for me to have. This was the future I'd worked towards all my life, the one I'd known I would have for as long as I could remember. But I was still hoping there would be time for something else.

"You've been dating a year. A year! You should know already. If you aren't interested, let him find someone who is."

In some ways, she sounded like Mom, the way she reduced my relationship with Bryan to marriage. But she also wasn't wrong. I should know already. "Hey, what if he's the one who's not interested?" I grinned and hoped it didn't look too fake.

Shruti rolled her eyes. "Anyone who put up with you for a year is interested."

I threw a pillow at her head, but she caught it before it hit her.

There was nothing wrong with Bryan. Nothing I could point to and say, *Here's a good reason*. He was kind and trustworthy and responsible. We got along well. It must be some sort of precommitment nervousness, a perfectly normal feeling before making a big decision.

"Anyway," said Shruti. "If you aren't going to tell Mom and Dad, then you need to let Mom set you up with people."

"Ugh."

"It'll be way more questions if you don't."

I didn't want to tell her that she was right. Every aunty who ever spoke to me would politely ask about school and then immediately mention a boy they wanted to introduce me to before I could answer. If they were this direct with me, the pressure on my parents had to be intense. But the moment they knew, the future between Bryan and I would become inevitable. The small bubble of safety around us would pop.

The coffee date was okay. He (Vikram?) bought my coffee and then also got some cookies for me without asking. We started with stiff conversation about school and work, topics that were already spelled out on our biodata, but then he launched into explaining his goals in life and the steps he was going to undertake to achieve them in exhaustive detail. I nibbled on a cookie, taking tiny bites to try and stretch out the time it took me to eat it so he wouldn't have any excuse to order another cookie and extend the date. How long did I have to sit here to show I'd made a good faith effort? An hour? Could I get away with forty-five minutes?

A hand waved in front of my face. "Payal?"

"Oh, sorry! What were you saying?" What had he been saying?

He straightened his blazer. He'd dressed up for this meeting. Shruti had loaned me a denim pencil skirt and I hoped it was okay. "I was asking about when you graduate."

"This is my final year."

Silence. After a moment, he raised his eyebrows and nodded, trying to prod an answer out of me. "And then?"

"And then…" I looked past him to the dark green wall. The paint had pulled off in one spot, showing a flake of brown paper and white plaster. "I guess I get a job."

"Have you thought about where?"

"I think my dad expects me to work for him. Unless I find a different position."

"My sister works at Deloitte."

"Oh." Was he making an offer? Could I ask him to ask his sister to put a good word in for me? Was he expecting me to ask? But if I asked, would I have to go on another date with him?

"Is that a company that interests you?"

"It's very prestigious. Lots of people in my class want to work there after graduation."

"But not you?"

I could feel the fake leather of the chair sticking to my legs. I'd thought this skirt was conservatively long, but it had slid up when I sat down. "I guess it's somewhere I should apply."

"And then what? Where do you see yourself in five years?"

"I don't know." I traced my fingers around the rim of my coffee cup. "The usual." This date was starting to feel like a job interview. I felt embarrassed saying the word marriage around him. What if he got the wrong idea? And if I talked about Bryan, would that get back to my mom? "Make my parents happy and settle down. You must get the same lecture."

He pulled his thick eyebrows together for a second. "If you don't mind me saying so, you seem a little—" He tilted his head to one side and then the other, critically examining me. "A little lost."

"Lost?"

"Aimless." He nodded to himself, satisfied with the word. "Where is your drive? What do you want to do with your life?"

I snorted. "Does it matter?"

"Of course it does."

"Your parents aren't on your case all the time? They aren't always telling you what to do? Lecturing you about every choice you make?" *Forcing you to go on dates with random people?* I smiled a little at this thought.

"No." My face must have shown my disbelief. "Well, of course they do, but so what? They only want what's best for me."

I wished I could remember what it was he'd spent so long explaining, his goals and how he was going to reach them. Or even his name. Was it Varun? "But what would happen if they didn't want what you wanted? Like my brother. He moved to LA to become an actor." I waited for the shock, but there was none.

"Good. That takes drive. You should be more like your brother."

"You're saying your parents wouldn't get upset if you wanted to be an actor?"

He brushed this off. "Success erases upset."

I raised my eyebrows.

"Okay, okay, they wouldn't like it. But still, your brother has direction. A plan to succeed. If you fail to plan, you plan to fail."

There was no point talking to this guy anymore, whatever his name was. If I wanted a lecture on my failures, I could have stayed home. I made an excuse about meeting a friend and stood up, trying to pull my skirt back down as gracefully as I could.

I checked the time as I left, and only thirty minutes had gone by. I'd have to stay a bit longer so that Mom didn't lecture me about giving Vinay or whatever a fair chance. I didn't know what to do with unexpected freedom. It wasn't nearly long enough to see Bryan. None of the stores in the plaza where the coffee shop was looked appealing. A grocery store? A dry cleaner? A Freshii franchise? I wandered back into the coffee shop and hoped the staff wouldn't think I was an airhead, and bought another cookie for myself. I sat back down at the same table.

The cookies had come in a paper bag. I smoothed it and

folded it on the diagonal to make a square, the carefully creased and tore off the excess. I split the back in half along its folds and then made a crane to pass the time. Then a second crane. I lined them up beside each other. A crane wedding. It was inevitable. Why was I delaying the inevitable?

Bryan wanted us to get married. I had no reason not to marry him. He'd been nothing but kind, even putting up with all the crazy rules and restrictions to work around my parents. And if I didn't get married, what would I do? I'd have to break up with Bryan and stop hanging out with his friends. I'd end up living with my parents and working for them too. Shruti would leave when she got married and it would be just be me and them, forever.

I set the cranes apart, but they looked out-of-place on the table, all alone amid the cookie crumbs. I put them back together and got up to go home. Surely enough time had gone by.

* * *

I knew Bryan was going to propose when he suggested dressing up and going somewhere fancy for dinner instead of our usual movie or hanging out with friends at a pub. I'd tried to talk him out of it, but he'd insisted, saying he wanted to try this restaurant. It was unlike him to insist.

Shruti went through her closet with me, but there was nothing I liked.

"Come on," she'd said, holding up a flouncy pastel chiffon dress. "This is so pretty."

"I should probably buy new clothes," I said glumly. I hated shopping. "Maybe an outfit I could wear to interviews?" Exams had just finished. I should have been applying to jobs already, but I just couldn't get motivated.

"Like a sheath? I might have a dress like that." She dug into her closet again.

Having overheard us, Mom poked her head into the room. "Why do you need to go to interviews? You'll work at the office."

My heart beat faster; had we said anything about Bryan? She didn't know we were dating, or at least, she was pretending she didn't know.

I hadn't actually told Dad I was going to work for him, but I was running out of choices. My entire graduating class had already lined up placements and internships. There wouldn't be much left.

The restaurant was plushy, one of those places that could be jammed full, but you could hardly hear the other people. The seats were all wood and velvet, the tables covered in pristine white cloths.

"Pretty great, isn't it?" said Bryan. He looked over the menus for a moment. "Should we get some wine?"

"Since when do you drink wine?"

"It's a special occasion."

I studied the wine list, but except for the prices, it was meaningless to me. Bryan also looked confused, but we'd heard that Merlot was supposed to be good, so we picked that. Hopefully the server wasn't secretly laughing at us.

There wasn't much vegetarian on the menu, so I went with a pasta and hoped I didn't splatter sauce on the tablecloths. I still didn't always feel graceful with a knife and fork.

Bryan seemed distracted all through dinner. He'd be jittery with his mind elsewhere one minute, and then staring too intensely into my eyes the next.

I started telling him about a commercial Amit had landed, plus a few lines on *ER*, which had now convinced my parents that maybe Amit wasn't crazy to go to LA. "They keep telling all their friends to get ready to tape the show and bragging that they sent him to drama school. Like they hadn't been against it the whole time." Bryan didn't react; he was distracted again. "Are you alright?"

"What?" The intense stare was back. "This place is fancy, isn't it?"

I sighed slightly.

As the server cleared our plates, Bryan asked if I wanted to get dessert.

"I think I'm good."

"Are you sure? I hear there's a dessert special here that's awesome."

"I guess."

"Great!" He caught the server's eye and nodded. The server nodded back and quickly left. He was going to hide the ring in the dessert and the thought gave me a sinking feeling. What was wrong with me that I wasn't excited? This was supposed to be one of the happiest days of my life.

"Pi." Bryan reached across the table and took my hand. "Do you ever think about the future?"

The pasta lay heavy in my stomach. "Of course I do. We've talked about it."

"Yeah, but what do you imagine when you do?"

I knew the answer because it was the same answer that Bryan and I had always discussed, the dream we'd imagined together, and all of a sudden the thought of it made me tired.

"I guess I'm going to work for my dad," I said. I looked at his nose instead of his eyes. I knew I wasn't answering the question quite the way he'd hoped.

"And then?"

We'd talked about getting married so many times, but now that it was happening, I felt like I was signing my life away. Bryan was the kind of guy you were supposed to marry. I liked his friends. We had all the same goals. We were good friends—wasn't that approach supposed to be the secret to a long-lasting marriage? He checked all the boxes for being the right person. "We've talked about all this before."

"Yes." His face softened. "Our dream. Isn't that the dream?"

"Yeah." The dream we'd talked about, the one I ought to have, the one Shruti and my parents wouldn't shut up about. This was just nerves, wasn't it? Was I simply not ready? But that was ridiculous, what reason was there not to be ready? I'd done everything I was supposed to up until now. And even if I wasn't ready, what could I do about it? I was the one who always insisted we do things in the right order, that we should get engaged after we finished school. He'd be angry that I was leading him on all this time, wasting his time when he could have met another girl who'd be excited about tonight instead of trying to find a way out.

"Pi." He got up from the table and came around to my side, and got down on one knee. If I stopped this now, we'd both be humiliated. A sinking feeling wasn't a logical reason.

Violin music started up, and two waiters walked in, one carrying a small pie with a ring on top, and the other holding a sign that said: "Marry me, Pi!" There was a flash as another waiter snapped our photo.

"So?" He stared at me expectantly. "Pi, I love you. Will you make our dream come true?"

The entire restaurant was staring at me. It was like there was no sound. No air. Just Bryan looking up at me with a goofy smile on his face, waiting for an answer. There was nothing I could point to as a reason not to go ahead—he was a good guy. We never even fought. I'd never said a word about the growing fear that maybe I could never be normal, maybe the way my life mapped out in front of me wasn't the life I should lead, but how could I justify that to anyone? To my parents? To Bryan? He'd always been there for me, right from the very beginning when he'd gotten me out of that terrible party without my parents finding out. He could always figure out answers when I had nothing but questions, and there he was kneeling in front of me, waiting for me to give the one answer to put all the plans we'd talked about in motion.

"Yes," I said.

* * *

Bryan had wanted to stay out longer, but we hadn't prearranged a cover story, and my parents were expecting me back at home. After he kissed me on the doorstep, I took off the ring and put it in my purse. I didn't want questions from my parents. They'd meet him soon enough.

I let myself in. Dad was in the kitchen, looking over a report and eating a biscuit. "Did you have a good time?"

"Yeah." I glanced down at my dress and started explaining it away. "Denise wanted to try this swanky restaurant."

He didn't look up from his report. "Where is Denise working?"

"I think she found a job at KPMG."

"Very good." He put his report down. "I'm worried about your future."

I pulled out a chair and sat with him. He passed over the package of biscuits, and I took one out and laid it on the table. I wasn't hungry.

He looked down his glasses at me. "What are you going to do now that you're done with school? You can't just stay home and do nothing."

"I can apply to KPMG. Or Ersnt & Young. Or Deloitte." All the big accounting firms. All the places where employees wore suits every day and spoke in serious tones, the places where school expected me to go next. Practically my whole class was going to one of those jobs.

"If you wanted to work in one of those firms, you would have applied before. They want people who have drive."

I studied the tile floor, the faint veins of grey running like long rivers through the faux marble tiles. Even the floor had a direction.

"You need to do something," he said. "Even Amit is busy. I never understood why he wanted to spend his life serving food and chasing a foolish dream. But maybe now that he's really going to be on TV, who knows? Although it's very unsteady income."

Maybe Dad would finally stop talking about Amit and see that I'd done a whole accounting degree for him. "I could help out at the office for a while," I said cautiously. "You're right that I shouldn't do nothing."

He patted the top of my head and stood up to leave. "Who knows, you might like it."

"Maybe." I could stay on temporarily, at least until I found something else. It would look better on a résumé to be working.

He nodded, and as he left, he smiled the smile of a man who'd successfully cleared his to-do list.

Later, alone in my room, I tried on my ring. I held out my hand, admiring it. It was a single diamond in a platinum setting. I turned my hand to different angles under my desk lamp to admire the light sparkling from it. I told myself it was a beautiful ring. Shruti would love it. Mom might even like it, even if she'd think it was too plain compared to Indian jewellery. She'd be pleased I was getting settled, unlike Amit, whom she nagged about not making enough effort to find a wife. She might even like Bryan. He wasn't Indian, but it was the kind of compromise that a lot of her friends' children made.

Now that the decision was made, I felt calmer. It must have been nerves. The timer had started and my future was clearly laid out in front of me. There were no more question marks, no more doubts. I'd work for my father and marry Bryan and have a normal, happy life. I wouldn't have to figure what else might bring me joy, and then do it without failing or disappointing anyone. Without having to reassure my parents that everything would be okay, and reassure myself at the same time.

Tomorrow, I'd tell Shruti. Maybe her excitement would ignite mine.

I'd have to work out a plan for introducing Bryan to my parents as my boyfriend, and then have Bryan officially propose with their blessing after that. Indian parents didn't understand dating, and it made them uncomfortable, but getting married put them on familiar territory. We'd have to decide what kind of wedding we'd have. Mom would want an Indian wedding, and Bryan's mom would probably want a ceremony that was more traditional for them. Maybe we could do both, find a way to combine it, though I didn't know of anyone who had. I could wear a sari and a white wedding dress. I got up from my desk and walked across the room like a bride would to see if it would help me feel like a bride would feel. Step-together. Step-together. I held an imaginary bouquet and envisioned myself in a big white dress with a long veil. That's what a normal bride looked like. I smiled at myself in the mirror. *I'm engaged. This is a joyous occasion.*

But as I got ready for bed, I had a strange feeling like my life was over. That once I walked down the aisle, I'd have taken my final steps along a path I couldn't choose to leave. There was no logic to this feeling; I was doing everything the right way, the way I was supposed to. Everyone would be happy for us. What was wrong with me?

CHAPTER EIGHTEEN

December 2010, Mumbai

"THE DARKER IT GETS, THE MORE your husband loves you," said Kajal. She stood over me and Shannon, watching the mehndi artists pipe intricate filigrees of fresh, green-brown mehndi on our palms. I bit back the urge to tell her that every person at the sangeet had come by to tell us the exact same thing.

"Really?" said Shannon. "In our culture, it's all about the size of the diamond." They chuckled, and I stayed silent. Shannon had made this joke before too.

Kajal held out her hands, both of which were covered in large, delicately shaded flowers. There were touches of silver paint highlighting the design and matching her champagne and silver sari. The mehndi had already lost its shiny wet look and turned a darker brown. She pointed to the cracks, where the mehndi revealed orange-stained skin underneath; it would later darken to a red-brown. "Colour is already starting to come. Mine loves me very much."

"Payal, look at this." Shannon grabbed Kajal's arm with her un-mehndied right hand. "Hers looks so different than ours. It's beautiful."

"This is Arabic-style," said Kajal. "Yours is traditional style."

"What if you're divorced?" I asked. "Does the mehndi tell

you about your first husband, or your next one?" I laughed a bit, trying to pretend I was only kidding. Shannon shot me a sharp look, but said nothing.

Kajal smiled. "Mehndi is not an exact science."

Shannon laughed. "Neither are diamonds." The mehndi artist finished Shannon's hand, and Kajal nodded approvingly. Shannon moved to try and stand.

"Just one hand?" said Kajal.

Shannon gathered up the bright yellow fabric of her chaniya choli in her clean hand, and tried not to step on it as she scrambled to her feet. "I have enough trouble managing in this as it is." She stepped into her white sandals. Another woman gracefully sat down cross-legged in the space where Shannon had been, and Shannon's mehndi artist took up her hand and immediately began drawing. I watched for a moment, and then felt cold mehndi being piped in the ticklish centre of my palm; my mehndi artist had started in on my other hand.

"I only wanted one hand," I said.

"Do both," said Kajal. "It looks nicer."

"How am I supposed to eat?" I wouldn't be able to use my hands until the mehndi dried, lest it smudge. Mehndi stained everything it touched and once ruined, it was unfixable.

"Someone will feed you," said Kajal.

"Amit can help you," said Shannon. She held up her mehndi-decorated hand. "I'll send him over after I show him my mehndi."

"The darker the mehndi, the bigger the diamond?" said Kajal.

"I want to see Amit's face when you tell him that," laughed Shannon. They walked away chatting, leaving me alone among the other women who were busily talking to each other in Gujarati. Every woman, old and young, was getting mehndi done, comparing how dark it was, and making the same comments about their husbands' love, almost as if the conversation was part of the pre-wedding rituals. Was that all that mattered? What about whether or not you loved your husband, or if you had just mistaken a sense of belonging as love? All my life, I'd seen women examining their mehndi, hoping it would come out as dark as a bloodstain, that it would mark their skin so deeply that they could count on it to never fade. But it was only decoration.

When my hands were finished, I clumsily got up, trying to both avoid smearing the wet mehndi and ripping out the carefully tucked pleats of my sari. I surveyed the room. Shruti sat surrounded by aunties, her forearms resting on her belly with her mehndied hands in the air while Naresh fed her snacks. Malika was on stage, sitting in a large, decorated chair, limbs splayed out, getting mehndi on her hands, arms, legs, and feet. Shannon stood among a group of Indian people, engaged in conversation while Kajal orbited her, basking in the reflected attention.

I joined Amit, who was standing to the side watching Shannon. "Hey," he said. "Did you get mehndi done?" I held up my hands. Amit took a step back in mock terror. "Don't get that gunk on me."

"What do you think?" I asked.

"Very nice," said Amit, without really looking. His eyes were still on Shannon, who was now showing off her mehndi to a fresh group of aunties. "I'm glad she's enjoying herself. She was really anxious about meeting everyone."

"Really?" I couldn't picture Shannon anxious. I looked around, a sea of Indian relatives and one tall white woman. "She stands out."

"Most of these aunties have never seen a person with red hair before in real life." He smiled in Shannon's direction. "Imagine if Bryan were here too."

I didn't respond.

Amit looked slightly embarrassed. "Sometimes a break helps. You might go back and everything is just fine."

I opened my mouth to explain and then changed my mind. "Sure."

Amit lightly punched my arm. It was the closest we got to affection. "Hey, you want something to eat?"

I held up my hands. "You'll have to feed me."

"I'll be back." He used a Terminator voice and headed off.

"Hasta la vista, baby," I said. But he'd already gone.

I looked at my hands, the designs still wet. Mom had insisted on doing a big mehndi event before my wedding day, to decorate my arms to my elbows and my feet halfway up my calves with intricate designs. I'd hated sitting there helplessly, like some kind of a living doll, waiting for people to feed me, to help me drink, to take me to the bathroom, everyone fussing over me.

A slim woman in an elegant sleeveless salwar kameez tapped my arm with her elbow. I didn't recognize her until she reminded me of her name. Sushma. Chandu Mama's neighbour's daughter. "We used to play together sometimes when you came to visit."

"Right," I said. I hadn't seen her in years. She blurred into the vast cast of people we had to visit in India.

She turned to my mehndi. "Can I see?" I showed her. "Very good." She gave an approving head waggle and then showed me hers.

"Enjoying yourself?" I asked.

"Weddings are always fun. Have you seen Reshma Aunty?"

"I haven't seen her in a while."

She looked unperturbed. "She's supposed to introduce me to someone."

"Who?"

"I don't know. Some boy."

"You aren't married?"

Sushma laughed. "Oh no. You sound like Aunty."

"But you're planning to get married soon?"

"It's just an introduction." She tried to push hair off her face with her upper arms, with little success.

"That's how it starts." I glanced over at Shannon, who was now seated on one of the black folding chairs that surrounded the room next to a woman in a rose-pink sari. They were deep in conversation.

"I'm just meeting them to please my mother. I'm too busy to get married." She gingerly used her fingernails to tuck loose strands of hair behind her ears. "I have a coaching centre, doing tuitions for students. Math, science, business, language, art…"

"Your own business?" I wondered briefly about introducing her to Shannon. I pictured them chatting away about being businesswomen while I stood quietly to the side, wanting to be among them.

"It's more fun this way. I am my own boss."

"Are you still living at home?"

She laughed again. "Centre is in Bangalore. I'm only visiting."

"Your parents let you move to Bangalore? By yourself?"

She did another head waggle. "This is a new India. If you work hard, you can have everything. Even my parents know this."

"But you're still meeting someone to please them."

She quirked a smile. "Old India is still here."

An aunty tapped Sushma on the shoulder, and they walked off. I could hardly remember her, but I hadn't quite remembered her being so bubbly. The new India suited her.

I studied the patterns on my hands and then looked over the colourful crowd. In less than a week, I'd be back home, and then I'd have to deal with Bryan. The idea of talking through all our issues made me tired.

What would it be like to live alone in our condo? Was Sushma living alone? She sounded happy, but I wondered if she was ever lonely. People in India seemed to move around with large packs of relatives. How had she struck off on her own? Was this more of the new India?

Amit came by with a plate of pakoras. "Want one?" I nodded.

He picked up a pakora, dipped in in the sweet brown chutney and held it up for me. I opened my mouth and he yanked it away, stuffing it into his own mouth and grinning while he ate.

"Will you grow up?" I was both hungry and irritated.

He pretended to think about it. "No one's made a good case for it so far."

"So that's why you're not marrying Shannon? It's too much like being an adult?"

His face went uncharacteristically stony. "No, it's that as grown adults we made a decision for ourselves."

"Sorry," I placated. "I was kidding."

He wordlessly fed me a pakora and we ate in silence.

"Can I ask you something?" I started, but then carried on anyway. "Shannon told me she didn't want to get married, but like, surely you've thought about it?"

"Nobody lets me forget in this family," he grumbled.

"But how does it work if she doesn't want to?"

Amit shrugged. "It works because it works."

"But how can you go on like that? What about security? Or commitment? Just taking the next step?"

Amit cocked his head. "Is that why you got married?"

"This isn't about me."

"You sure about that?"

I huffed in frustration.

Amit continued to eat, evidently forgetting that I couldn't feed myself without ruining my mehndi. After a moment, he spoke. "Are you really asking, or are you trying to talk me into a wedding?"

"I'm really asking."

He looked thoughtful. "Of course, I assumed I'd get married one day. You don't grow up in an Indian family without that idea in your head. But like, Shannon doesn't." He shrugged again. "It's just no contest. Shannon wins."

"But what about Mom and Dad? Or what everyone else says and thinks?"

He smiled, genuinely for a change. "Shannon still wins."

The music in the hall picked up: harmonium, tabla, and singing from the musicians seated on the platform at the front of the hall. On stage, Malika was getting up from her chair, carefully and with help so not to smudge her elaborate mehndi. The clear space in front of the stage was starting to fill with women in saris and chaniya cholis and salwar kameez, all coloured cloth and sparkling jewellery. They arranged themselves in slow, hesitant circles as they found rhythm and unity together. I spotted Shruti among them, moving gracefully despite her belly. Garba was starting.

Kajal returned. She nodded her head toward the front of the room. "Are you coming?"

"Maybe," I said.

She turned to Amit. "When are you and Shannon getting married?"

"I love India," said Amit. "Nobody hesitates to tell you what they think."

Kajal laughed. The silver embroidery on her sari sparkled under the lights. "Everything is ready, Amitbhai. Everyone is here. We could have two weddings for the price of one."

Amit laughed back, at ease with all the marriage talk from Kajal. "Oh, but then how can we convince you to visit Canada if you don't have a wedding to go to?" He offered her the plate of pakoras.

"I can't," she said. "Mehndi."

"How long does it take to dry?"

"It's dry. But I don't want it to get greasy."

"Kajal didn't come to my wedding, Amit," I said. "What makes you think she'll come to yours?"

"We couldn't get a visa," protested Kajal.

Amit held out a pakora for Kajal.

"What, none for me?" I said.

"You know what you did," said Amit. But he was smiling.

Kajal chewed quickly and swallowed. "Amitbhai, that isn't nice. She can't with mehndi on her hands."

"Who made her get mehndi?" But he fed me another one.

"Everyone gets mehndi," I smiled. "Even Shannon got mehndi."

Amit chuckled. "It's good to be a guy."

"You could get some too," suggested Kajal. "Men are doing this now."

"I'll pass."

"Don't you want to know how much your future wife loves you?" teased Kajal.

"Who could help but love me?" said Amit.

"Lots of people," said a voice from behind them. Shannon. Amit reached for her undecorated hand and smiled, his face brightening. Shannon smiled back, her face radiating more brightly than her red hair and yellow outfit. A wave of sadness passed over me. Had Bryan and I ever looked at each other like that?

"Shannon, we're trying to convince Amitbhai to get mehndi done," said Kajal.

"That would be fun!"

Amit's face lost some of its glow. "I have an audition right after we get back."

"Oh, it won't last that long," said Kajal.

"An audition?" I said. "Does Dad know?"

He made a brushing motion with his hand. "It's nothing. Just a favour for my agent."

I didn't think Dad would see it as nothing.

"It won't last?" said Shannon. "I wanted to show it off at home."

"Old-fashioned mehndi, yes, it used to last two, three weeks," explained Kajal. "But not anymore. They add things to it so that it comes dark fast. Smell."

We held our hands to our faces and breathed in a spicy scent.

"Eucalyptus," said Shannon.

"Yes," said Kajal. "The colour comes good very quick, but it fades away fast."

"Sounds like a commentary on modern relationships," said Amit drily.

Kajal began teasing him. "If you're worried about Shannon, get mehndi done, then you can know for sure."

Shannon spoke up before Amit could say anything else. "I have a better idea. Amit can get me some food."

Kajal was puzzled. "But if he gets you food, that shows how much he loves you."

"But I'll love him forever if he brings me some food. I'm starving!"

Everyone laughed. Amit fed Shannon the last pakoras from his plate and then left to get more. Shannon spoke to Kajal. "So are you going to show me how to do this dance or what?" She looked over at the front of the room, where mostly women but a few men were stepping and clapping in concentric circles.

"I thought you were hungry."

"Teach me while we're waiting."

"I know how to do this too," I said. It had been a long time since I'd done garba, but I could feel the three step rhythm in my legs.

"Then show me."

"Wait," said Kajal. She checked the mehndi on Shannon's hand and then both of mine. The shiny wetness was gone, and it was cracking in places. She waggled her head approvingly. "Clap slowly. Later, we can put some lemon water so it comes really dark."

Shannon laughed. "You all take this very seriously."

"Husband's love is a serious thing."

Of course, mehndi was just henna, just a dye. The eucalyptus oil, the lemon water, leaving it on without washing for as long as possible—they were all tricks to set the dye. A chemical reaction. So much effort for some immediate proof of love. And yet I wished for some simple test, some trick I could try so that I would know for sure how I felt about Bryan, and how he felt about me, and what we would do now. Had I ever really loved him? It wasn't that I didn't have feelings for him, but was what I felt enough? We'd been checking off all the boxes on a life that should have made us happy, but it hadn't worked. I would go home soon and we would talk about it and probably do marriage counselling because that's what you're supposed to do. But still, somehow, the only thing I knew for sure is that I'd fundamentally failed to get something right here, and that I didn't know what it was.

Kajal started teaching Shannon garba, counting loudly to three as she went through the steps. On one, she took a jumping step forward with her right foot, clapping her right hand over the left softly to preserve the mehndi. On two, she brought her left foot forward behind her right, clapping left hand over right. On three, she took a turning step backward, clapping right over left again. "One, two, three," she called out in time with the music and claps from the dancers at the other end of the hall. "Now bend on the first step, it looks nice. Bend, two, three. One, two, three."

I remembered learning garba as a small girl, and also dandiya raas: a dance with sticks that inevitably followed the garba. At the edge of my childhood memories was a picture of family and family friends doing raas at someone's apartment. There weren't enough dandiyas to go round, so people used rolling pins and wooden spoons and rulers. I remembered that I had been good at it, and that I had loved it, but I could never talk about it at school the next day. How could I explain it?

The music was as familiar as nursery rhymes, and I could feel the beats in my legs, but I had trouble coordinating the movements. I felt inept and uncomfortable, like a towel dried stiff instead of soft and pliable, and I kept leading off on the wrong foot. Shruti had kept up going out for Navratri every year even still, but I hadn't gone in ages. The muscle memory was sluggish.

Shannon picked it up quickly, and soon she and Kajal went to join in the dance. I opted to wait for Amit to bring back food, not wanting to make a fool of myself. Soon, even Shannon's height and hair and skin colour blended in as the aunties happily welcomed her.

"Payal! Do you remember me?"

An older man was standing in front of me. I recognized his face but couldn't recall his name. "Of course I do!" I hoped he wouldn't test me.

We chatted for a moment about the usual: how long it had been since I'd been in India, how long for Amit, how long for Shruti. "Where is your husband?" asked the uncle.

"He couldn't come." I was tired of making up stories and pretending that he'd ever intended to come.

We stood in silence, and then a series of drumbeats sounded from the front of the hall, and the tempo of the music picked up. After one quick beat, all the dancers changed rhythm and danced faster. Some people had dropped out of the circle and I caught glimpses of Malika next to Shannon and Kajal, moving harmoniously with the other women, stepping and clapping and bending along with the others and the circle turned at a steady pace. Elsewhere I saw Shruti, still keeping up with the faster beat, although off to the side I could see Naresh looking on, a worried expression on his face.

The uncle spoke again. "Tell him next year he must come to India. And he should bring his parents too. How can Ammaji have any peace not knowing her own daughter's son-in-law?"

I said something noncommittal and excused myself from the uncle, who seemed satisfied that he'd said his piece. Standing around in the hall was only going to invite more conversation from random uncles and aunties. I left and found myself outside the elevator bank; there were six floors in this banquet hall, and a different wedding in progress in each one. Glittering people and their broad smiles were everywhere, the scent of food and flowers, and the music from different musicians escaping from every room and mingling discordantly with conversation and excited greetings of the guests. I pulled out Kajal's phone and called Bryan, but no one answered. I was a little relieved; I didn't know what was left to say.

The elevator opened, letting people out, and on a whim, I went in and pressed the button for the lobby. I hoped it would be a little more space, but mostly, I needed to be away from the party for a while.

But the lobby was more congested than I'd expected. Bhangra music throbbed through the space as strangers in bejeweled or be-sequinned wedding clothes gathered around something. Curious, I threaded my way forward to see. A man was standing, pointing to a folder and trying to make himself understood. A man dragging a large roller suitcase and dressed in jeans and a crumpled shirt. A white man. I stepped forward and realized that it was Bryan.

CHAPTER NINETEEN

December 2010, Mumbai

I DON'T KNOW HOW I GOT THROUGH the crowd so quickly, only that the next thing I knew I was standing in front of my husband. Part of me was relieved to see him, a familiar reminder of home like seeing signs written in both English and French. He reached out to hug me, and I held my dry, mehndied hands in front of me. "Careful!" My voice was sharper than I'd intended. "You'll smudge me."

He stood back, and we stared uneasily at each other. I waited for him to explain himself, but he said nothing. He gripped the handle of his roller bag tightly.

"What are you doing here?"

His eyes were red with travel and tiredness, and the light and colour of the hall seemed to flood out the pale blue, as if there were no colour to begin with at all. "I wanted to surprise you."

"You succeeded." I didn't know what to do with him. Take him back to the flat? Bring him to the sangeet in his jeans and crumpled shirt and introduce him? How had he even gotten here? I wanted to ask, but the crush of people surrounding him, this novelty of a sweating white guy, driving their stares into us under the cacophony of excited conversation, was making me edgy.

Your husband just surprised you, Payal; this is a grand romantic gesture. Stop being so defective. Be happy.

I held my mehndied hands out in front of me and guided him to the elevator to head back to Malika's sangeet. There were a lot of people there too, but at least they were my people.

Once the elevator doors shut, Bryan started to talk. "This is crazy. I can't believe how many people are here. Are these all your family?"

I wrinkled my nose. "No, there's like half a dozen wedding parties happening."

The first person we ran into was Chandu Mama, who scarcely blinked in surprise before he slapped Bryan on the back and shook his hand vigorously. "You came to India! Now you can meet the family." He signalled to one of my cousins to find Ammaji.

Bryan stood there, slightly stunned. "Is everyone here family?"

"Family, friends of family, family of friends...."

Shannon and Amit came by and greeted Bryan with enthusiasm, while Shruti waved tiredly from a nearby chair where she sat beside Naresh with her feet up. Seeing some familiar faces made Bryan visibly relax. I glanced at the front of the room. Malika was still surrounded by women doing garba. She probably couldn't see us at all.

Ammaji arrived and was introduced. Bryan reached forward to hug her, and was given a one-armed version from my surprised grandmother. She was chattering excitedly in Gujarati.

"Touch her feet," I told Bryan.

"What?"

"Just bend down and touch her feet. It's a gesture of respect."

He looked around, slightly bewildered, and squatted down. I cringed slightly at how bumbling he looked. We'd always bent at the waist without thinking twice about it. He tapped one of Ammaji's feet lightly and looked up at me. "Is that good?"

"Yes, get up now."

He faltered as he rose. Ammaji folded her hands and bowed slightly. Bryan nodded back. I relaxed a little; things were a little better than they seemed.

Shannon asked. "How did you find this place?"

"Oh man," said Bryan. "I went through hell to get here."

Chandu Mama interrupted. "Why didn't you tell us you were coming? I would have sent the driver."

"Driver?" Bryan looked slightly awed. On top of his jet lag, he seemed almost punch-drunk. He pulled a creased card out from the side pocket of his black roller bag. "I found this." It was glittering gold, with red elephants and red writing on it. Malika's wedding invitation.

"You just got on a plane and flew here?" I said.

"Oh man, I had no idea how hard it would be to get a ticket," he said. "I kept talking to the agents at the airport and they finally worked it out." He wiped off some of the sweat beading up on his brow. The hall was air conditioned, even a little chilly, and still he was sweating. "Anyway, I took a taxi here. I showed him the invitation, then he went around asking people about it. He'd stop the car and talk to other taxi drivers, over and over again. And it was like we were turning around and turning around forever. I have never been so scared in my life. Like, was I being kidnapped?"

Chandu Mama laughed a little bit. "Good thing this is India, not Pakistan." Shannon pursed her lips at the casual Islamophobia, but said nothing. I knew better than to react, lest everyone around me start berating me with explanations as to why this was an entirely reasonable thing to say.

"You should have heard my mom before I left," said Bryan. "*Be careful. It's a foreign country. You never know.*"

I stared at his milky white face, nearly alone in a sea of varying shades of brown.

Ammaji spoke. Chandu Mama translated. "She wants to know how you like India."

"I just got here." Bryan seemed stupefied as he tried to take in the dozens of people gathering around him, the crash of the wooden dandias as they smacked together in time with the music, the pungent waft of food on plates people carried around the room. "I can't believe how many people there are."

I wished he would stop saying that.

Chandu Mama laughed again. "Yes, yes, India has excess of everything. This is why you must come more often, so you get used to it."

Ammaji spoke, and Chandu Mama translated. "She says you must come back every year."

I made a polite excuse about food, and using my elbows I pushed Bryan into a relatively quiet corner. "What are you doing here?"

"We needed to talk," said Bryan. "To work this out."

"You couldn't wait until I got back?" My breath was coming short and shallow. "What did your mother say? You're missing Christmas. She's going to flip."

"This is important." He paused, and for a moment I couldn't hear the music or the constant hum of conversation. "You were right. I should have been here. When you love someone, you show up for them."

Amit's voice echoed in my head. *Shannon still wins.* I had an urge to wash away all the mehndi on my hands immediately, so that nothing would reveal that Bryan loved me, but the stain was already there. "We're supposed to talk seriously in the middle of a big Indian wedding?"

He reached out to hug me, and I ducked away. Confusion flooded his face, and I gestured around at all the people, hoping he'd get the message. No public displays of affection. But also, I didn't want any. My mind had gone into overdrive trying to process how to deal with Bryan's surprise appearance. *You're being ungrateful.* He had come all this way. He had figured out the flights and even getting to a wedding hall in suburban Mumbai, despite everything being vastly different. I couldn't have done that. I'd have been terrified. He'd gone so far out of his comfort zone, further than I'd ever gone, just for me.

"Maybe," said Bryan. "We could find a time to find that fertility clinic. Just to talk to them, but without your mom there. Just so we both understand all our options."

Come on, Payal, he did all this for you, you owe him.

"Maybe," I said. "Since we're both here."

"I'd like that." He reached out for my hands, but I pulled them away, not wanting to disturb the careful, intricate work.

* * *

After the sangeet, we all gathered at Chandu Mama's flat, except for Malika, who had been packed off to get a good night's sleep before the wedding. The last few days had been an exhausting line up of parties and pre-wedding events; hopefully any of her pre-wedding nerves would crumble under a desperate need for sleep.

The rest of us sat in the living room, and though it was late and we were all tired, none of us were ready to sleep. We were all in our fancy clothes except for Bryan, who was still travel-crumpled. The women in the room were slowly undoing themselves, taking off heavy jewellery or pulling bobby pins out of their hair. Ammaji, who could not be convinced to go to bed, sat in the middle of it all, exclaiming at Bryan, who kept smiling at her and looking at me for translations. I gave a tiny shrug in response.

Chandu Mama explained. "She's very happy he's here. She thought she would die before she met Payal's husband."

Kaushik added: "We are all very blessed you are here. Now, the real wedding can begin. Everyone is together." The rest of the room chattered their agreement, using a mix of English and Gujarati. Despite the late hour, Bryan was plied with more and more snacks as everyone gathered around him, asking him questions about himself and his parents. Bizarrely, though the travel had been exhausting and stressful, and though he seemed to start at every car horn or yelping dog from outside, Bryan seemed to be enjoying himself.

I sat on the periphery with Shannon, who was yawning. "This is a lot," she said. "How does everyone have so much stamina?"

"Fuelled by chai," said Amit. "And wedding-mania."

"Maybe you could make a tea for the shop?" I said. "Indian wedding chai?"

She smiled. "I like it." A pause. "Was your wedding like this?"

"Kind of." It was smaller. It had been a small wedding by Indian standards, but still a huge one by Canadian ones. I hadn't wanted a big wedding, but there was no avoiding it. Mom had been adamant, and no amount of showing her wedding magazines explaining that it was my day would convince her otherwise. She had social obligations to meet, people she had to invite because she'd been invited to their children's weddings, people who needed to be there because if you invite one family, you must invite all the related families, a big production to put on because people would talk and compare weddings. A lot was expected from her, and therefore me.

"Payal's wedding was great," said Amit. "Big party, great food, everyone having a blast—it was very un-Payal-like."

"Hey!"

"Can I help it if you're the responsible one?"

"Yes."

Amit laughed. I stuck out my tongue at him.

There was a brief quieting of conversation in the room, and into the quiet, Bryan's voice seemed to boom. "Payal and I were kind of having a fight. That's why I was wasn't here earlier."

Everyone spoke at once, and above it all thudded my heart as I tried not to panic. I wanted to explain, it only became a fight because Bryan refused to come to India, but I also wanted to tell him to shut up and drag him away before he said anything else, and also I wanted to laugh it all off like it was some kind of a silly joke, even though no one would believe me.

Someone must have asked my mom about it, because her voice cut through the others. "Of course I knew. They are having problems having children." Her face was squinched up in irritation. I couldn't tell if it was because she wasn't in control of the situation or if she was simply bothered at being questioned at all.

They all turned towards me, and I stared at the smooth white floor and answered as noncommittally as possible as questions and advice rained down. Have you seen a doctor? Was it a good doctor? I know a very good doctor, he helped Bhauna Aunty's son. These things take time. We must do puja at the temple for you. Have you tried homeopathic medicines? Ayuerveda? These Western doctors don't know anything. And this Western diet is all wrong for health. Indian diet is the best. Have you been taking too much stress? Good thing you're on vacation, huh?

I snorted at the mention of stress, but no one noticed. Shannon squeezed my hand and thankfully did not mention a tea.

Eventually, Bryan's voice cut through the clamour. He began explaining the difficulties we'd had in North America, answering questions as he went through our entire fertility journey. It was the Christmas party all over again. I tried to catch his eye, to signal to him to stop talking, but he never looked directly at me. Had nothing changed?

As he spoke, my relatives began to murmur amongst themselves. I caught some of the English words among the Gujarati, and pieced together that they were gossiping about other people they knew who'd seen fertility doctors, or needed egg donors, or adopted a relative's child if they were unable to have their own. Everyone knew somebody. No one talked about it except in gossiping murmurs. My heart sank, realizing that I would be just another whispered story to pass along.

I thought of Malika and her parents. Everyone knew what Ashok Masa working in Dubai all those years really meant. Maybe some of them even knew about his other family. No one talked about it, and they pretended nothing was wrong. Who were they kidding? But I pictured Malika's face, with its angry tears, after meeting her father and half-sister, having known nothing about it all this time.

There was a brief lull in the conversation, and this time my mom spoke into it. "I took Payal to a clinic soon after arrival." Geeta Mami asked her a question in Gujarati, and she and Mom discussed rapidly before Mom switched back to English. "Medically, I'm sure everything is excellent. But the system is all wrong. You don't meet the donor, you don't know what kind of family they come from." She shook her head. "I'm not comfortable with this."

I opened my mouth to tell her this was a decision between Bryan and me, but Bryan jumped in and starting talking first. "Same here. Especially with total strangers involved."

Chandu Mama spoke. "In the old days, if husband-wife couldn't have a baby, maybe brother and wife has a baby and gives it to them. He nodded vaguely toward my brother and Shannon. Amit seemed entirely nonplussed, but Shruti instinctively put a hand on her belly.

Reshma Masi spoke up: "Even today, people still do."

Mom nodded in agreement. "This is a good system. You know the baby is coming from a good family, one you know."

Bryan wasn't doing anything to shut this down. "This is kind of a private matter," I said loudly. I tried murdering Bryan with a look, but he still lived. He smiled in my direction, without actually looking at me.

Reshma Masi waved this off. "It's only family here."

Mom added. “Who better to help you? Everything that affects you, affects us.”

“I kept telling you,” said Bryan. “We shouldn’t keep this a secret from our families. I don’t know what you were worried about.”

Everyone began nodding to each other in approval, and the murmurs began anew as discussions started among them.

I whispered to Shannon. “Am I the only one who finds this strange?”

She looked uncomfortable. “I don’t think we should judge another culture’s values.”

“It’s my culture. I’m judging.”

“It’s hella strange,” said Amit.

I turned to him. “Can you help me stop it?”

He gestured at Bryan. “You’re going to have to go to the source.”

Of course Amit was no help. What did I expect? I tried to catch Bryan’s eye, but he was looking around, trying to follow the little bits and pieces of conversation, until Chandu Mama spoke up loudly, quieting them all. “Egg donor system is better. You go to doctor, get it done, nobody knows, nobody talks. Other way, everybody knows but has to pretend nobody knows.”

Geeta Mami protested in Gujarati and then Reshma Masi nodded emphatically. “Exactly. How can you trust the family is good?”

“Egg donor can be related too,” said Kaushik. I wondered how he knew that.

Everyone looked at Shruti. “Perfect match,” said Reshma Masi.

Mom spoke in Gujarati, but I caught the word ‘expecting’ in English.

“I’d be happy to help,” said Shruti. “After the baby is born.” She looked over at Naresh, who nodded quietly, his face unreadable.

"That would be amazing," said Bryan.

"I thought you said this thing made you uncomfortable," I said.

The room went quiet as the rest of the family listened in, but for a change, I didn't care. Bryan had turned our half-formed plans upside down, and now he'd involved my whole family, and I still didn't understand what he was doing here in the first place.

"It was the stranger part that bothered me."

Mom clapped her hands. "Exactly what I thought. How can you trust a stranger? How do you know if you pick one and they give you a different one?" She pointed at me. "You should listen to your husband."

I started to tell her that if I'd listened to my husband, I wouldn't be in India in the first place, but Reshma Masi spoke over me, and the hurt tone in her voice obliterated any chance of being heard. "This is a very good doctor." She named people she knew who'd been to see him. It occurred to me that Mom had gotten the clinic recommendation from her, that she'd been talking to her about our infertility problems. Was nothing private? Did everything belong to the whole family? Was nothing mine alone?

Shannon gave my hand another squeeze, but I snatched it back and glared at Bryan, who was grinning like an idiot.

Mom was placating Reshma. "Even with a very good doctor, known is best." Everyone in the room agreed. "But I was thinking, instead of Shruti, maybe Malika. That way, we can do the donation now."

"Mom!"

"Bryan is here, you're here. We can get the whole process done in one trip."

Amit spoke up for a change. "Won't Malika be on her honeymoon?"

"She can postpone it."

My head spun through the millions of details that Mom

had no idea about. The need to time the process carefully, the invasive testing, the daily injections. Least of all, Malika being just barely married and being put through all this. The idea of doing it right now was so ludicrously impractical that my mind could barely register the question of whether or not I even wanted to do this at all.

Amit and Shannon got up to say their goodbyes; their driver had arrived to take them back to their hotel. The rest of the room took this as a signal to start getting ready for bed, although Mom and Reshma stayed where they were, talking in Gujarati, their conversation getting increasingly heated.

Bryan got off the couch and sat next to me, the cheese-eating grin still on his face. "I told you we should talk to people. Look how everything is coming together."

I wanted to punch him. "This is insane," I hissed. "You didn't want to do this at all."

He rubbed his eyes, and I saw how red with tiredness they were. "I wanted to talk about it."

"We haven't talked." I flung my arm toward Mom and Reshma Masi. "They talked."

"I know you have issues with your sister, but you have to admit, she's the perfect choice," he said. "She has your genes. It just makes sense."

Was this what he had in mind all along? He'd never said so. Or had I just not been listening, like I hadn't listened when he told me he wasn't coming to India? "They aren't talking about my sister now. They're talking about my cousin."

Bryan nodded slowly. "Maybe that's still a good compromise. We know her, and you don't have to deal with your sister-issues."

"You want to do this right now? Bryan, you know how impossible that is."

"Maybe it's possible?" said Bryan. "I could freeze my, uh, contribution."

"You drop in like a lightning bolt for a wedding and now you want to go home with a baby?"

"It's getting our lives back. Getting the future we dreamed of back. Don't make this sound crazy."

"It's crazy!"

Everyone in the room had stopped talking, even Reshma and my Mom, and they were looking at Bryan and me. Fuck.

Mom broke the silence. "You both must be very tired. Bryan especially." There was an immediate hubbub of the last few people sitting around gulping back their tea, and reorganizing who would sleep where now that Bryan was here, of moving people and clothes and furniture around. Before I knew it, I was lying in bed beside Bryan, wide awake and listening to the dogs barking and the horns honking and the low rumble of his snoring.

CHAPTER TWENTY

December 2010, Mumbai

THE MORNING OF THE WEDDING was busy with people: people making chai and food, people pleating and folding our saris, people doing hair, people doing makeup. I went through each task in a fog, glad that so much of it could be done without needing my active participation.

Like the other married women, I wore my wedding sari. Red with gold embroidery. The last time I'd worn it was Shruti's wedding. All around me, women were dressed as I was, in red saris with gold embroidery, except for Ammaji, who wore her usual white homespun, but with a red border, embroidered in gold.

Kaushik had found Bryan an Indian outfit to wear and taken him with the other men to get ready in a neighbouring flat. I hoped he was managing okay. We'd been launched straight into getting ready for the ceremony. There had been no time to talk. Bryan had slept soundly while I spent the night mostly awake, trying to comprehend how he could have changed his mind so quickly.

All that was left was to put on my jewellery, which was my wedding set of gold and diamonds that I had seen twice: when I wore it at my own wedding, and then when at I wore it at Shruti's. Mom and Dad had insisted I get this made and then Mom promptly took it from me to store in her safe deposit box with her other jewellery. "You won't keep it properly," she'd said.

I put on the necklace and the matching bracelets and the ring. I tried putting in the earrings, but they wouldn't fit; my holes had closed over enough that the thick, screw-style posts of Indian earrings wouldn't go in. I put them back in the case, and joined the rest of the family in the living room.

Kajal was the first to notice. "Where are your earrings?"

"They wouldn't fit in my ears, so I left them."

Mom retrieved them from the bedroom and tried to shove them in, pulling hard on my earlobes and pressing the gold posts into them. I gritted my teeth against both the physical pain and being peppered with comments. "Why didn't you tell us? We could have re-pierced your ears! We could have had your earrings remade as clip-ons!"

"It's no big deal," I said. "No one's looking at me anyway." But no one listened; they interrupted getting ready for the wedding to search through jewellery boxes for unlikely clip-ons or thinner posts or other ideas that might work. After several people tried jamming a few other earrings in my ears, they finally gave up. Mom grumbled at me for not having checked earlier. I was too tired to feel guilty about it.

The drivers and taxis were ready to go, and we had to leave. I pulled my theft-proof purse over my head and one arm, the practical black nylon jarring against the elegant sari. One by one, we packed ourselves into the musical elevator, trying not to crush our saris while getting as many people downstairs at once.

Outside the building, the men were already waiting. Bryan wore a cream-coloured kurta with a long sapphire blue embroidered vest, his own blue eyes faded to nearly white in comparison. On his feet were black dress shoes, rather than the sandals most of the other men wore. He turned around, somewhat self-consciously. "How do I look?"

His hair was still gelled into spikes. I half-smiled. You

could take Bryan to India and put him in Indian clothes, but he stayed Bryan.

We piled into the cars, trying to fit everyone in without wrinkling our clothes. The air conditioning blew at its maximum, and it was still warm in the car from too many bodies squeezed in together. I remembered doing this years ago on visits to India, when cars in India were less pervasive, squeezing even more people into fewer vehicles, women sitting on other people's laps, people in the back bench sitting as far up as possible so that others could squeeze in behind.

The bride's side of the family filled the outdoor wedding site and milled around sipping chai or nibbling on snacks while they waited for the groom. He would arrive along with members of his own family, who would dance alongside the procession. I reminded Bryan of this part of Indian weddings as we wandered away from my relatives.

"I'm glad we skipped that part in our wedding," said Bryan.

"It's not like it would have killed you to dance." It was one of the few concessions my mom had made, largely because she realized the futility of getting Bryan's family to dance in the street to the beat of a tabla.

"It could have."

We stood around in an uneasy silence. In my head, I ran through ways to bring up the sudden about-face from last night, and then opted to wait for him to begin the conversation.

Instead, he asked. "When does all this start?"

I shrugged, but I was still annoyed, since these were the factors we'd had to sort out for our own wedding. Shouldn't he know this? "It depends on astrology. And also, the time needs to be counting up, not down."

"What?"

"Imagine a clock. When the big hand is going down towards six, it's unlucky."

The sun was bright and hot and Bryan already looked a little bit red. "Did you have to take classes on all this? I don't know how you keep track."

I shrugged.

We could hear the drums and the music. The groom had arrived. The wedding guests began to gather, and we grouped in with them.

"Where's the bride?"

"She comes later." I hadn't seen Malika at all. I wondered if she was nervous. At the end of today, she would be married to Raj; I still worried if that would be enough for her.

What would happen if my mom or her mom started pressuring her to be my egg donor when she'd been scarcely married a minute? When she was still trying to find her own way with so many other voices around her, telling her to find fulfillment in making everyone else happy?

"It's a crazy plan, you know." I spoke softly. "We can't do all this before we leave India. Mom doesn't have the least idea of what's involved. We can't dump all that on Malika right after her wedding."

"So that can be Plan B," said Bryan. "Plan A, we sort out with Shruti once we're home again."

"She doesn't know how involved the process is either."

He nodded. "But you know she'd do it anyway."

I did know. No matter how invasive, how expensive, or time-consuming, no matter how much medical drama was involved, Shruti would go through it all for me, because we were family, because we were two parts of a larger whole that looked out for each other and took care of each other. And now, everything felt inevitable, like a marble rolling downhill, nothing to stop it from free-falling into a pit.

The drum noises were getting louder, and Mom emerged to lead Bryan and me to the wedding mandap. We took off our shoes and sat cross-legged on the floor on the mandap stage with all of the other close relations, me on one side with all the women, blending into a sea of red and gold saris, Bryan the sole white face among all the men on the other side.

Malika arrived, arranged in a palanquin and carried in. I looked for signs in her face that she was happy, but her expression was obscured under her elaborate sari, makeup, hair, and jewellery.

The tablas stopped and, for a change, the wedding guests were silent. We watched while Malika and Raj carefully placed heavy garlands of flowers around each other's necks. A smattering of applause swelled into fuller cheers, and the wedding guests resumed their chatting and eating while Malika and Raj took their seats on the mandap to complete the wedding ceremony. The next important step wouldn't be for a while.

Near me, Reshma Masi was beginning to cry. An aunty pulled a tissue from her sari blouse and handed it to her. Reshma Masi held it still against the tears leaking out of her eyes in an attempt to keep her makeup looking fresh. Shruti sat off-stage in her red and gold sari on a chair; between the sari and the belly, getting up and down from the floor of the mandap was cumbersome. Shannon sat next to her, watching raptly.

Would it be distressing for Shruti if we took her egg and let it grow into a baby in my body? Cousins were considered the same kind of relationship as brothers and sisters in our culture; would Shruti see the relationship between her child and any child I had with her help as an extension of that idea? She probably would. In any case, if she felt bad about it, she'd never admit it. Mom, I knew, would pretend the egg donation never happened, even though all of us would know. They'd all pretend like it never happened, except maybe Mom might see this as another reason why I should be more like my sister.

An aunty I didn't recognize tapped me on the shoulder, pointing worriedly to my ears. I shook my head and tried to gesture that it was fine. She became insistent. I pointed to my ears. "The hole is shut. Closed." So much for no one noticing. I wasn't sure if she heard me, or simply gave up on trying to explain the problem to me, but eventually she settled down.

The wedding dragged on and the women, seated cross-legged on the mandap, began to move around, some eventually getting up and leaving for tea or a snack or to chat with a guest before returning. I couldn't see Bryan anymore, wherever he was on the other side of Malika and Raj. He was probably getting uncomfortable sitting on the floor for so long. I hoped Amit or Kaushik had reminded him that he could get up and leave whenever he wanted.

Malika and Raj sat in their chairs, sometimes leaning in to chat quietly with each other in between various instructions from the pandit. There were rows of chairs in front of the mandap, and beyond them tents covering long tables of food and tea and cool drinks. The chairs were sparsely populated, but women in saris and men in a mix of sherwanis, kurtas, and business suits kept coming in and out from under the food tents. Throughout the field, they stood in clumps; talking, eating, and laughing.

Bryan wasn't wrong. Shruti was the perfect choice, and Malika a good alternative. So why wasn't I excited? I rearranged my legs, trying to take the pressure off my sit bones and not crumple my sari. Was I just stuck on the Shruti of it all, that my sister's apparent superiority to me now extended to her ova? What was wrong with me? Why wasn't I jumping on the chance to have all our dreams come true, to go back to Bryan and me being on the same page, to dismiss this trip as a blip, and to go back to the life as I'd expected, instead of staring down a lonely, formless future?

Mom tugged at me. "Go get some food."

"I'm not hungry."

"Take Bryan to get some food."

I rose and tried not to step on the hem of my sari and rip out the safety-pinned pleats as my legs un-cramped. I could imagine the horror: no earrings and can't walk in a sari either. I got off the mandap and made my way around to the other side and gestured for Bryan to join me. He hesitantly came over to where I stood, and I pulled him away toward the back of the field where the food tents were set up. The sun was bright and blinding.

"It's kind of bizarre," said Bryan, as we walked. "It's a wedding and no one pays attention to the ceremony."

"It's a long ceremony." People kept glancing in our direction, pointing to Bryan and openly commenting on his blond hair and pale eyes. Bryan didn't seem to notice. I held up my pleats and dodged people as we made our way to where chai was being poured.

"I guess it seems a little rude," said Bryan.

"It was the same at our wedding."

"Was it?"

It was, and it wasn't. Bryan's side had mostly stayed seated and watched. We had found an English-speaking pandit who explained things and kept the ceremony to a tight seventy-five minutes; a rarity, since some pandits seemed to add things as they went along. "You're in a different culture," I said tiredly. "Adapt."

We picked up small cups of tea and wandered out into a clear space.

"Do you think we'll have time to visit a clinic before we fly back?" asked Bryan.

"I thought we were leaving Malika out of this."

He nodded. "But we could check the place out, and maybe I could still freeze my part in case. Just as a backup if things don't work out with Shruti. That way, I wouldn't have to come back." He took a sip of chai.

"Shouldn't we talk about this more before we jump right in?"

"We talked last night."

Unseen, under my sari, I stomped my foot in frustration. "You talked. My mom talked. And now we have all these new plans and I'm supposed to go along with it because you're here?"

He changed his stance and when he spoke, an irritated edge had entered his voice. "You were the one pushing visits to some unknown clinic in India. And you were the one who kept hammering on about how I had to come to this wedding. And okay, fine, I didn't get how important that was to you. But I'm here, and we finally found a way that we can have the life we wanted." He gestured impatiently, slopping tea out of his cup without noticing. "What the hell is going on, Pi? If you're this pissed at your sister that you're going to sabotage your life, you need therapy. Because this is straight-up crazy."

We were surrounded by hundreds of guests, forming and reforming small groups as they talked and greeted one another, looked for people they knew, or headed back to the food tables to try another dish, carried out on a small napkin or disposable plate and eaten by hand. I caught snippets of conversations as the wedding guests walked by, a mix of English and Gujarati, a mix of gossip and food commentary. Once in a while, a guest would turn to watch the ceremony for a few moments. Bryan only watched me, his white skin blotchy from the heat, the thin fabric of his borrowed kurta beginning to cling to his sweaty neck.

Last night, everyone had steamrolled over me, including Bryan. They decided everything for me without my even participating, although somehow Bryan got a vote. I felt claustrophobic. There were too many people in the venue, too many people at this wedding, too many decisions being made, taking up all the space so there was none left for me. Bryan was too close and despite the many safety pins holding my sari just so, it felt as if I couldn't move, that I dare not move, lest the fabric wrapped again and again around me would slide off and leave me exposed. We'd been standing under the shade of the tent canopy and yet the light seemed too bright, and I could feel beads of sweat edging along the heavy makeup covering my face.

I was hardly aware of the crash as I dropped my tea cup, nor the hot chai splashing against the gold border of my sari, nor Bryan taking my arm and guiding me to a chair. The world had gone translucent and purple-edged. I felt a coolness against my neck; it crinkled, a bottle of water. The next thing I could make out was a rust-coloured sari over a tall, pale figure. Red hair. Shannon. And beside her was Amit.

I could hear Bryan's voice, but couldn't see him. "Pi? Pi?"

"Stop calling me Pi." The words were like marbles in my mouth. "That's not my name." No one understood what I was saying. My hands were enfolded into mehndi-decorated ones and squeezed tight, anchoring me so I wouldn't get lost. Shruti.

"Pi! Are you all right, Pi?"

"Go away." The words still weren't coming out in a way that anyone could understand. "Leave me alone."

Shannon put the bottle of water in my hand. "Drink." She hunkered down in front of me, holding Amit for balance, trying to read my face.

I was starting to focus again. Shannon's eyes, green and fringed in thin copper lashes, stared into mine. Somehow, she understood. "Bryan." She looked up at him and smiled sweetly. "Why don't you get Payal some more tea? And maybe something sweet to eat? I think her blood sugar must have dropped a bit, and that will make her feel better." Bryan was off in flash, his kurta and vest flapping behind him. She gently pushed the water bottle to my mouth again and told me to drink. The water was lukewarm and stale-tasting, but the world around me started to clear up. I could see the embroidery on Shannon's sari, the freckles on her collarbone just visible over the neckline over her blouse. Her eyes flicked off to the side to confirm no one was in earshot, and she spoke in a low voice: "What do you need?"

"I'm fine."

"Bullshit."

I looked from her to Amit, and back to her again. Shruti gave my hand another squeeze. "It doesn't matter," I said. "It's impossible."

Amit leaned in. "Come on, Payal. Before Mom notices and gets involved."

There were too many people around. Too much noise. The thrum of conversation from wedding guests, the rumble of street noise beyond the walls, the music, the droning prayers from the pandit being broadcast over loudspeakers from the wedding ceremony that most people were ignoring in favour of food and gossip. "I want to lie down somewhere quiet. Alone. But it's the wedding and we have to be here and I don't know what's going on with Bryan and we still have the reception." I began babbling, not even sure what I was saying anymore, and everything began to spin and go translucent again.

Shannon lay her hand on the back of my neck, a hand that felt strangely cool in the hot weather. "Shh. We can work this out."

Bryan arrived with tea and some kachoris on a plate. "I hope this is sweet."

Amit leaned over to look. "It isn't."

"Damn."

"It's okay," I sipped at the tea, sweet and mildly spiced. I breathed in the scent of ginger and cardamon. For a second, everything was quiet.

* * *

I was lying on a bed inside Amit and Shannon's hotel room at the Taj, and for the first time since arriving in India, I couldn't hear any noise. Shannon and Bryan had been dispatched to Chandu Mama's to pick up my clothes for this evening's reception. Amit had gone to sit in the lobby. We had left the wedding early, before the ceremony was complete; Amit had worked it out with Mom and Dad.

I didn't know what to do in the room by myself, aside from stare at the ceiling and drink in the quiet. I had a queen-sized bed all to myself. It might only be for a few hours, but I had to make the most of it while I could, since after that it was back to the wedding reception, back to my uncle's flat, and back to Bryan. Back to Canada, back to settling the final details of our house and back to the moving ahead with fertility treatment, this time with Shruti or maybe Malika along for the ride. Shannon's copy of *Lonely Planet India* was on the nightstand. I picked it up, and it fell open to the chapter about the Taj Mahal. *One of the Seven Wonders of the Modern World.* Shannon must have read that chapter over and over. Somewhere, Malika, who had been so excited by the idea of visiting the Taj, was moving between one wedding preparation and the next, being dressed, made up, styled, bejewelled, and cried over by her mother. And after that, she would leave her mother to be dressed, made up, styled, and cried over by her mother-in-law and husband. Would she find joy? Would I?

The door clicked as the lock turned and Amit walked in. "Sorry. Just wanted to get my laptop."

"You're going to work?"

He scoffed. "My agent sent me a script. Another possible role."

I sat up on the bed with the guidebook open on the taupe coverlet. "I thought you were only going to that first audition as a favour."

"I don't know. There's some promising opportunities out there."

"Are you going back to acting?"

He sat on the bed beside me. "I'm not sure. I thought there was nothing left for me, but maybe there is."

"More roles as doctors and terrorists?"

"Cheap shot." He picked up a pillow and tossed it at me, but I batted it away. "Things are a little different in Toronto versus LA. Like, not perfect, but hopefully different enough."

"But what about Dad?"

"I went to theatre school. He knows I was never going to be an accountant."

"He's been keeping the office next to his empty all this time for you. Meanwhile, I've been busting my ass in a job I never wanted because you had to go fail at acting."

Amit's eyes narrowed. "Right. Poor Payal had to make money and be the favoured child."

"You have no idea what it was like when you left for LA. You didn't see the way they were beating themselves up, wondering what they did wrong. Who filled the cracks you left behind?" I slid off the bed and began pacing. I was antsy, new feelings rising up. "People have been making things easy for you your entire life, and not once do you think of anyone else. You get what you want, and never mind other people."

"Right." Amit sat on the bed and edged closer, tossing the guidebook behind him. "Bookkeeping for Dad instead of acting is exactly what I always wanted to do. All the classes and auditions were just a long con."

"It's all about you. Nobody else has problems."

Amit looked confused. "Bryan showed up, you two need to talk. What does that have to do with me?"

"Everybody got on my case about using Shruti or Malika as an egg donor. And you didn't say a single word."

Amit moved to another part of the bed. "You didn't speak up."

"I did. They just kept going like I wasn't even there."

He adjusted his position again. "You can fight your own battles. You don't need me to do it for you."

"You could still help. Look around you, see if you can do something. Like Shannon does."

His face softened slightly, and he looked pensive for a moment. "What did you want to be, instead of an accountant?"

I sat at the edge of the bed. "I don't know," I said. "I wanted the chance to find out." I played with the gold border on my dupatta. "But I guess the dreams they had for newborn me weren't so bad, right? I mean, it's not like these aren't things that everyone wants."

"Not everyone," said Amit.

Shannon said she didn't want to get married, but I wondered if that also meant they didn't want children too. I sighed. "I'm tired of running around trying to fulfill everyone else's dreams."

"So do something that makes you happy."

"Isn't that selfish?"

"Is it?" asked Amit. "We're supposed to be miserable forever because of what everyone else wants?"

Bryan had dreams. My parents had dreams. What did I have?

I sighed again. "I want to get out of here."

Amit looked at the door and then back at me.

"No," I said. "Out of this wedding. Away from Mom. From Bryan. I just want to get away."

"You're a grown adult."

"How will it look, leaving in the middle of a wedding? Abandoning Bryan."

"That sounds like something Mom would say," he teased.

I crumpled onto the bed.

His face went serious. "I can talk to them."

"Right, you can just wave a magic wand and, poof, it's fine, no one will worry at all."

"You're always accusing me of getting away with everything." He opened his laptop. "Why not take advantage of it?" He fussed through connecting to the Internet in the room. "Where do you want to go? Maybe Shannon could talk to her supplier if you wanted a room here."

I pulled Shannon's guidebook closer, and the pages fell open to the chapter about the Taj Mahal.

CHAPTER TWENTY-ONE

December 2010, Agra

IT WAS COLD IN AGRA. I had expected the same tropical heat as Mumbai, but instead I was shivering in my gold high-heeled sandals and the too-long dress I'd hurriedly picked out from Shannon's suitcase. In the rush off the plane and finding a hotel at the last minute, I hadn't noticed the cold. Possibly, it was because I was convinced my mom would jump out from behind other people to drag me back to Bryan and Mumbai.

But on the drive through the near-empty streets in the tuk-tuk, I could only huddle against the wind. I got a pitying look from the tuk-tuk driver, who was bundled in layers of mismatched sweaters and a woolly hat. He dropped me off near the Taj complex, pointing down the road and speaking in slow Hindi. I nodded as if I understood.

There were other foreign tourists walking along the wide road: more white people than I'd ever seen in India, but even more Indian tourists. Corrugated tin shacks were set up along the sides, filled with souvenirs—magnets, pens, t-shirts, mini Taj Mahals—but there weren't many touts so early in the morning. Those who were there sat around small open fires, warming their hands. There was a slight fog dulling the pale dawn light.

It was the emptiest place I'd ever been to in India. I could have opened my arms out wide and not touched anyone. I could hear silence between wisps of conversation. I could hear the sound of my feet on the dirty paved ground.

The entrance to the Taj Mahal wasn't open yet, but there was already a long line up against the red brick wall that surrounded the complex. I stood in the shorter queue, but after a moment, a man spoke to me. "Madam? Ladies queue." He pointed to the longer line, which I realized was all women.

I'd never seen much of tourist India before. India to me had always meant visits with relatives and shopping. It was horns honking and engines revving and hot sun and people and sitting around being polite, a place that felt oddly familiar in its discomfort and yet was completely out of my element. In India, I always felt like my day-to-day life was no longer in my control.

From the line, I noticed a small grey monkey crawling along the top of the wall. I stared. The monkey, unconcerned, carried along on all fours. From the corner of my eye, I could see some people looking to see what I was staring at, but they quickly looked away, disinterested. I'd never seen a monkey outside of the zoo, and here was one, attracting about as much attention as squirrels did back home.

At that moment, I wished that Bryan was with me so that I could tell him about the monkey. He didn't know where I was. I'd made Amit promise not to tell him in case he got some idea about following me. Amit wasn't to tell anyone where I had gone, only that I'd definitely be back. I had no idea how he'd get away with this, but he assured me he'd figure it out when he helped me into the taxi to the Mumbai airport. I still had Kajal's old phone with me, but I'd turned it off. I didn't dare face the barrage of messages and calls that would come in if I turned it back on.

The line trundled along. I could picture Bryan ensconced in my uncle's flat, being fed chai and snacks and having everyone sympathize with him, and also grilling him over my whereabouts. Maybe they'd take him shopping to distract him, as well as themselves, by going to the mall, or to various shops where they could get shirts custom-tailored for him. They'd appreciate the opportunity to dote over him. Relatives would come by to chat with him and bemoan the circumstances of my disappearance, chat with him about the clothes he'd bought and the food he'd eaten and about his parents and sister, and then wonder at what was wrong with me? My mother would keep asking, *What would people think?* What would people think of our family? What would people think of my being such a terrible daughter, running off from her husband? What would people think of my having run away from my cousin's wedding?

I shivered and hugged myself and put my cold, clammy hands under my arms to try and warm them up. Bryan would spend time with my relatives in India in exactly the same way he spent time with his family in Toronto, living the same kind of life we'd been planning for ourselves. He'd enjoy the time in India with my relatives more than I would, and he'd enjoy the life we'd planned more than I would.

The line shuffled forward. The gates had opened and things were moving. I was actually doing this: visiting the most famous tourist attraction in India on my own, having run away from my parents, my husband, all their expectations. The world had not ended. No matter what happened next, I had chosen this, I had ignored all the expectations people had of me, I was here.

"I'm happy," I said, and then realized I'd spoken aloud. I looked around nervously, but aside from a glance or two, everyone was too focused on moving with the line to pay any attention to me. I looked back at the monkey, sitting on the wall, gnawing on something in its hands.

Everything I'd been doing in my life had been in pursuit of fulfilling a formula, and suddenly I felt ridiculous that I'd never stopped to consider the reality of it, that none of it made me happy. "I don't want this life," I said out loud again, pleased to notice that no one was paying attention to me.

I shivered again, both from the cold and then thought that if life had gone the way I had planned, we'd already have a baby. How much more impossible would this moment be?

My body felt jittery, but not with anxiety. Energy was building in my toes, in my legs. After passing through the metal detectors, I took a dozen sedate steps toward the Taj Mahal and then spun around once, spreading my arms and doing my best imitation of jazz hands. A few people looked at me and smiled.

I took spinning, dancing steps toward the gate. There was no beat to follow, only the energy bubbling up. The heavy, clumping steps of garba, the circle of women dancing and clapping in unison—none of that had a place here. There was only me, moving, no music and no rhythm, no proscribed pattern of steps. I tried jumping and turning in the air like a figure skater, and stumbled in my heels, but I only laughed out loud to myself.

"Ah, you're grand!" A man's voice, a vaguely Irish accent. I didn't even look in the direction of the voice, but called out "Thanks!" and carried on.

Some of the early morning fog had burned off, but the air was still misty. A small group stood in front of the gate, listening to a guide explain that they were on the direct centre line. The gate was enormous, red sandstone inlaid with white marble in perfect, gently pointed arches. But I couldn't see the Taj yet; the gate was too thick.

I was getting a little out of breath and I stopped for a moment near the group of tourists, and eavesdropped on the guide.

"Some say, this is the most romantic place in India," explained the guide. His group dutifully listened and took photos. "The Mughal Emperor Shah Jahan had built it for his third and most beloved wife, Mumtaz Mahal. It was her tomb."

The guide went on to explain Shah Jahan's grief and the twenty-two years he'd spent building the tomb in her honour. I walked away when the guide started in on the architecture and construction details.

The legend of Shah Jahan's love seemed impossible. Emperors in those days married for political reasons. She was his third wife and had probably spent most of her life pregnant or bearing children. However long they'd been married, no amount of love could make up for the daily grind of expectations and duty and family and trying to do everything you were supposed to do.

And yet, he'd built this for her alone. I couldn't imagine spending twenty-two years building a monument to Bryan. Twenty-two years of grief was not something I could imagine with Bryan. For all the grand gesture of flying to India so that we could talk, we had only ended up in the place he'd evidently wanted in the beginning, with Shruti as my future egg donor, so we could get on with our lives: our new house, with our new kids, and our friends. His friends. It occurred to me that I didn't miss them.

Another guide was in earshot, and I listened in as he spoke to a group who was waiting impatiently and not listening. "Originally, there was to be a second Taj: black Taj, across the river. Exact mirror copy. Black marble instead of white. This, Shah Jahan's tomb. But Shah Jahan, end of his life, imprisoned in Agra Fort by his son, Aurangzeb. And Aurangzeb said, no black Taj, cancelled. Too expensive. And so Shah Jahan's tomb in Taj Mahal. Beside Mumtaz. Only thing not symmetrical, not perfect." The guide smiled as he noticed some people in his group starting to pay attention. "Aurangzeb was not favoured son." There were scattered chuckles in the group. "He was not supposed to rule." The guide made a slashing motion against his throat. "But favoured son, Aurangzeb cut his head off. So who else to rule?"

Amit and Shruti were lucky I had no desire to chop off their heads in pursuit of gaining control of Dad's accounting empire. I made my way through the gate, smiling at the idea.

The gateway was thick and it took my eyes a moment to adjust to the darkness, and then, all I could see were people. Their voices echoed inside the stone gate, and I walked on and stepped out into the light and saw something extraordinary.

The pale mist had lifted like a bridal veil and beneath it, the white, impossibly symmetrical building glowed, as if Mumtaz Mahal's love shone through the pure marble.

I'd been to India many times, and not once had I seen this. I could wonder about the reality of Mumtaz Mahal's life and marriage, but in front of me was the building Shah Jahan had built for her, a building so beyond any expectation, any duty, so far away from the ordinary day-to-day business of living.

We weren't emperors. We would never aspire to a custom marble mausoleum, even if that were remotely affordable. But Bryan could select a cookie-cutter house in Pickering, picked from the same plans as everyone else, and feel like a success.

In all my striving to be the most normal Canadian I could be, while still keeping my parents' approval, I'd been acting out a role. And the next step would have been to drag a new person into this pretend life, and act out a role for them too, raising them to believe there was nothing more to life than meeting other people's expectations. And for the first time I knew, in my chilled bones, that it was time to stop.

* * *

In the multitudes of brown people around the Mumbai airport, I spotted Shannon easily. It took me a moment to realize that there was no one else there but Shannon. Not my parents or my uncle. Not Bryan. She gave me a hug and bustled me into the car before telling the driver where to go.

"Is everyone mad?" I asked.

"More worried," she said. "But they had the wedding to deal with and all the family around. Amit tried to calm them down a little."

I'd gone back to the airport right after seeing the Taj in the morning. There was nothing in Agra that would compare. I tried to picture it in my mind, the white marble glowing through the mists, both ephemeral and eternal at once. But the first image that came to mind was the monkey crawling up the wall, unconcerned by the extraordinary monument nearby.

"How's Bryan?" I asked.

She didn't answer right away. "You'll have to ask him yourself."

"But how does he seem?"

She considered. "Like he's putting a good face on things." She pulled a bottle of water out of her bag and took a sip. "Ammaji was the most worried."

Ammaji. She would never understand why I ran off, and I could never explain it to her. I wasn't even sure I could explain it to Bryan.

We drove through a traffic jam where the horns blared particularly loudly. Shannon scowled slightly. "I don't know how people live here. It's so loud all the time."

"I thought you loved India."

"I do." She grimaced a little at a sustained horn blast from a neighbouring car. "But it's so loud, I can hardly think."

"It was quieter in Agra."

She raised her water bottle to me. "Cheers to that." She took a sip. "I have some news to think over, but maybe it'll have to wait until we're out of Mumbai."

"What news?"

"About the shop." She started on a long, convoluted explanation before getting to the point. "Someone wants to buy the business."

I knew the numbers. The shop was profitable. "The price is

really good. You'd make a lot of money—you could do whatever you wanted after that."

"I know." She stared out the window. Just outside the car was a man on a bicycle, with dozens and dozens of large filled sacks strapped to it. I didn't know how he was even staying upright. "But I don't know if these guys would really take care of the business—they sound like they want to turn it into the McDonald's of tea shops. And the shop is my baby, you know?"

I plucked at the dress I was wearing: one of Shannon's. It was too big, but it was comfortable. "Do you want to stay a small local shop forever?"

"I wouldn't mind," said Shannon. "I kind of love being a neighbourhood shop. But I also think, there are other neighbourhoods where we could be the local tea shop. And these guys." She shook her head. "They see the numbers, but I don't think they get the shop. But maybe I just don't know how to let go."

I thought about it. For all of Shannon's silly tea names and the administrative chaos in her tiny basement office, she had good instincts for business. "What if you grew the business? Like what these guys are thinking about, but your way?"

"That's a huge leap," said Shannon. "Can I afford that?"

"I think you could make it work." I took a long deep breath. "You grew this shop from nothing. And it's been successful. Think about what you could do if you expanded. If these guys think they could do it for you, what stops you from doing it yourself?"

"You really think so?"

I nodded. "I've seen the numbers."

She smiled. "More to think about."

We got back to Chandu Mama's, and when we opened the doors to the musical elevator, Ammaji was waiting for us in the landing. Her eyes lit up when she saw me, even though she spoke in a scolding tone as she escorted us inside the flat. No one else was home. I bent to touch her feet, but she stopped me and pulled me over to the couch, where she sat, and then gestured for me to sit on the floor in front of her.

"Ammaji," I started. "I'm sorry. I'm so sorry."

I could feel her warm hands on my head, stroking my hair back gently. Then after a moment, I felt something cool on my scalp, and she began to hum as she massaged it into my head. The kneading was soothing. I could feel my eyes welling up again.

I breathed in slow to control the tears, and caught the scent of coconut oil.

CHAPTER TWENTY-TWO

December 2010, Mumbai

WHEN EVERYONE ELSE GOT HOME—except for Malika and Raj, who had left for their honeymoon—there was a commotion of relief and worry, questions and scolding. Bryan came to my side as soon as he saw me, but made no attempt to hug me or hold my hand. I could tell his jaw was clenched from the tightness in his face; he was angry but holding it in.

Mom, on the other hand, was holding nothing back. "How can you run away like this in the middle of the wedding?" She grabbed my shoulders and shook me a little. "You weren't even there for the pictures."

"Do you know what could have happened to you?" added Reshma Masi. "You could have been murdered. Kidnapped. Taken to jail."

"We were very worried," said Dad. "We had to tell everyone you were sick to explain where you were. How can you make us do this?"

"At least Bryan was there," said Mom. "Do you know how it looks? What will people think?"

"She's fine," said Amit. I caught his eye and he winked at me.

"And you," started Mom, turning on him. "How can you help your sister run away? What kind of idiot are you?"

"Elder brother should protect younger sister," added Reshma.

"She's a grown woman," said Amit.

"What kind of a grown woman runs away in the middle of her own cousin's wedding?"

"Malika was so worried," said Reshma. "How can you worry her so much on her wedding day? She can't begin her married life worried."

"I'm fine," I said. I was surprised at how calm I was despite the onslaught of guilt and accusations. Mom and Reshma Masi dominated the conversation, but it was clear they were speaking for the room. "I'm sorry I worried you. I just needed to get away."

"You couldn't wait until after the wedding? And going alone? Not even your husband with you?"

Bryan hadn't said a word. I glanced his way, but he wouldn't look at me.

After a while, even Mom ran out of things to say. The fuss died down. The exhaustion from last night's reception and today's lunch, and the past several nights of sangeets and parties plus all the worry on my behalf was pervasive, but now everyone could relax. Once Malika and Raj were back, there would be smaller gatherings as they went from house to house, visiting all the relatives for the first time as a married couple. And then a new life together would go on and become ordinary, but hopefully that would build day-by-day into a life they enjoyed.

I managed a reprieve by saying I was tired, and Mom sent me to the room she and I had first shared on my first night in India. I lay down on the bed, and I was alone again like I had been in Agra, but this time I was warm. Mumbai had that going for it.

Bryan came in a few minutes later. "Hi," he said, guardedly.

"Hi." Neither of us spoke for a few moments, and then I spoke again. "I'm sorry that I worried you."

The dam broke. "I came all the way to India to talk to you, and at the first opportunity—"

"We haven't talked!"

"—you run away! What the fuck happened?"

I looked down at the bed, at the soft thin sheet I'd slept under that was folded neatly in a square. It had been washed many times, sent out to the same launderer and scrubbed and dried and ironed and returned, over and over again. "I'm sorry."

He dropped on the bed beside me. "I don't understand."

"I needed to get away."

"From what? We had a plan for having kids at last. I came to the wedding here. We were finally on track."

I pictured a train, relentlessly chugging forward, mindlessly barrelling through obstacles in its path. "What if I don't want to be on this track?"

"What do you mean what if? Do you, or don't you?"

I ran my fingers along the soft square of folded sheet and for a second bent it diagonally, the first step in folding a crane. It was too thick and it would be too soft to hold its shape anyway. How many cranes had I folded in a lifetime of wishing for something else?

Bryan nudged me, waiting for an answer. His eyes were the palest blue. I didn't quite know if I never wanted the life we had or not; I just knew that I didn't want it right now, and he did. And no matter how kind and understanding he tried to be, I couldn't be the reason that got in the way of his life and his dreams.

"Bryan," I said. "I don't."

I looked away as his face crumpled and felt mine do the same.

* * *

Bryan and I got through the rest of the day. That evening, as the members of my family scattered about the living room, I stayed as far off to the side as I possibly could to avoid further comments from my mother. I knew, though, that the offer to move back home after we got back instead of sharing the condo with Bryan was still open, although I didn't think I would take it. I needed more space to think for myself, and that was too hard around Mom.

Bryan had latched onto Kaushik, comparing the rules and skills between hockey and cricket. We'd agreed to pretend our marriage was fine until we got home in a few days when we could talk more. Not even Bryan wanted my parents and uncles and aunts involved in this.

Kajal and Shruti had Saanvi on the floor, talking about pregnancy and baby care while Naresh waved toys at the baby and smiled big. I could always stay with them for a bit, and help out when the baby was born. Motherhood would always be complicated for me, even if I decided I wanted it, but in a few months, I'd be Payal Masi. A new role for me that I could define for myself.

Amit and Shannon were back at their hotel, getting ready to travel to Agra and then Dehli. Shannon was already planning a trip to South India for the next time they came.

They would let me stay with them for a bit, I mused, but dismissed the idea. Their place was small and I'd only squeeze them out. But they could help me find a place of my own. I'd never rented an apartment before. I imagined a space that was entirely mine. I didn't know yet what I'd fill it with, but the possibilities were there. I felt good about my future. Things would be rocky, but for the first time, it felt like I had choices.

Dad tapped me on the shoulder. "I want to talk to you."

My good feelings for the future evaporated. "What is it?"

He took a large sip of tea from the cup in his hand. "I was talking to Amit," he said. "He told me he's going to keep pursuing acting. He'll do some part-time office work here and there, but he's looking for local acting work."

My heart felt tight in my chest. I stared down at Dad's tea, the still smooth surface of it in the cup. "What does this mean for the business?" I asked. Even though I knew.

"Shruti will be gone soon. She might do some part-time work later. But we'll need to hire some staff. You can't do it all."

Even though he didn't mean it as a dig, that he was only talking about the practical realities of running a business, I wanted to insist, yes, yes I could do it all. To prove to him that I was capable, good enough. I nodded, not quite trusting myself to speak in response.

He patted my shoulder. "I'm glad I've always been able to rely on you."

It was the closest he'd ever came to saying he was proud of me. "Dad." I stopped, hesitating.

He looked at me with the straight, steady gaze of a man who'd had many difficult conversations with employees. "What is it?"

I couldn't live my life waiting for words he might never say, words that might never have occurred to him to say. For him, there was never pride in doing what was expected of you, only disappointment in not doing it.

He spoke. "Tell me as a friend, not as your dad."

I took a deep breath. "I didn't want to disappoint you like Amit had. But now..." There was a time when I wanted to do anything but accounting, but I'd never fully formed a picture of what that looked like. "I don't know. This is the only thing I've ever done."

"But you want to do something else?"

I nodded. "I don't know what yet."

Dad looked over at the rest of the living room, at Ammaji half-asleep on the sofa, at Reshma Masi still weepy after Malika's wedding, reminiscing with Mom and Chandu Mama, and Geeta Mami handing out snacks and more chai. "You don't have to keep running the business."

"But you're retiring," I said. "You'll lose everything you've built without me."

"I don't have to retire," he said.

The world around me reeled. I took a deep breath to steady myself. "You can't work forever."

"I can't do nothing all day."

A wild thought occurred to me, and I blurted it out. "If you're holding out for Amit—"

"It was good Amit came to learn a little bit." He gave a slight smile. "It was good working with my kids, working all this time with you. Good to imagine the business staying in the family." He chuckled softly. "Besides, Amit is a lousy accountant."

"I can still take over." It still felt too selfish to let my father's dreams, his legacy, die out for my sake. But I also knew that I'd only be pretending to take over, because I would resent it, and it would all still slowly fade away.

Dad smiled gently. "Payal, you don't want to."

I didn't know what to say.

"We can always sell the business," he said. "I can keep a few clients to stay busy. Shruti can help me with the computer now and then. You and Amit can take the money and do what you want. We'll keep some money aside for Shruti and the baby."

"But it's your company, your legacy," I said. His dream.

Dad shrugged. "I came to Canada, and started this company from nothing. Amit went to LA and started his career from nothing. Maybe it's your turn to start something from nothing."

CHAPTER TWENTY-THREE

May 2011, Toronto

IT WAS MOVING DAY. OUR CONDO WAS half-packed. Exactly half. I was packing up all my things to move out to a new apartment not far from the future location of Shannon's second tea shop. Shannon had decided not to sell, but she didn't know if she'd be able to manage expanding on her own. I'd gone into a partnership with her to open and run the new location, and map out a system we could replicate elsewhere. In time, maybe we could spin off franchises of our own. And then maybe I could do this for other businesses as well. Or something else. In any case, it was a start.

Shannon and Amit were helping me pack up, although Amit had spent more time talking about the new play he was in than actually helping. Even Shannon was tuning him out. Maybe she missed the quiet of the days where Amit sat around in Dad's office doing very little, but she'd made a special tea blend for the cast and crew. TheatricaliTEA. I had to admit, it tasted pretty good.

The office was no more. Dad had moved his desk and the photographs he'd always hung over it home, and set up a small office for himself there. The sale of the business was going smoothly. Dad had sounded positive, talking about maybe learning to play golf at last, but I wasn't sure how he really felt. Still, our little accounting empire was winding down, and neither Amit nor I were trying to chop each other's heads off, so in the end we did better than the Mughal emperors.

I had clean newsprint and boxes. Shannon and I sat and wrapped things while Amit carried them down to the cube van I'd rented. Most of the furniture was staying. I'd bought a bunch of flat packs from IKEA and borrowed the rest from Mom. So it was clothes and books and papers, and a lot of the kitchen items.

Bryan had gone out. He didn't want to be around for any of this. He was keeping the condo, but things had been tense and angry since we decided to sell the house: the one we'd never lived in. He'd been bitter at the lawyer's office when we'd signed the final paperwork to let it go. He'd left from the appointment and disappeared for two days. When he returned, he alternated between snapping at me and slumping on the couch, looking mournfully at the house's listing online.

Shannon opened a cabinet and found photo albums. Wedding photos. "Are you taking these?"

I started flipping through. Photos of me in my red wedding sari the first time I'd worn it. Would I wear it again at the next family wedding if I wasn't married anymore? My mom would have to worry about that.

Amit leaned over. "Hey, look. That's when I had my goatee."

"I'm glad I wasn't around for that," said Shannon.

I kept flipping. I was beaming in the photos. I had been happy, but it had been for the wrong reasons. There was Bryan and his parents, his sister and Greg with a tiny Ethan and baby Madison. There was Amit and my parents, but no Shannon. Shruti and Naresh, separately since they weren't yet engaged and we had to keep up a pretence for appearance's sake. No relatives from India—visas had been difficult to get—but Ammaji had called during the wedding reception: the closest she would come to being there.

I smiled to myself. All of this had meant something, even if none of it belonged in my life now. I shut the album and gave it to Shannon to pack. Bryan and I hadn't decided who would get the wedding album, but I'd been the one to destroy the future he'd dreamed of. I couldn't bear to think of Bryan, in the midst of his hurt and anger, throwing it away.

When we'd come home from India, I'd noticed our tiny Christmas tree was still up, unlit and tucked again in its sad corner, the decorations we'd hastily put on before the disastrous party untouched. It had sat like that all through Christmas.

Bryan flopped on the couch and turned on the TV. Infomercials. I left the bags by the door and sat with him. Neither of us spoke for a while.

"Is it really so bad?" said Bryan. "Being married to me? Or our life together?"

I shook my head. "I just don't know how to be myself in all of this."

"Can't you find out while we're still together?"

I didn't want to say it so baldly. "I just need to live my own life for a while."

"So move out for a month. Three months. Then we can work out the rest."

It all sounded so reasonable. But I took a deep breath and closed my eyes and pictured the Taj Mahal through the morning mists. I didn't yet know what I wanted, but I knew for sure it was not this. "Bryan, I can't."

He said nothing. The flickering light from the TV reflected off the tears on his face. Noticing me looking, he wiped them away with his sleeve and laughed bitterly. "I guess it's a good thing we couldn't have kids."

I snorted, but wondered how much more lost I'd have been if I had gotten pregnant right away. How much longer would it have taken me to realize I didn't know how to be myself?

Shannon rode with Amit in the truck and I drove over to the new apartment near St. Clair West. The transit construction that had plagued the area had finally finished, and the neighbourhood was starting to come to life again. It was good to be somewhere that was rediscovering itself too.

Aside from the bed from my room at my parents' place and the flatpacks of furniture still stacked in their cardboard boxes, the apartment was empty. The parquet floor shone like gold. Shruti had come over and helped clean a few days earlier, while I hung out with my new nephew. He'd squinted at me suspiciously while I sang whatever nursery rhymes I could remember, and tried to convince him to sleep.

There were no granite counters or engineered wood floors like in the house, but the apartment had big windows and a long balcony, and it was my space alone. Mom was still miffed I hadn't moved home. "Why do you want to live alone? Stay at home and we can take care of you." But she had stopped saying "What will people think?"

Now that Bryan and I were splitting up, there was nothing people could say about my living alone that was worse than what they were saying about my getting divorced. I would have to ask Amit sometime if the same had been true when he first became an actor.

I'd have to send Malika some pictures when I had my furniture set up. She was enthused about my apartment, but also worried for me. She'd asked me if I was scared to live alone on our Skype call a little while ago.

"No," I'd said. "But it's new. I've never lived alone."

"It's exciting," she'd said. "It's like on television, having your own apartment, friends coming by and visiting."

I told her I agreed, not wanted to pierce her fantasy, since aside from Amit, Shannon, and sometimes Shruti, there was no one to visit. Yet. But Malika seemed content with Raj, and was getting used to living with her in-laws. She showed me some new outfits she had so she looked more like a bride. I remembered my mom complaining I hadn't dressed enough like a bride after I'd gotten married, and I still had no idea what that meant. But she and Raj were planning trips around India together, starting with the Taj Mahal. I was glad she had some say in her life.

Mom came over the next day and surveyed all the work Amit, Shannon, and I had done setting things up the day before, before she re-organized my kitchen over my protests. She reminded me that I wasn't as good a cook as Shruti and then filled my fridge with yogurt containers filled with Indian food. She said nothing about Bryan or the divorce, which seemed to be her way to cope with the situation: by pretending it had never happened.

But it had. After she left, I was alone in my mostly functional apartment. It was quiet. Quieter than the hotel room at the Taj hotel with the faint sounds of traffic, or the hotel in Agra, where the window air conditioner had whirred loudly enough to drown out the honking cars and barking dogs. Quieter than the condo that Bryan and I had lived in, even in these last few weeks, while we'd lived together but had all but completely stopped talking to each other, though I was aware of his presence constantly. Even in the middle of the night, when I lay awake with worry and fear over what I would do in the future, unable to get comfortable on the couch, I could hear him breathing in the bedroom.

Before today, I had tried to picture my life after Bryan, and all I could picture was a blank wall, one that I was approaching with terrifying speed. I didn't know if I would get over it or through it, only that it loomed so large that I could not see what lay in my future beyond it. I knew there would be this apartment and the tea shop, but I couldn't see it. All I could see was a blank, and I'd been terrified of that blankness all my life.

But now I was past the blank wall and living in the apartment. Tomorrow, I would visit the new shop to check on its progress.

I didn't know yet how I would fill the rest of the blankness, but it was no longer terrifying.

Shannon had strung Christmas lights near the ceiling, and so I turned them on, filling the room with soft white light, and went out on the balcony. It was only a few stories up and looked over the parking lot. I thought of the monkeys in Agra; they would have no trouble climbing up here. There was a light drizzle chilling the air, but I stood out there anyway. I couldn't see the lake, or the CN Tower, or the stars; only the lights from all the buildings all around me were visible. So many people, going about their own lives, making their own choices. Now I was among them.

ACKNOWLEDGEMENTS

It's a surreal experience to achieve a lifelong dream. What do I do now?

I'll start by thanking Evelyn Elgie, for selecting this book from a pile of manuscripts and being one of its biggest fans. Ev, among the many, many things you do, you are a maker of dreams. Thank you for loving this book and sharing my bewilderment at those who did not.

My amazing cover was designed by Pei Yuan Li. I loved it so much I had it printed on a t-shirt. My anxiety at having to promote this book was immediately calmed upon meeting publicist Melissa Ren, who was so clearly on top of everything. Many thanks to the entire team at Inanna; small press is a labour of love, emphasis on the labour.

My deepest gratitude to my substantive editor, Susan Musgrave. The experience of repeatedly sending a manuscript to one of Canada's most esteemed writers so she could note every single lazy writing crutch I had was extremely humbling, and even a little personally embarrassing. But her care and diligence made this book so much better. My ego will recover.

I was a huge reader as a child, but it never occurred to me that I could be a writer until my grade 9 English teacher, Rosemary Corbett, pulled me aside before class to apologize for reading my short story out loud to the previous class without having asked me first. She was later my first creative writing teacher for OAC Writers Craft.

I was nearly thirty when I took my next creative writing class, at Humber College, where Brad Reed called us writers and told us how writing had saved his life, and that being a writer mattered. I cannot recall exactly what he said, only that in his class I had the profound feeling that I was doing exactly what I was supposed to be doing; this feeling has sustained me through the years of rejections and self-doubt and fear that every newer writer has about not being good enough.

The first success I ever had as a writer was a short story I sent to The Toronto Star Short Story contest. It did not win. But I later heard from one of the judges, Jessica Westhead, that my story had been her favourite, and it had made her cry, which was frankly better than winning. Through the years, Jess has been an unfailing source of advice and support, and I maintain that she is the nicest person in all of Canlit.

This novel first came into being with the guidance of Gail Anderson-Dargatz; I'd have spent many more years not knowing what I was doing without her. It was then rewritten multiple times amid an extremely chaotic period in my life under the patient mentorship of my thesis advisor, Nancy Lee. When my thesis was done, and I decided my novel was a failure, Nancy encouraged me not to give up on it. I was too demoralized to believe her, and too new a writer to understand that this feeling happens for everyone. Fortunately, the comments from my second thesis reader, Kevin Chong, helped me realize that I'd accidentally written the book I'd intended to write.

After shopping the book around way too soon, my chats with Shelley Tepperman helped me figure out a plan to revise it. I then stalled on this plan until it was completely derailed by the death of my father, the birth of my daughter, and a global pandemic. Once I could write again, the combined efforts of Nicola Winstanley, Lesley Finn, and Karen Palmer cleared up all my structural problems, and the advice, encouragement and co-working time with Jill Margo, Rami Schandall, Laure Baudot, Sarah Ojamaë, Sidura Ludwig, and Kelsey Andrews kept me going.

I come from a long line of accountants, but needed to ask my cousin, Mihir Shah, some accounting-specific questions to write this book. Much to the chagrin of my mother, I speak virtually no Gujarati, but thankfully my cousins, Vaishali and Karthik Shah, and my aunt, Rekha Chheda, were able to provide Gujarati-to-English help.

My sincere gratitude to the Canada Council for the Arts, the Ontario Arts Council, and the Toronto Arts Council for their financial support. Grants for artists return more than their value in economic activity, and the more we advocate for arts education and funding, the better we all are.

Thanks to Sarah Selecky, whose magical dining table writing classes in Parkdale inspired me to pursue my MFA, and who gave me the opportunity to teach creative writing for ten years; teaching and coaching writers has been such an incredible joy. My students have been taught me so much, and I hope they have writing in their lives.

I can't name all the writers who have cheered me on, helped me out, commiserated with me, or reassured me. There are far too many. But I'd like to make note of a few: Michelle Good, Michelle Barker, Chris Tarry, Mark Cutts, Jean Sheppard, Anil Kamal, Claire Cameron, Kirti Bhadresa, Hajera Khaja, and many members of the Toronto Women Writer's Salon.

Most of all, I would not be the writer I am without Kim McCullough, the other half of my writing brain. May no one ever read our chats.

My personal cheering squad of non-writers is surprisingly large for a person who avoids people. Some notable mentions: Manish Champsee, Jean Doyle, Shilpa Kothary-Shah, Molly Rotering, Monique De Yong, Patricia Klayh, Karen Ryan, Lauri Cox Connor, Susan Gress, Annie McCliment, Janet Grove, Lisa Venuti, Dana Davies, Mary Johnson, Mariska van der Western, Kelly Lee, Dean Hartshorn, Michaela Logan, Rima Chaddha

Mycenyk, Jennifer Johnson, Elina Valentine, Kim MacDougall, Linnea Duckworth-Jeannette, Bevin Campbell, Kate Brittain, and Sara Speltdoorn.

Many thanks to my husband, Gordan Stuhne, the Shane Hollander to my Ilya Rozanov, for the years of support, including breakfasts, lunches, many dinners, tea, snacks, childcare, and never once questioning why I was playing games on my phone and not writing. Thanks as well to my kids, Dorian and Renata, for simply being awesome.

If I have missed anyone, my apologies. I will get to you in the next book.

To quote Snoop Dogg: "Last but not least, I'd like to thank me. I want to thank me for believing in me, I want to thank me for doing all this hard work. I want to thank me for having no days off. I want to thank me for never quitting. I want to thank me for always being a giver and trying to give more than I receive. I want to thank me for trying to do more right than wrong. I want to thank me for being me at all times."

Writing is a book is a long and difficult road, full of more reasons to quit than to continue. As much as I know I didn't get here alone, I also know that I wouldn't be here without my own sheer bloody-mindedness to keep going. For this quality and more, I must thank my mother.

AUTHOR

Sonal Champsee's work appears in anthologies, magazines and newspapers, such as *The New Quarterly, Today's Parent*, and the *Toronto Star*. Her debut novel, *Everyone Can't Be Wrong*, was a finalist for the 2022 HarperCollins/UBC Prize for Best New Fiction. Sonal lives in Toronto, Canada.